# THE
# AFTERMATH

D0595864

ALSO BY R. J. PRESCOTT

*The Hurricane*

# THE
# AFTERMATH

## R. J. PRESCOTT

**FOREVER**

New York   Boston

Copyright © 2015 by R. J. Prescott
Bonus chapter copyright © 2016 by R. J. Prescott
Excerpt from the *The Hurricane* © 2014 by R. J. Prescott
Cover design by Louisa Maggio
Cover copyright © 2015 by Hachette Book Group, Inc.

Forever
Hachette Book Group
1290 Avenue of the Americas
New York, NY 10104
hachettebookgroup.com
twitter.com/foreverromance

Previously published as an ebook
First trade paperback edition: August 2016

Printed in the United States of America

RRD-C

10 9 8 7 6 5 4 3 2 1

Forever is an imprint of Grand Central Publishing.
The Forever name and logo are trademarks of Hachette Book Group, Inc.

The Hachette Speakers Bureau provides a wide range of authors for speaking events. To find out more, go to www.hachettespeakersbureau.com or call (866) 376-6591.

The publisher is not responsible for websites (or their content) that are not owned by the publisher.

Library of Congress Cataloging-in-Publication Data

Names: Prescott, R. J. (Novelist), author.
Title: The aftermath / R.J. Prescott.
Description: First trade paperback edition. | New York : Forever, 2016.
Identifiers: LCCN 2016009274| ISBN 9781455593118 (softcover) | ISBN
    9781478909873 (audio download) | ISBN 9781455593101 (ebook)
Subjects: LCSH: Women mathematicians—Fiction. | Boxers
(Sports)—Fiction. |
    BISAC: FICTION / Romance / Contemporary. | FICTION / Contemporary
Women. |
    GSAFD: Love stories.
Classification: LCC PR6116.R46 A69 2016 | DDC 823/.92—dc23 LC record
available at https://lccn.loc.gov/2016009274

# THE
# AFTERMATH

# PROLOGUE

## CORMAC O'CONNELL—
## TWELVE YEARS EARLIER

"Whatcha cryin' for?" I asked the skinny blond kid. He was sitting with his legs dangling over the side of the riverbank. I could tell he'd been crying because he was sniffling and rubbing his eyes with the back of his arms.

"Feck off," the kid told me. Fucking charming. I'd only been in my new school a couple of weeks. Since me da left, Ma had been moving us from place to place, looking for a replacement husband I guess. I didn't want a replacement da. I just wanted to stay in one place for a while so she could clean herself up. Some clothes that fit me would be nice as well. I was getting sick of scavenging about in Ma's loose change when she'd passed out after a drinking binge, then stretching the money between food and charity shop clothes. Every new school meant new kids making fun of the way I looked. I didn't like talking much so, when they started on me, looking for an easy mark, I punched them in the face and stopped them talking. I was a pretty big kid, and you didn't have to punch that hard to shock most people.

"There's no need to be a dick about it. I was only trying to help," I said to him. I don't know why I was wasting my time with this kid, 'cept maybe because he was Irish too. I'd heard him and a couple of other boys talking in class, and they all had Irish accents. Outside of my parents, I'd never met any Irish before. He looked me up and down then stared at me hard. Finally he said, "You can sit down if you want." I don't know why I shrugged and took a seat next to him. I wasn't looking for a friend or anything. I was just curious I guess. This kid usually looked like he didn't have a care in the world.

"Where are you going?" he asked me.

"Me ma's out so I was going to try and get something to eat." I didn't explain that I was looking for some food to steal. There was no money left in Ma's pocket when I found her passed out this morning.

"You can come to my house for dinner if you like. Me ma always cooks enough for about five people when she's stressed."

"Okay," I agreed. I didn't know this kid or his ma, but no way was I turning down a free meal, especially if it was hot.

"Why's she stressed?" I asked. He kicked at some stone embedded into the grass, and I didn't think he was going to answer.

"We just found out that me da's sick. His chest is bad from breathing in some shite at work. Doctors don't think they can fix him," he explained quietly.

"That blows," I said. I didn't know what else to say. There was a gravel path behind us so I gathered up a pile of stones and dropped them down between us. He looked at me sort of confused

"See those beer bottles down there?" I asked indicating the empty bottles someone had thrown down the bank. "You wanna see who can smash them first?"

"Why?" he asked.

"Why not?" I answered. "Breaking shit always makes me feel better. Might work for you too." I don't know if it did, but he didn't talk about his da anymore. Instead he talked about his friends and the stuff they got up to, what comics and television shows he liked. I didn't say much. The picture on our television was shite, and I didn't have money for food let alone comics. I liked that he didn't push me to talk. Hell, when this kid got going, you couldn't get a word in edgeways anyway. When I'd smashed all the bottles, 'cause he couldn't throw for shit, we got up and walked back to his house for dinner. I was so hungry that I was practically dragging him. "What's your name anyway?" he asked me.

"Cormac O'Connell. But everyone just calls me Con."

"I'm Kieran," he replied. "And me mates at school are Tommy and Liam. You can sit with us tomorrow if you like," he offered.

"Okay," I said. "What's for dinner?"

"Chicken, roast potatoes, and veg, I think," he told me. He turned his nose up at the last part, like veg was something disgusting that he was forced to eat. My mouth watered, and I dragged him a bit faster.

* * *

That was pretty much the day that Kieran Doherty became my best friend. The sicker his da got, and the worse things got for me at home, the more trouble we got into, mainly 'cause we were letting off steam. That and I never let anybody fuck with us. Hitting someone who deserved it made everything seem better. I couldn't or wouldn't hit me ma, and Kier couldn't hit the people who made his da sick, so we hit anyone else who gave us shit.

"You ever been to that gym John Callaghan trains at?" I asked Kier one day.

"John Callaghan in year six?" he said.

"You know any other John Callaghans?" I replied sarcastically.

"Seven others, including him," he shot back straightaway, and I rolled my eyes.

"I heard the guy who owns the place is Irish too. You reckon he'd let us train there?" I asked him.

"Why would he? We can't pay him nothing," Kieran said.

"We could sweep floors and do jobs and stuff," I suggested.

"I don't see why he'd go for it, but we could try," he agreed. The idea of actually learning to box properly made me excited, and I couldn't remember the last time I'd been excited about anything.

The next day we headed to John Callaghan's gym after school, and after hanging around outside for a bit, we built up the courage and went in. It was four in the afternoon and already pretty busy, mainly with older boys like John, who was already changed and going at it on one of the heavy punch bags. I itched to join him. Finally some guy noticed us and stared suspiciously.

"What do you two want?" he asked us.

"Can we train here?" I called back.

"No, you're too young. Owner's rules are you need to be at least sixteen." I wanted to tell him to fuck off and that we were sixteen, which we weren't, but I couldn't risk pissing the owner off if they were friends.

"That's it then," Kier said as we walked back down the steps.

"Fuck him," I said. "He doesn't own the place. We'll just hang about for the owner to get here. I'll offer to do jobs for him and see what he says." 'Course we weren't known for our patience, and by the time the guy actually showed up, we were scrapping outside the doors.

"What the feckin' hell are you two little shites doin'?" the owner asked us.

"We want to train here," I told him. "We ain't got money but we both hit good and we work hard. We can sweep up and do jobs and stuff to pay our way," I told him in one great big rush, trying to spit it all out before he stopped me.

"I don't train kids. You've got to be sixteen to fight here," he said and walked past us, through the doors.

"Can we go home now?" Kier asked. "I'm starving." Kier's ma cooked like nobody I ever met. She let me eat with them almost every night and I think she must have known how things were at home. She never said anything but she

came to parent teacher meetings for me or, if the school ever
called, backing up my story that Ma was really sick. Never
one to turn down a meal, I went with him but dragged him
back every day for a week until the owner, Danny, gave in
and let us train there once. After that he couldn't get rid of
us. One night there and I was totally addicted. After a couple of months, John was scheduled to fight one of the boys
from a gym across Canning Town. The night before the fight,
Danny told all of us to grab our coats, and he dragged us to
church. We knew some of the other kids had to go to church
before a fight, but he'd never asked us to go before.

"What're we doing here?" I asked.

"He goes to church to clear his head and get ready for the
fight. You want to be part of this gym, then you go too or
you don't get to train. That's the way this family works."

It was clear that Danny wasn't messing around. So I sat on
the bench with my hands in my pockets looking bored, and
Kieran sat next to me the same way. Finally Father Pat came
out to get me.

"So, Cormac, Danny tells me that you like to fight," he said
as he showed me to my seat.

I wanted to tell him that of course I liked it, why else
would I hang around at Danny's, but I didn't think Danny
would appreciate me being sarcastic to Father Pat and I
couldn't afford to piss him off.

"You can call me Con, Father. Everyone else does," I answered. "And yes. Makes me feel better."

"About what, son?" he asked.

"About everything," I answered.

"I understand that it's getting you into a bit of trouble at school though," he added. I shifted about on my seat wondering how he could have known that.

"I don't need school anyway. Me and Kier are going to leave as soon as we can. Get a job in construction before I become a boxer full-time."

"I see," he said with a smile. "You have it all worked out then." I nodded in answer. "Being a professional boxer requires a great deal of discipline you know," he told me.

"I ain't afraid of hard work. I can train as hard as the other boys do," I argued.

"I'm sure Con. But that's not what I meant."

I frowned at him, pissed off that he thought I wouldn't be as dedicated as the older kids. I could kick half their arses now.

"You know, there's a story of an old Cherokee man who told his grandsons, 'There is a battle between two wolves inside us all. One is Evil. It's anger, jealousy, greed, resentment, inferiority, lies, and ego. The other is Good. It is joy, peace, love, hope, humility, kindness, empathy, and truth.' The boy thought about it and asked, 'Grandfather, which wolf wins?' The old man quietly replied, 'The one you feed.' I don't know who said it, but it's a good story."

"I don't get it," I answered, confused. "What does it mean?"

"It means, Con, that you've been dealt a bad hand in life. But one day, you have to decide what kind of man you want to be. You have to choose which wolf you feed."

# CHAPTER 1

It never occurred to me that mail was something to fear. Not until the day I came home and found Em sitting on the floor, her arms wrapped around her knees, and a ripped open white envelope on the bed behind her.

"Sunshine, what's wrong?" I asked. She swallowed hard and sniffed a few times like she was trying to hold back tears long enough to talk to me. I reached for the envelope, thinking it would give me some clue as to why she was so clearly freaked out.

"Don't," Em croaked. "Please," she added pleadingly. I knew then, as a tear rolled down her cheek, that whatever was inside had to be bad. Contained within a folded sheet of plain white paper were about a dozen or so photos. They were different sizes and all taken at different times, but Em was in every one of them. The earliest photo was of a smiling, happy nine-year-old. Just a normal kid out riding her bike. When the next one showed the same kid, fast asleep in her bed, I felt sick to my fucking stomach. The older that Em was in the pictures, the more invasive they became and none of them looked like they were taken with her knowledge. The last photo was really grainy, like it had been through a window maybe, or with a really bad camera, but it showed, in intimate detail, her frail, bruised body taking a shower.

"Motherfucker," I yelled, wanting to fucking hit something. Anything. I grabbed the envelope looking for some clue who'd sent it, like I didn't fucking know. Frank was still in prison, pending trial, so someone on the outside must have sent this for him. The postmark on the envelope read London, which didn't tell me much. The knuckles on Em's hand were white where she was gripping hold of her legs so hard.

"Shit, love. You okay?" I said, hating that she looked so fucking scared. She nodded unconvincingly, but didn't answer. I gathered up the pictures and stuffed them back into the envelope, not wanting her to see them anymore, but I knew we'd need to give them to police as evidence. The idea of her being on display like that to the police and the prosecution lawyers was as bad as knowing what she'd been through. Sitting down next to her, I wrapped my arm around her tiny body and pulled her into my chest. She was stiff as a board and shaking slightly. Rubbing up and down her arms, trying to get her warm I waited for her to talk to me. That was the way of it sometimes with Sunshine. She needed to think shit over before she could get it off her chest.

"I didn't know about any of them. He's been taking pictures of me for years. How could I not know? How could I let that happen?" she asked me.

"You didn't *let* anything happen. He's a violent, abusive rapist who's sick in the fucking head. He did what he did because he's a fucking whack job. Nothing you said or did gave him permission to do this." I could see by her face that the pictures shamed her. Fuck that. There wasn't a single fucking thing for her to be ashamed of.

"It was bad enough dealing with what happened, but he could have hundreds of these pictures and God only knows what he does with them. As if that's not bad enough he knows where we live. Even in prison he can get to me. I'll never be free of him, will I?"

"Sunshine, even if it means killing him, I swear he will never touch you again. This is just a sign of desperation. In a few more months he'll be too concerned about how to pick up the soap in the shower without getting arse raped to worry about getting you back. He's going away for a very long time and there's fuck all he can do about it. This kind of shit just gives the barristers more ammunition against him." I did my best to reassure her, but I was as freaked out as she was. The fact that he could get hold of the pictures and post them from prison had me worried about what else he could do from the inside.

She wiped her eyes and leaned across to give me a quick kiss.

"You're right," she told me. "A few more months and this will all be over." It had to be, because I hadn't been exaggerating. If Frank came after her again, I'd kill to keep her safe.

* * *

Three days later I held up my right hand so Danny could tape my knuckles, while the grip of my left hand tightened on the bench. Why did the door have to be red? Of all the fucking colors a door could be, this one had to be red. Changing rooms were pretty much the same in every place I'd ever fought in. This one was practically identical to the changing room I'd had when Em was kidnapped. As my mind played over that night, I started to lose focus.

"You've got this fecker, Con, but don't go soft on this guy. It might be an exhibition fight but Temple wants to hurt you. He wants a show. The cocky little fucker is top of his game and needs the world to know he's staying there. He's gonna treat you like a stepping-stone, so you show him you ain't one, okay?"

I didn't hear a word that Danny said. I couldn't take my eyes off that fucking door. My certainty that Frank was going down had picked Em up a bit, but truthfully, Frank's letter had properly fucked me over. He'd taken Em once on fight night, and just because he was in prison didn't mean he couldn't send someone else to finish the job. He'd found a way to get those photos to her hadn't he? Once I walked out the door and into that ring, who would protect her?

The slap to my face woke me up. "Where the fuck is your head, Con? You're fighting in fifteen minutes, and right now I wouldn't put you in the ring with Kieran's feckin' grandmother," he roared. I hung my head knowing he was right. Six months ago, I had nothing to lose. Now I had Em and I knew what losing her felt like. It made me afraid, and going into the ring like this was a bad fucking idea.

"Kier, he's not going to hold it together."

Kier swapped places with Danny and carried on taping. "What's going on, Con?" he asked me.

"This place looks the same as the one where she was taken. I can't think about anything else," I told him. Maybe I should have made some shit up, but Kieran knew me well enough to call me on my bullshit if I lied.

"It's not the same, Con. You know that. Frank's in prison, and Em has more bodyguards than Justin Bieber. You can do this. Stop worrying about what will happen when you lose everything and start getting mad at the fuckers trying to take it from you. She's right here and she yours. So what happens when someone messes with what's yours?" he asked.

"I decimate the fuckers," I answered. He was right. I needed to get my head out of my arse. I was hard as fucking nails and no one was fucking with my girl.

"What happens if some guy wolf whistles or tries to grab her arse tonight?" he goaded.

"I'll decimate the fucker," I told him more forcefully, feeling the adrenaline starting to kick in.

"And what happens," he said finally, "if someone tried to take her?"

"I. WILL. FUCKING. DECIMATE. THEM." I enunciated slowly, completely pumped now.

"Thatta boy," he replied with a smile. "He's ready," he said to Danny, who'd swapped places with Kieran to put on my gloves. My knee was bouncing, and I was impatient to get out of there. Pumped and primed, I wanted to hurt someone. The second he was done, I jumped up from the bench and started going at the pads with Kier. Cross, cross, jab. Cross, cross, jab. I cleared my mind of everything but the pads. How to move my body to land the perfect punch was instinctive. Years of relentless training did that. There wasn't a how or a why when I fought. The only thing that concerned me about the guy I was fighting was where to land my fist to cause the maximum pain. But this time was different. This time my opponent had a face, and it was Frank's. It burned me that, with everything that went down, I hadn't had the chance to lay a fist on him. I was a valve with no release, and if I didn't vent that rage and fear soon, I was going to explode, and there'd be casualties in the wake. Danny watched me spar and didn't look happy. As far as he was concerned, getting in the ring carrying any kind of baggage was a bad fucking idea. It was why he made us go to church before a fight. Inside those ropes I was supposed to be an emotionless machine and I hadn't been that in a long time. One of the management team opened my door. "Con, it's time," he told me.

Kieran held out my robe, and I stopped bouncing just long enough to slip it on. Danny opened the door and cringed as my music pumped loudly through the speakers. Fort Minor's "Remember the Name" didn't do it for him at all, but Kieran had picked it years ago, and it sort of stuck. The bass was making my blood pump and I strutted out of the room like I was invincible.

"You ready?" Kieran asked.

"Hell, yeah," I replied. I burned with the need to hurt someone, and the thought of releasing all that rage on Rico Temple got my blood pumping.

"I hate that cocky little shit as much as you do," Kieran admitted. "But fight smart. Don't just go barreling in there trying to hurt him. He's got a lot more fights under his belt than you do, so you need to think about how you're gonna do this," he told me. I rolled my eyes, not really caring about his advice. Making him bleed was all I could think about. Danny reached up to grab my chin and turned my face so that I was staring straight at him. It took some effort given our height difference.

He looked more pissed off than I'd seen him in a long time. "I'm your coach, and Kieran's your corner man. That means you listen to what we have to say. If you don't fight smart like Kieran said, this guy's gonna walk all over you. Now I want you to fight the first three rounds defensively. Keep your guard up and wear him down. Round four or five, when he's up on points, you let him have it. Then take him by surprise when he thinks you're done." I nodded my head as I bounced. I knew he was right but I struggled with the craving to hurt someone. "And for fuck's sake, don't knock him out. This is an exhibition match. Anything more than heavy sparring and you'll be disqualified."

"Sure thing," I answered as I shifted my weight from foot to foot. Then it was time. At the sign from the management guy, I jogged slowly toward the spotlight.

As I reached the ring, I climbed in through the ropes, with Kieran and Danny right behind me. Kieran helped me off with my robe, and I looked past him, anxious for Temple to join me.

Even standing in this ring was cathartic. In a few minutes, I'd be able to unleash all my hatred in the name of sportsmanship, and what's left of me after belonged to my girl. My music ended as his began, and I snorted. He'd chosen some stupid rap shit and was strutting toward me like he had the fight sewn up. He hadn't fought with me yet. I was gonna knock the cocky right out of him, and he'd kiss the canvas in gratitude for the lesson. I bounced around shaking out my arms and looking like I hadn't got a care in the world. Rico Temple was nothing to me. I had enough inside to take down ten of him with how I was feeling. Danny smacked my abs to draw my attention and shoved my gum shield into my mouth.

"Stick to the plan, keep your guard up and pick your punches. You ready?" he asked. I nodded at him but my mind was already on Temple. Squeezing my shoulder reassuringly, he climbed out of the ring. The referee called us to the center, and the self-assured smirk on Rico's face was already pissing me off.

"Gentleman, when I say 'break' I want a clean break. In the event of a knockdown, you will be directed to go to a neutral corner. You're both professionals so I expect a good, clean fight. No hitting below the belt, and protect yourself at all times. Okay, touch gloves and come out at the bell."

I held my gloves out, staring Temple in the eye as I willed him to know that I was gonna end him. He ignored the gesture and saluted me mockingly. The crowd was already booing at the bad sportsmanship. It didn't matter. I wasn't feeling very fucking sporting anyway. I tried to keep my expression neutral and remember what Danny told me about the game plan. Then the bell rang out, and it all went out of the window. Every bit of training I'd ever had, all the advice I'd ever been given, every ounce of common sense I'd been born with and it was all gone at the bell. With the sound ringing in my ears, Temple became Frank, and I threw myself at him. He didn't expect me to come out so aggressively, and I landed two crippling body shots and a right hook to the head before he got his guard up. I wasn't pacing myself or holding anything back for the rest of the fight. All the power I had went into every punch as my stress melted away. I managed to herd him into a corner and was going at his ribs as hard as I did the bags at the gym. Em was the most fucking precious thing in the world to me, and I imagined this was the fucker who nearly broke her. He spent most of his life tearing her down and beating her, and when I swore she'd never feel that way again, he took her from under my nose. Not this time. This time I was gonna end him in the ring and he'd never get to her again.

The referee pulled me back, and Temple shook it off. A few minutes ago, he looked cocky. Now he looked mad. "Tone it down. This is supposed to be an exhibition match," the referee warned me.

It was all the time Temple needed to recover. As soon as the referee moved away, he smacked me in the cheek with a killer left jab, throwing my head back and nearly dislodging my gum shield. Without pause, he served back to me exactly what I'd just delivered. I couldn't stop him, but I didn't really feel much pain either.

Pushing him back in the corner, I started going at him again until I was almost windmilling. My adrenaline level must have been through the roof because I felt like I could pound on him all night. In my peripheral vision, I saw the referee moving toward me on my right, and I knew he was going to warn me again when a left uppercut came out of nowhere and had me seeing stars. The referee stood between us giving me a moment to recover, and any warning died on his lips. We were both breaking the rules and spirit of an exhibition bout, but the referee had no fucking clue what to do. He couldn't disqualify us both, and the crowd was fucking loving it. He threw his arms down to signal that we could fight but both of us were a little bit wary this time. In that moment, I literally wanted to end the arsehole. As we squared off against each other, I dived at him again, no longer caring that I didn't have an opening. He fended off all my body shots, and I wasn't holding back. The more he held his guard, the angrier I became. When the bell sounded to signal the end of the round, I could have roared in frustration. Kieran put my stool down in the corner, and I sat down. *Hard.* Leaning forward, I was dying to get back out there, and I willed the sixty seconds to go by quickly. Kieran shot water into my mouth, while Danny laid into me.

"Are you deaf or feckin' stupid, Cormac O'Connell?" he asked. "'Cause I distinctively remember telling you how to fight this match. You don't look like a professional boxer out there. You look like an arrogant kid who's about to have his arse handed to him." I didn't answer back but it's not like Danny would've given me a chance anyway. He was on a roll. "You listen to me if you want to save this fight. Now he knows what you're made of but he has to be betting that you've worn yourself out. So you go back to the original game plan. Protect yourself and let him think you're spent, then let him have it." I nodded at him but I couldn't concentrate, and I was already looking for Temple behind him. Danny looked at Kieran and shook his head, like they were having some kind of silent conversation. I didn't give a fuck what they were both bitching about. Whether I did it Danny's way or my way, I had this in the bag.

The bell rang, and I stood up to fight. I was watching Temple's shoulders, trying to read his next move when he came at me. His hook-hook-jab combination was predictable. The left hook that caught me square in the eye wasn't. I stumbled about a bit on my feet, dazed but not knocked out, but it was enough for the referee to give me a standing count. As I waited impatiently for the count to be over, I could see the judges scribbling furiously. That hook had cost me, but Temple was going to pay for it. Charging at him the minute I had the go-ahead, I unleashed a volley of body shots. Most of them were blocked, but the ones that did get through must have been rib bruisers. Thinking that I had him trapped on the ropes, I was stunned when he jerked up and reversed our position. Every single one of his hits, even the ones I blocked, hurt like hell. I'd been motherfucking rope-a-doped. Like Ali had done with Forman, he used my anger to provoke me into attacking. The ropes were taking the strain of my ineffectual hits while my energy level plummeted. The referee pulled him off with a warning when he cut above my eye. We danced around each other for a few more seconds, but when the bell rang again, we both sat down looking like we'd done ten rounds, not two. Going against the norm, it was Kieran who gave me the pep talk, while Danny sorted out my cut. For the whole sixty seconds, Danny didn't say a fucking word. He simply squeezed my shoulder as a silent gesture of support as he climbed out of the ring. The next ten rounds were absolutely brutal. We both punished each other, and the whole thing was more like a street brawl than a professional boxing match. The only reason the ref never called it was because we were both as bad as each other. When the bell rang out for the final time, I was banged up and exhausted. The cut had reopened, and the blood was streaming down my face. Both Kieran and Danny were uncharacteristically silent as they patched me up. After a few minutes, the ref called us back in the ring. I looked for Em in the crowd as he called out how the judges had scored the fight. I wasn't really listening until he finished. "Ladies and gentleman, your winner by unanimous decision. Rico Temple." He raised Temple's arm in the air as I locked eyes with my wife. She looked sad, and I guess she thought I'd be worried about the loss. I wasn't. In my head, I'd just gone twelve rounds against Frank. All I felt was relief and the burning need to do it all over again.

# CHAPTER 2

I woke up on a knife edge of pain and pleasure. After the boys had all but carried me home last night, I sat in an ice bath, which was almost as bad as the fighting, then collapsed on the bed with my girl in my arms. On the one hand, my sore, achy body felt like it had been hit by a bus. On the other, the love of my life was asleep on my chest. Did she look perfect first thing in the morning? Hell no. My wife had naturally curly blond hair, meaning that she got bed hair like you wouldn't believe. She was a light sleeper, no doubt a consequence of always worrying about Frank finding her, and sometimes she drooled in her sleep.

Was she perfect? No, but she was perfect for me. Waking up to feel her warm body safe and curled into mine was like a little piece of heaven and lying here with her in my arms gave me peace. The sun streamed through the window where we'd forgotten to close the curtains, lighting up her hair like a halo. 'Course she chose that moment to snore and wake herself up, which made me chuckle. I loved the way she gave my chest a loving rub as she checked for drool.

"Mornin', Mrs. O'Connell," I told her, tilting my head up to capture her bottom lip between mine.

"You're very chirpy for someone who just got their arse handed to them," she teased.

"I let him win," I replied.

"Is that right?" She questioned me with one eyebrow raised.

"Sure. With a face that ugly, someone had to throw him a bone," I told her with a smile.

"I knew you were all heart." Any reply died on my lips as she raised herself up on all fours and kissed me. I moaned into her mouth as she brushed past my thickening cock. She'd slept in one of my T-shirts which swamped her so much that she looked like she was sleeping in a tent. Reaching behind her, I grabbed the back of it and tried to pull it over her head. I was so smooth that I ended up tangling her arms and hair in it so, by the time it was off, she'd collapsed on the bed in fits of laughter.

"Do you know what it does to my hard-on when you laugh while we're making love?"

"What?" she asked curiously.

"Absolutely nothing. Now get your sexy arse over here and kiss my war wounds," I replied, hauling her to me.

"Are you sure you're up for this?" she asked. I didn't bother answering. It wasn't even a real question anyway. I stroked my way gently down her naked spine, knowing how much it turned her on. The skin on her back was so soft that my big calloused hands must have felt like sandpaper. If her low moan was anything to go by though, I was doing okay. My face was killing me, and there was only one muscle left that didn't hurt, but none of that mattered with Em's body this close to mine. When her tits brushed up against my chest, I slid my hands inside her panties to cup the globes of her arse. She squirmed as she rubbed herself up against my cock. I wanted to flip her onto her back and suck on her until she was screaming my name but given that I could barely lift my own arm, I satisfied myself by sliding my hand around to her front and slipping a couple of fingers deep inside her. Watching her ride them, her head thrown back in ecstasy, was one of the most erotic things I'd ever seen. If I wasn't careful, I was gonna shoot my load before I even got my boxers off. With my free hand, I reached out to cup her breast and maneuvered her nipple into my mouth. Twisting my tongue around that firm, moist nub made her ride me harder. When I nipped her slightly then salved the bite with my tongue, it tipped her over the edge. Intensifying her orgasm, I rubbed gently over her clit until she literally couldn't take any more pleasure and collapsed hard against my chest, making me moan in pain.

"Shit! Sorry baby," she apologized, climbing quickly off me.

"Don't worry about it. I'm fine," I reassured her.

"Are you sure there isn't anything you'd like me to kiss better?" she asked me, provocatively.

I fucking loved seeing Em like this. Alone with me, she was sassy and confident and sexy as fuck. She only had to pretty much walk past me and I got a hard-on. Watching her tease me in just a tiny pair of panties and not trying to hide or cover herself up had my cock hard as a diamond and my blood pumping. Leaning down to kiss her way across my chest, her thigh pressed against my cock, and I had to fist the sheets to stop myself from flipping her under me and sinking deep inside her. By the time she'd shown appreciation to every one of my abs, I was on fire. She gently lifted the elastic of my boxers and pulled them down, so I lifted my arse off the bed to help. Seconds later, her lips were wrapped around my cock, and I groaned. Loudly.

"I fucking love you, Mrs. O'Connell," I told her as she took me deeper into her mouth. I was seconds away from coming when someone started pounding on the door. Em paused. "Ignore it," I told her, and she carried on.

"Con. Quit fucking Em and open up. You two have been going at it for ages," Tommy shouted as pounding started again. Angry whispered voices argued with him, and I could hear a scuffle, so the boys must have been trying to rein him in.

"I'm gonna fuckin' kill him," I told Em as she started giggling.

"Sorry, love. I'll make it up to you later," Em promised me.

Of course that didn't help me while I was lying here too stiff and achy to move with my cock stood up like a tent peg. Em kissed me passionately, which took the edge off my bad mood over the interruption, then jumped up to let the boys in. Pulling on some shorts, her bra, and my T-shirt, she still looked far too gorgeous to be answering the door to those horny maniacs. At least it was my T-shirt she wore. I fucking loved seeing her in my training clothes. I sighed loudly as I tried to think about washing machines, Father Pat, having a medicine ball dropped on me, literally anything I could to stop my cock standing to attention. Hearing Em's laughter, I knew Tommy was hitting on my girl, which was all the push I needed to get my arse out of bed. Every bone in my body hurt, and I swear some of them even creaked as I sat up. Five years ago, I would have jumped out of bed after a fight, even with a hangover, and run five miles easy. Now I could barely sit up. These days, I was fighting world-class boxers and my body knew the difference. I pulled on clean underwear and my favorite worn jeans, buttoning them as I went. The guys were slouched in the few chairs around the flat. As I suspected Tommy leaned against the counter next to Em with his arms crossed over his tightly fitted T-shirt as she made them all bacon sandwiches.

"Take your eyes off my wife's arse, boyo," I warned Tommy.

"Geez. You're so fucking possessive," he answered me back. "You're married now, Con, and I totally respect that." Everyone stopped and stared at him, not quite believing what they were hearing. "Besides, if I was going to check out anything, it would totally be your tits. You have an absolutely banging rack, Em," he whispered conspiratorially to my wife.

"That's it," I shouted and, pain forgotten, dived across the tiny sofa to smack him. Liam and Kieran intercepted, talking me down before I got anywhere near him. The gutless fucker dived behind Em, who was laughing her arse off.

"Seriously, Tommy," she wheezed between breaths, "do you have a death wish or something?"

"He knows how much I respect you. I don't know why he keeps getting his knickers in a knot all the time." Tommy whined like he had no idea what my problem was. My problem was that Em treated him like a little brother she needed to protect when she actually needed to let me teach that little fucker a lesson. After sorting everyone out with their breakfast, she sat down in my lap when the boys finally let me up. I gave Tommy the stink eye, which he completely ignored, but any remaining rage faded away when my gorgeous wife wrapped her arms around my neck, bringing me close enough to smell the slight vanilla scent of her skin. Em loved the smell of vanilla. Candles, body wash, shampoo were always the same. For me, if sunshine had a smell, it would be vanilla.

"Em, don't suppose you've been baking lately?" Liam asked hopefully, breaking the tension.

"Red tin on the countertop," Em answered with a grin.

"Don't eat them all, you greedy bastard," I warned him. Danny banned me from all of Em's cakes during training, and I knew Sunshine had baked those ready for me to eat as soon as the Temple fight was done. Liam opened the tin, and the guys dived into it like it was filled with the phone numbers of Victoria's Secret models. Rescuing a lone chocolate chip muffin, Em fed it to me so that I didn't need to let go of her. She smiled as our collective groans explained how fucking delicious they were.

"Jesus, Con," Liam piped up when the last muffin had

been demolished, "you are one lucky bastard." I smiled widely as I tucked Em into me more closely, knowing that he was right. Having her curves pressed so close was rapidly redirecting the blood flow around my body. As much as I loved the guys, the sex ban had been in place for the last four weeks, and I had a lot of time to make up for.

"So what brings you ugly lot here?" I asked.

"Fucking charming," Kieran replied. "Anyone would think we're not welcome."

"Ignore him, Kieran," Em said. "All of you are always welcome here. Now who's for a cup of tea?" she asked, slipping off my lap. I rolled my eyes at their collective grins, knowing how much they loved Em mothering them. She moved over to the kitchenette, and I waited for the kettle to start boiling before I turned to Kieran.

"What's going on?" I asked him quietly. I didn't want to alert Em but something must be up for them to be coming round this early after fight night.

"Danny wants to meet you," he explained. I figured this would be about the loss last night. It wasn't uncommon for Danny to want a postmortem of what went down.

"Fine," I huffed. "I'll stop by the gym tomorrow."

"No, Con. He wants to see you now. He sent us to come and get you."

"Shit," I said, because there really wasn't anything else to say.

* * *

Liam dropped my sorry arse at Driscoll's Gym then took off with the guys leaving me with no backup. They knew I was about to get a bollocking for my shitty performance and were too chicken shit to stand in the line of fire. Sitting down in the crappy chair opposite Danny was like sitting in the headmaster's office all over again. I'd been in this seat and under his spotlight many times before for drinking too much and fighting outside the ring, but it was the first time I'd sat here since I'd met Em.

"I'm sorry Danny. I don't know what to say..." I started.

"I don't need you to say anything, Con. I need you to listen. Last night weren't just a feckin' shambles, it were the first time in a long time that I thought about jacking in the boxing for good."

I sucked in a breath. That was a serious thing to say. Danny ate, slept, and breathed boxing. I wasn't sure he could ever walk away from it, and I wasn't sure what I would do if he ever did.

"All because I didn't run the fight like you told me to?" I asked, pissed that he was completely overreacting just because I'd gone off the reservation once.

"No, Con. Because if you were any other fighter, Rico Temple would have killed you last night." It was on the tip of my tongue to argue with him, but the look on his face told me to shut the fuck up.

"Look, I know that everything that happened with Em screwed with your head, but last night I watched fear and anger eat you alive until the only thing I could see was a beaten-up, scared-shitless kid. So you wanna tell me what the fuck's going on?" I hung my head in shame, knowing that he was right and ran my hands through my hair in despair.

"A few days ago Em got a letter from Frank. There was no note, just an envelope full of pictures. Turns out the sick fuck had taking photos of her for years without her knowing."

"Shit," he mumbled, looking as devastated as I probably did.

"You told the police?" he asked.

"I took it down to the station yesterday. It's being tested for fingerprints but unless they find any, there's nothing to tie it to Frank. This shit's got me worried, Danny. I can't get her through this while he's messing with her head. And where does it stop? Even when he goes down, we don't know how long he's gonna get and it's clear he can still get to her from the inside. So how's this gonna end?"

"It ends when you say it ends, son. Frank's in prison and he's gonna be there for a long time. He'll keep messing with your head as long as you let him. Bring me or Kieran any suspicious mail and let us vet it. Don't set up voice mail and tell Em not to answer any calls where she doesn't recognize the number. Cut the cancer out of your lives and start living. Otherwise Frank wins. The best way to stick it to him is to lead a long and happy life with the woman you love." This was Danny's epic advice but he didn't know what it was like to have failed someone you loved and having them hurt because of it. It would always be my sin to bear and I couldn't fuck up again.

"That's easier said than done, Danny. I'm fucking terrified of letting her down again," I admitted.

"Son, fear lives in the dark. Drag it into the light and you'll see there was never anything to be afraid of in the first place. You tell Em how you're feeling?" he asked, frowning.

"No. She doesn't need to know all the shit going through my head. It's my job to take care of her. She needs to know that I've got this handled," I said.

"Bollocks. She ain't some wallflower that needs wrapping up in cotton wool. That girl had the brass balls to stand up and walk away from that fecker long before she had you behind her. I'm telling you straight that you keep bottling shit up like you have been and not talking to her about it and you'll end up losing her. Holding on to this anger is gonna eat you alive. So I think it's time we brought someone in to fix your noggin and while we're at it, you need a manager."

"I don't need a manager, Danny. I've got you, and I sure as shit don't need some fucking pansy-arsed head doctor," I shouted at him.

Taking the cigarette out of his mouth, he turned toward me, his face a picture of anger. "Don't you fuckin' bark at me," he yelled. "If I tell you we need something then we fecking need it."

"Why can't you manage me?" I asked, unhappy with all of this.

"What the fuck do I know about managing? It's a full-time job, and I'm out of my depth. I'm a trainer not a manager. We're going into the big leagues now, and we need someone who knows what they're doing," he said.

"I can't afford to pay someone," I admitted. There were

lots of things that I needed before I could afford to hire someone full-time.

"Don't you worry about that," he reassured me. "I need someone to organize fights for some of the kids. I've got some good prospects round here so don't be thinking you're anything special," he warned me, which made me smile grudgingly. "Pretty soon you'll be able to afford your own guy, but for now you can borrow mine. I'll keep him on staff until you can afford to take him on."

"Fine," I huffed, "but no fucking shrink."

Danny sighed deeply. "There ain't no shame in it, boy" he reassured me. "You want Em to get counseling for what she went through, right? You gonna think less of her for doing it?"

"Of course I won't," I said, pissed that he would even suggest it. "But it ain't the same. You know it ain't. Real men don't see fuckin' shrinks."

"What a load of shite." He laughed. "Real men ask for help when they need it, and we're both in uncharted territory here, kid."

I didn't agree with him but I didn't argue either. It still sounded like the worst idea he'd ever had, but I couldn't lose him as my trainer, and if this was his price, then so be it.

"Sorry I yelled at you," I mumbled, hating that I needed to apologize.

"So you fucking should be," he admonished, never letting me off lightly. "I may be a few years older than you, but I can still kick your scrawny Irish arse, so don't you forget it!"

I compared his frail frame next to my six-foot-five-inch body and smiled. "Whatever you say, Danny."

# CHAPTER 3

As planned I met the boys later at Daisy's, Em was busy wiping down a table when I crept up behind her and tickled her. Shrieking, she jumped then turned around and smacked me with a wet dishcloth.

"O'Connell, you scared the life out of me."

"Sorry, baby, I couldn't help myself." Wrapping my arms around her tiny waist, I hauled her in for a kiss. The way that some guys kiss their long-term girlfriends or wives is an absolute travesty. A kiss should never be routine, like saying hello or good-bye. Kissing the person you love should be sign language for the soul. It should say I love you, I need you, and I'm happy to see you or sorry to see you go. If you can't kiss like that, you should really keep your fucking lips to yourself. When I was done, Em rested her forehead against mine and closed her eyes, like she was already missing the press of my lips against hers.

"Baby, I'm supposed to be working. You're going to get me in trouble," she complained, but made no move to separate us.

"You don't mind me stealing a kiss from my girl, do you, Rhona?" I asked another waitress as she passed me carrying a huge tray.

"As long as I get a turn when she's done," she joked.

"Here, let me get that," I told her. Letting go of Em, I grabbed the tray, which was much too big for Rhona, and strode into the kitchen. I frowned as it occurred to me that Em must carry trays like these. They were much too heavy for her too.

"You don't have to do that, Con, but thank you," she told me. Pressing her hands against the small of her back, I could tell that the early evening dinner rush was taking its toll.

"No problem," I told her. "I'm happy to help. Hey, Mike," I said, nodding to him as he flipped burgers in the corner. He smiled as I salivated over the food laid out on his grill. I'd been dreaming about having a Daisy burger for weeks. Walking back out to put my order in with the boys, I saw Em loading up another full tray as she hurried to empty a table. Kieran had already snagged one for us, and he looked like the wait for me to come over so he could place his order was causing him real pain.

"Aren't you a bit short tonight?" I asked Rhona, watching her scurrying to help Em.

"You can say that again. Katrina and another waitress didn't turn up for their shifts. It's just us for tonight."

Nodding at the guys, I made my way over to our table.

"What's up, Con?" Liam asked.

"Can we order already?" Kieran whined, and Tommy added a "pleeease" in the style of an annoying six-year-old.

"Sorry, boys, you're going to have to wait a bit. They're slammed so I think we should give them a hand."

"Seriously!" Kieran complained. "I'm fucking wasting away here."

"Don't be a dick," Liam answered. "You're seriously going to sit there and chow down while Em's rushed off her feet?"

We all turned in unison to watch Em, and as soon as she stumbled trying to shift her weight to lift the heavy tray, I didn't need to ask the boys again. They fell over each other to get out of the booth and help her. Kieran reached her first and effortlessly lifted the tray and took it to the kitchen.

"I'll do drink refills," Liam offered.

"I'm the most likeable one of you ugly fucks, so I'll take orders," Tommy offered. Grabbing a pen and pencil from the counter, he walked over to a table of elderly ladies and turned on the charm. "What can I get for you fine and lovely ladies this evening then?" he asked, which made them giggle like schoolgirls.

Wrapping an arm around my waist, Em kissed me on the cheek and whispered in my ear. "It's lovely of them to help, but how many orders do you think they're going to mess up?"

"Don't worry, love," I replied. "I doubt many people will argue with them about it." Between us, we were good at either scaring or charming people. There wasn't much middle ground. Kissing my cheek, she left me to collect a food order at the ring of Mike's bell, and I started clearing another table.

Two hours later, I had a whole new appreciation for how damn hard waitresses work. The balls of my feet ached, and I'd had a fuck-full of watching people leave shitty tips for damn fine service. None of us spoke to each other as we studied the menu. We were all going to order the same thing—we always did—but it was good to check it out just to be sure.

A juicy, succulent Daisy burger was placed down in front of me, and three more followed for the guys.

"On the house," Rhona said, "for getting us out of a jam."

With a cup of tea and a sandwich in hand, Em squeezed onto the bench beside me. Pulling her closer, I kept one arm around her and used the other to lift up my burger, demolishing a quarter of it in one bite. She giggled as I moaned appreciatively.

"Sunshine, you should never have introduced me to these things. I'm addicted," I told her.

"A little of what you like now and then does you good," she told me. Giving her a squeeze, I plowed straight back into my food.

When she froze with her cup of tea halfway to her mouth, I looked up to follow her line of sight. Standing in the doorway was a middle-aged, dowdy-looking woman with plain clothes. She nervously clutched an old cloth shopping bag as she scanned the café, her gaze only stopping when it met Em's.

"Who's that, babe?" I asked, knowing from how she was acting that I wouldn't like her answer.

"My mother," she whispered.

* * *

The woman walked slowly toward us in a way that reminded me of Em when I first met her. For a moment, I felt a swell of pity when I thought about her experiencing everything Sunshine had. Then I woke the fuck up.

"Hello, Emily. You look beautiful," she spoke quietly.

"Hello, Mum," Em replied.

"What the fuck are you doing here?" I said angrily, as I tried to urge Em out of the booth. My huge body was wedged in the seat, and with Kieran and the guys to my right and Em to my left, both unwilling to budge, I was trapped.

"I'm sorry," she muttered, staring at the ground. She seemed to be searching for her words and was visibly shaking. "I know I shouldn't be here but I was wondering if I could speak to you alone for a few minutes."

"No fucking way!" I answered without thinking. This bitch had done enough damage. Frank might be behind bars, but the bitch was still messing with Sunshine's head just by being here.

"It's okay, baby." Em soothed me with her hand on my knee. "Let's just listen to what she has to say."

I didn't like it at all, but my girl knew her mind, and she didn't question any decisions I made about my useless bitch of a mother. I nodded to show I was okay but clenched my jaw shut, trying not to interfere.

"You've got five minutes, Mum. The guys will leave but O'Connell stays with me." This calmed me down slightly, but not by much.

"Okay," her mum agreed quietly.

Tommy, Liam, and Kieran shuffled out of the booth, taking the last of their burgers with them and shooting daggers at Em's ma the whole time. Once they'd left, she sat down gingerly at the table.

"What are you doing here, Mum?" Em asked suspiciously. "I haven't seen you leave the house in years."

"Frank's trial starts soon, and his barrister asked me to come down to London so he could go over my evidence."

"I hope you're not here to ask me for anything," Em answered. "If you want to stand up for him and lie in court, that's up to you but that animal deserves to go away for life, and I'm going to do everything I can to see that happens." Her spine stiffened as she spoke, and I couldn't have been more proud of her.

"Yes, no, I mean that's not why I wanted to come here," she answered, getting all flustered. "Frank has asked me to give you something but that's not why I came," she clarified.

"I knew you were here for him. Just give me whatever that psycho wants you to deliver and leave," Em said angrily.

"Please, Emily," her mum pleaded.

"Please what, Mum?" she replied. "Please be nice, please don't argue, or please forgive you for doing absolutely nothing while that man beat and raped me?" She didn't shout. She didn't even raise her voice at her mother. Instead she was eerily calm. Tears were streaming down her mother's face, and with a resigned sigh, Em rubbed her own tiredly with her hands.

"Just go home, Mum," Em said softly. The woman pulled a

long white envelope from her tattered bag and slid it across the table toward us.

"You have no idea how sorry I am for my part in what happened, and I don't ever expect you to forgive me, but I'd like to explain myself to you someday, and I'd like the opportunity to know you. I don't expect you to hear me out anytime soon, but can I come by the café from time to time, just to say hello and see you?" she asked hopefully.

"I don't know. You've had years to get to know me. I can't help feeling that whatever you're doing is in Frank's best interest."

"Believe me, if Frank knew I did anything other than follow his instructions, I'd be beaten black and blue when he next had the opportunity."

After a long pause of me clenching and unclenching my fists and silently willing her to tell her mother to get fucked, Em finally answered. "Fine, but only now and again, and I'm not talking about Frank," she agreed.

"What the fuck, Sunshine?" I asked her. Her only response was to link her fingers through mine and squeeze my hand tightly.

"I understand," her mum replied, "and thank you."

Slipping quickly out of the booth, her mother paused to stare at Em like she was trying to memorize her face, then dropped her gaze to the floor and walked out of the café. As soon as she was gone, Em slumped against me. Letting go of her hand, I wrapped my arms around her and pulled her in for a hug. I knew, even before she hiccupped, that she was crying because her tears began to soak through my shirt. My heart broke for her. Sunshine rarely ever cried. She was a pro at bottling up her feelings and going quiet when something was bothering her. But her ma had cut old wounds wide open, and now her pain was bleeding out. I didn't have it in my heart to complain about her giving in to her mother and allowing future contact. That conversation could wait for another day. Right now, Em needed me, and I knew only too well how deeply the wounds inflicted by a bad parent ran.

"Come on, love. Let's get you home. I'll run you a nice hot bath, you can put on a shitty chick flick, and we'll fall asleep cuddling. I saw the ghost of a smile as she sniffed back the tears and wiped her face with her hands.

"That sounds nice," she said. "Let's open the letter first though. Whatever's inside won't be good and I just want it over and done with," she said, looking at the envelope in disgust. The fact that Frank had even held it made it tainted. I wanted to snatch it away and open it when I was on my own, shield her from whatever was inside. But Danny was right. No way would she put up with that shit. Quickly, like she was ripping off a Band-Aid, she tore open the letter and pulled out a sheet of paper, folded around a single photograph. She glanced at it briefly before allowing it to fall to the table and burying her face in the crook of my neck. She didn't make a sound but the warm, wet tears against my skin broke my heart. I picked up the note with shaky hands to see what had moved her so badly. In bold black type was printed the message:

You are MINE. You have always been MINE.

The picture it came with made me want to vomit. She must have been about seventeen when it was taken. In it, she was unconscious on the floor so I assumed he'd knocked her out. What made me sick was the hand in the photo that had pushed down her shirt and her bra to caress her breast.

"What else did he do when I was asleep or unconscious? How many other photos does he have? Or worse, what if there are videos?" she mumbled into my neck.

I squeezed her to me tightly but I didn't have a single word of compassion to give her. What could I possibly say that would make this cluster fuck any better? The only thing I knew how to do when people tried to hurt me and mine was to hurt back. Without that option, I was helpless. And it was fucking killing me.

After wiping away the tears, Em went to the bathroom to clean herself up. Before she came back, the guys jumped in and I slid the letter and picture into my back pocket. There were some things they didn't need to see.

"What the fuck did she want?" Kier asked.

"She's delivering a letter Frank's sent from prison but apparently that's secondary to her being sorry for everything and wanting the opportunity to get to know her daughter better."

"You've got to be shitting me," Liam commented.

"What do you want to do, Con?" Tommy asked me.

I sighed deeply as I answered him. "It's her ma so it's her choice. But if that bitch thinks that I'll allow her to break Em a second time, she's got another thing coming."

"The sooner Frank's trial is over the better," Kieran said. "I don't think any of us will rest easy until this thing is done."

"There's something else," I told them. "Turns out that Frank took pictures when he abused Em. Now he's sending them to her to mess with us." A collection of "fucks" sounded around the table before Kieran spoke up.

"And her fucking mother is delivering them?" Kieran asked angrily.

"The last one was mailed but without Frank's fingerprints, there was nothing to tie it to him. Unless her ma testifies that Frank gave her this letter and that it hasn't been tampered with, the police ain't likely to be inclined to do anything about this one either," I said.

"So what now?" Liam asked, like I had all the fucking answers.

"We sit tight and wait for the trial. There's nothing else we can do."

# CHAPTER 4

"Con, this is Heath Earnshaw. Heath, this is Cormac O'Connell, otherwise known as Con." It wasn't often that I met people my size, but this guy that Danny introduced was almost exactly my build. With his brown hair that was almost military short and tanned skin, he could have been my stunt double. I didn't mind new people training at the gym—Danny always kept the number under control so it didn't get too busy—but something about the way he'd introduced me to him had me instantly suspicious, like I should know exactly who he was. He held out his hand and said, "Nice to meet you." Great. He was American as well. Em loved American accents, and I was insecure enough to be pissed off about him being here. My girl only had eyes for me, but that didn't mean that I wanted anyone trying to turn her head.

"How are ya?" I asked him, shaking his hand. Okay, so it might have been a firmer handshake than I'd usually use but

I was starting this pissing contest like I meant it to go on. He gave me a knowing smirk, like he was mildly amused by my childishness, and stepped back.

"Heath is your new manager. I'll carry on training ya but Heath here will be helping with your training where he can and organizing and promoting your fights." You had to be kidding me. I ground my teeth together, not wanting to disrespect Danny, but I was pissed that he thought Heath could handle my career better than he could.

"Can I have a word, Danny?" I said, needing badly to let off steam. Danny sighed, like he knew I was going to be a pain in the arse.

"Fine," he barked. "My office now. You too, Heath. This involves you." It was on the tip of my tongue to say that I needed a private word with him, but fuck it. I was pissed, and this kid was getting both barrels. As soon as the door closed, Danny pulled out a rollie and lit it. Inhaling deeply, he blew out the smoke, sighed, then let rip at me. "Right then. You've got something to say, Con, let's have it."

Crossing my arms across my chest defensively, I looked at the guy, whose face was completely stoic, then turned to address Danny. "I don't get why you think a kid, that's only a couple of years older than me, can manage my career better than you. And why an American?"

"Heath? You wanna answer that question?" Danny said.

Heath's stance mirrored my own as he tried selling himself to me. "I've been boxing since I was sixteen and promoting for almost ten years, eight years of which I've been contracted to one of the most premier sports agencies in the US.

I hold several amateur boxing titles and I have a business degree from UCLA."

Okay, so his résumé was pretty impressive, but fancy degrees didn't do anything for me. "Boxing isn't just a sport for me. It's a fucking religion. And the team I've got around me now? They're not just a team. There's no freeloaders or fair-weather players here. Every one of these boys is fucking family. Now you swan in here and expect me to let you into my family and trust you with my future. Well excuse-the-fuck out of me for being so skeptical."

"I'm not asking you to welcome me with open arms. Just give me a chance. If you do that, I'll show you what I have to offer," he replied.

"What can you do for me that Danny can't?" I asked pointedly.

"Honestly? Everything. Danny, I respect the hell out of you. What you've done, not just with Con's career, but for all the kids is amazing. But neither of you know anything about contracts, fee negotiation, promotion, merchandising..." He trailed off. "You don't have the connections to set up international and title fights, but I do."

"If you're so fucking awesome, why d'you leave your fancy job in the States?" I asked.

"My sister," he replied. "She got an internship at a company in the UK. My parents separated a couple years ago, and I didn't like the idea of her being on her own so far away, so I moved here."

Em chose just that moment to start her evening of bookkeeping for Danny. It killed me that she was still waitressing as well, but as long as we were saving for our own place, she refused to give it up.

"I'm so sorry. Am I interrupting something?" Em asked.

Danny smiled and beckoned her in as he poured her a coffee.

"Sunshine, this fella here is Heath Earnshaw. He's going to be Con's new manager," Danny informed her.

"Ah. Nice to meet you," she said to him, shaking his hand. "I'm Emily O'Connell, Con's wife." Earnshaw looked a little surprised, like maybe we looked too young to be married, but my chest puffed up with pride. With her corkscrew curly, wild blond hair, pale, soft skin, and petite frame that showed off killer curves, she was stunning. Her appearance wasn't what made her beautiful though. Warmth, kindness, and compassion poured out of my wife. She lit up any room she was in, and the fact that she had no idea how wonderful she was made her even more beautiful.

Earnshaw composed himself enough to give her a broad grin. Fuck him and his all-American white smile.

"I take it your mother was a big Brontë fan then?" she said.

"*Wuthering Heights* was her favorite book, but with a surname like Earnshaw, it would be a missed opportunity to call me anything else," he joked. Great, so they were making references to a book I'd never read, and I felt even more stupid and uneducated. If I hadn't heard of Brontë, I wouldn't even have known it was a book. I stood sullenly, though I did uncross my arms to pull Em's back into my front, then wrapped them firmly around her waist. I needed to stake my claim in case this guy started getting any ideas. I gave her a quick rundown of his background, and I silently willed her to be on my side.

"If you don't mind me asking, Heath, why take this job? Don't get me wrong, I think this is the best place in the world to work, but your background is corporate. With all your transatlantic contracts, surely London sports agencies would snap you up."

"Honestly," he said, relaxing to lean against the desk, "I'm sick of spreading my time among too many clients to meet targets. I want to be part of something special and I'm prepared to take a pay cut to see that happen. I've been following Con's career for quite a while. Danny's given me the most intensive interview I've ever had, and he's prepared to give me a go. I'd like for Con to give me a real chance to show him what I can do for his career."

Em and I both turned to look at Danny. "Don't you two look at me like that. I've said my piece, Con. Whether you use Heath or not, he's here to stay. I'll be your coach but I'm done as manager."

I looked at Em for her advice. Smiling she said, "I feel like I've just met Jerry Maguire."

\* \* \*

Em leaned against the desk, and I sat on her chair, resting my forehead against her stomach. She ran her hands gently through my hair like I knew she would, and instantly I felt better.

"What don't you like about him?" she asked me.

"He's not one of us Em, I don't trust anyone outside the family," I replied.

"You trusted me once. All of you welcomed me with open arms, and I wasn't family," she pointed out.

"You were always family. I just needed to persuade you to make it legal."

"Okay. That aside, what else?"

"He's barely older than me. What does he know about boxing that Danny doesn't?" I questioned.

"There's nothing Danny doesn't know about boxing. But, baby, Danny's an old man. He's a fish out of water with promoting and managing, and he's told you as much. Age and experience aren't necessarily the same thing either. Danny's been bookkeeping longer than I've been alive, and he trusts my work. You don't need to trust Heath. Trust Danny. Because I guarantee you, there's no way he would have recruited this guy and put your future career in his hands if he didn't see something in him."

I knew that what she was saying made sense, and she was right. I trusted Danny, and that meant giving this kid a chance. Didn't mean I'd have to like it though. Lifting my head, I pulled her down to sit in my lap. Nuzzling her hair aside with my nose, I gently kissed my way down her jaw. I felt her shiver all the way through to my bones. "Okay, Sunshine. If you think this is a good idea, we'll give it a go," I said with a sigh.

"What else is going on in that noggin of yours?" she whispered breathlessly as I drew lazy patterns on the inside of her thigh with my finger.

"You'll think I'm insecure and needy," I admitted.

"I already know you're insecure and needy. But I am too, which is why we're so perfect for each other."

"I don't like the idea of some cut, cocky American spending time with my gorgeous wife. Especially when you talk about books and education. You don't need any reminders that you could have done far better than me."

Wrapping her arms around my neck, she turned to face me. "What's a rope-a-dope?" Confused about where she was going with this, I answered her.

"It's when you trick a boxer into thinking he has you on the ropes, then you use up all your energy hitting him while he lets the ropes take the impact of the hits. When you're out of energy, he'll flip your positions and finish you off. It's what happened to me in the Temple fight."

"Who is the longest-reigning World Heavyweight title holder?" she asked.

She asked three more questions like that before I cottoned on. "You looked all that stuff up didn't you, to make me feel better about how much I know about boxing."

"No, love. I looked that stuff up because I get sick of feeling like an idiot around you and the other guys. A year ago, the only thing I knew about George Foreman was that he made grills! You're one of the most intelligent and logical men that I've ever met, and your opinion matters to me more than anyone else's. So don't belittle yourself by thinking you're any less of a person for not having a degree. It pisses me off."

"Yes, ma'am," I said, imitating Earnshaw's American accent.

Truthfully, I fucking loved how fiercely Em defended me. See-ing myself through her eyes always made me feel better.

\* \* \*

I spent the rest of the afternoon working out as much frus-tration as I could.

"Hey, Con," a familiar voice said from behind me. I stopped punching long enough to see who it belonged to.

"Albie, what're you doing here?" I asked, noting the train-ing bag slung over his shoulder.

"Danny had an opening for a couple of new members. University gym is packed during the day so Danny said I could train here," he explained.

"Good idea," I agreed.

"You looking to toughen up a bit? Student life making you a bit soft is it?" Kieran added, as he slung an arm playfully around Albie's neck.

"Rugby might not be boxing, but I'm doing okay," he an-swered and lifted his shirt. An impressive set of abs proved his point.

"Hey, fuckers, what'd we miss?" Tommy said, as he and Liam joined us, both acknowledging Albie with a nod.

"University gym is full so Albie's training here. Kieran's worried student life is making him soft and Albie proved he's got nothing to worry about. Oh, and I've got a new fucking manager from the US who's gonna get his fucking nose bro-ken if he looks twice at Em," I summarized. The group stared at me in silence.

"Don't worry about him, Con," Tommy told me seriously with a pat on the back. "If Em's gonna leave you for anyone. It's definitely going to be me."

"Come on," Kieran said to Albie, "I'll show you where the spare lockers are. You can train and watch Con put Tommy on his arse at the same time. It's quite entertaining actually."

\* \* \*

I stood under the piping hot water and willed it to take away my aches and pains. Danny had definitely been pissed at my reaction to Earnshaw because he trained me harder than he ever had, even before the Temple fight. I closed my eyes and thought over what Em had said. I needed to let this Earnshaw guy do his stuff. But knowing I needed to do something and actually doing it were two different things.

Earnshaw had a long way to go to prove himself to me. I just need to work on reining in my inner arsehole long enough to let that happen. When the water had worked well enough to turn the ache to tiredness, I switched it off and reached for my towel. I was so wiped out I hadn't even bothered to turn on the shower lights, the light from the locker room in front let me see well enough. There was no one here but me anyway. Danny wasn't done with me when Em had finished, so Kieran had given her a ride home. Only a couple of the guys had been training when Danny sent me on a five-mile run to finish out my day. He left just as I got back and I told him I'd lock up, so I was alone. At least that's what I thought until the lockers behind the shower banged loudly, like someone was being thrown against them. I smiled when I heard the unmistakable sound of two people kissing. Danny was gonna shit bricks if he caught one of the boys sneaking a girl in. A guy groaned in pure ecstasy as they bounced off the locker doors. Whoever they were, they were going at it pretty hot and heavy. Flesh smacked against flesh and teeth clashed as I stayed silent, hoping they'd be done quickly so I could get home to my girl. When I heard the sound of a second, much deeper groan, I froze.

"You feel so fucking good," the deeper voice whispered.

"Why did we wait so long to do this?" the other voice replied.

"Fuck knows," said the deep voice, "but I ain't waiting no more."

I gave them five more minutes of kissing and fuck knows what else. I was stunned to realize one of the guys at the gym was gay. I racked my brain trying to think of whose voice it could be. After five minutes of freezing my arse off, I didn't give a shit. When both their breathing became labored and belt buckles jangled as they were removed, I decided that enough was enough. Coughing conspicuously, I figured the polite thing to do was give them five minutes to leave.

"What was that?"

"Shit," the deeper voice answered as they scrambled to dress.

"Go. I'll call you later." They kissed briefly, and I heard one of them leave. "Okay. You can come out now." As soon as he said it, I knew who it was. Walking around the lockers, I confirmed my suspicions.

"Hey, Liam," I said with a nod.

"Bit cold are we?" he asked.

"Freezing my feckin' balls off actually. Speaking of which, Danny will have yours off if he catches you sneaking someone in here again."

"Fair enough," he replied. "Look, Con, what you heard . . ." He started to explain, but he was searching for words to tell me what I already knew.

"I take it you're gay then," I told him.

"I guess," he replied.

"You ever checking me out or thinking about me naked?" I asked him. He smiled at me in response and shook his head.

"You're not my type," he replied.

"Fuck you. I'm everybody's type," I answered with a smile. "As long as you ain't doing either of those things, me and you don't have a problem."

He nodded at me but still looked tense.

"You'll keep it to yourself?" he asked me. Scraping my hand over my unshaven chin thoughtfully, I leveled with him.

"Look mate, I'll be honest. I'm not keeping secrets from my wife. That being said, Em would take them to the grave."

He nodded in acknowledgment, and I watched the relief wash over his face as I promised to keep quiet.

"Seeing as we're getting everything out in the open at last," I said to him as his nervousness came back. "Who's your new boyfriend?"

"Mind your own business," he told me with a wry grin.

# CHAPTER 5

"Why the fuck are we looking at this shithole, Con?" Tommy asked me, as he climbed out of Liam's truck. Kieran and I already stood in front of a run-down old house. The windows were mostly cracked, and the small front garden was so overgrown with weeds that you'd need a flame thrower to actually get inside the place.

"It's not a shithole, arsehat," I said defensively. Tommy kicked at the rotten fence and his foot went straight through it.

"I beg to fucking differ," he argued back with a smirk. I frowned at him menacingly and, as usual, he ignored me. He never did have any sense of self-preservation. "It's probably full of druggies and squatters," he added.

"Will you shut the fuck up?" I said, angry that he was pissing all over my great idea. "I want to buy it for me and Em to live in."

Like some kind of comedy duo, he and Liam tilted their heads to the right, obviously trying to picture it as habitable. "I guess professional boxing doesn't pay as well as I thought," muttered Tommy. I sighed deeply, reminding myself that Em didn't like it when I gave Tommy a slap. Even if he deserved it.

"I know it looks a bit banged up, but the houses around all look well-kept. It's in a nice street, close to the gym, and there's a good school nearby."

"Why do you care about schools?" Liam asked.

"Shit, wait. Is Em pregnant?" Tommy chimed.

"What? No!" I added, as they bantered.

"Can you imagine how big their fuckin' kid will be!" Tommy said, ignoring me. Kieran didn't reply. He was too busy laughing at Tommy pushing my buttons.

"Right, that's it!" I announced, as I lunged for Tommy. "No one makes fun of my kid." The slippery little fucker dodged out of my way and hid behind Liam.

"So Em is pregnant then?" Liam asked, seriously.

"No." I sighed. There was a bit of me that couldn't wait to see her belly rounded with my child. It was too early yet though. "I just meant that it's a good place to call home, and there's a nice school nearby, if and when we do have a kid."

"Can you afford it?" Kier asked looking at the sales particulars I'd given him.

"It'll take everything we've got saved, but it'll be ours outright. There's no way either of us will get a mortgage for a long time, and it's cheaper than anything else I've found 'cause it's a repossession."

"Why's it so banged up?" Liam asked.

"Apparently the old owner didn't like the idea of the bank taking his house, and he fucked the whole place over with a baseball bat. Inside is worse than the outside." They all looked horrified, like that could even be possible.

"Don't worry, mate," Liam reassured me, with a pat on the back, "by the time we're done with it, it'll be Buckingham Palace."

I grinned, picturing it in my mind all finished and seeing Em's face as I carried her over the threshold of our first real home. "Listen, I know you guys all have jobs and your own training to worry about, but do you think you could give me a hand with the labor? There won't be any money left to pay anyone, and I'm going to need help with this."

"I'll redo the central heating for five minutes alone with your wife and one of her chocolate cakes," Tommy volunteered. Kieran, punched him in the arm for me.

"What? It would've hurt a lot more if he'd done it!" he said in response to Tommy's wounded expression.

"It's a good buy," Liam told me. "Property is a good investment so at least you know your money is safe. Plus you'll save rent on your crappy place. You do realize though that you could have the same size place with much less hassle if you bought a flat."

I looked up wistfully toward the house. "I know," I answered, "but I don't want a flat. I want a place that's mine from the roof to the foundation. I want a home."

Kieran nodded, knowing exactly what I meant. I spent what I guess would pass as my childhood bouncing between the haven of Kieran's ma's house and the pit that was my alcoholic mother's house. Em's shithole flat was the nearest thing I'd had to a home, but that was only because she was there.

Liam looked over the house with a careful eye, and I hoped he could see the potential that I could. Of all of us, he was the most experienced in construction. When I'd worked full-time, I did mostly carpentry. Kier was a general builder like Liam, while Tommy worked in plumbing and heating with his dad.

"We'll need to find an electrician," Liam pointed out. "This place is definitely going to need a rewire."

"How about Big Joe? I've worked with him before, and he's bloody good. I hear he's looking for a new gym as well since Joe's burned down. If we could talk Danny into letting him train at our place, he'd probably give us a good deal on the electrics," Kieran suggested.

"Wait, didn't Tommy fuck and dump his sister?" I asked.

"Who's Big Joe's sister?" Tommy said. Though I wasn't sure a first name would help him pick her out of the sea of women he'd slept with.

"Evelyn. Wasn't that the redhead you met in Brady's? The one who acts like you've got some nasty venereal disease whenever you see her, which you probably have," Kieran told us helpfully.

"Wait. I didn't fuck her, and I don't have VD."

"Yeah, try telling John that when we're doing up Con's house together," Liam chuckled.

"Fuck. Can't you find someone else?" whined Tommy.

"We'll see," I told him, though I liked the idea of working with someone who would keep Tommy's mouth in line. "If you didn't sleep with her, why does she hate you?" I asked.

"None of your fucking business," he returned.

Now I was intrigued. Usually Tommy didn't give a crap who knew his business. This girl must be special if he was clamming up. I shrugged like I wasn't interested. I'd just ask Em about it later. She'd get it out of Tommy soon enough.

\* \* \*

An hour later everything went to shit. I'd stopped by our place to grab a snack before going to collect Em from the café. Out of habit I emptied the mailbox but as soon as I saw the brown padded envelope I knew it was another gift from Frank. It was addressed to Em but I tore it open anyway. Out fell a polished wooden box and I opened it to see a diamond ring that looked pretty fucking expensive. In with it was another typed note that simply read:

I WAS SAVING THIS FOR YOUR BIRTHDAY

I never made it up the stairs. Slamming the box shut I headed straight for the police station.

\* \* \*

"Tell me you're fucking joking," I said to the pale-faced policeman opposite me.

"Please don't swear, Mr. O'Connell. We're on the same side you are, but there really isn't anything we can do. The hallmark on the ring tells us who made it, but we've telephoned the company and they sell thousands of these rings every year. They keep track of sales but not who purchased each individual product. We can test the box for fingerprints, but given that Mr. Thomas's fingerprints didn't appear on the letters you've brought, it's unlikely that we can trace this back to him."

"So he can just get away with harassing my wife like this?" I shouted.

"If you can get some proof that the harassment can be traced back to Mr. Thomas then we can assist you in taking out a restraining order, but that's really all we can do."

I pinched the bridge of my nose as I tried to refrain from telling him to go fuck himself. "Can you test it for prints anyway, please?" I said finally.

"Of course," he agreed, taking the ring box back. "I'll let you know if we find anything."

I walked out of the station and called Kieran from my new phone, a perk Em had insisted on after my title win.

"Can you do me a favor and give Em a ride home from work tonight? I need some time in the ring," I asked him.

"No problem. I'll see you later," he agreed and hung up. There was no way Em was finding out about Frank's latest stunt but fuck knew I needed to hit something if I had any chance of hiding this from her.

* * *

The thump of the bag echoed across the nearly empty gym. I'd been smacking the shit out of this thing for over an hour but it wasn't working. I was still as pissed off and as pumped up as when I started. To calm my rage, I needed the satisfaction that only the crack of knuckles across flesh would give me. Ignoring the gloves by my side, I stuck with the dirty wraps I'd found at the bottom of my locker. They didn't smell too good but they protected my knuckles at least. I needed Kieran or Liam to spar with me to take the edge off but the place was empty. Heath Earnshaw chose just that moment to walk out of Danny's office. He'd do nicely.

"Earnshaw," I called out. "You got a sec?" He looked shocked, if not a little bemused, that I was talking to him.

"Do you have any training gear with you?" I asked.

"Sure," he replied. "Why?"

"Wondered if you fancied sparring?" I asked innocently.

"Sure," he replied. "Just let me change, and I'll be there." I shadowboxed patiently while I tried to calm down.

He wasn't gone more than five minutes, but as he strolled confidently toward the ring, everything about him, from his tanned skinned to his all-American perfect white teeth got on my nerves. Even his training gear looked new and expensive compared with our raggedy old stuff.

"How long you been boxing?" I asked as we danced around the ring.

"Since I was about sixteen. My old man taught me."

"He anyone I would've heard of?" I asked curiously.

"Nah. He never did it to compete. He just wanted me to be able to take care of myself. I won a few amateur titles when I was a teenager but I was never good enough to go pro."

I started out with a few combinations to test his mettle. Kieran was a better sparring partner because he could read me. We'd had a lifetime of training together, and he often knew what punch I'd throw before I did. This guy wasn't half bad though. He picked up the pace, and we were throwing a few combinations back and forth when a rogue left hook clipped me with more force than he'd intended. It was unexpected and knocked me off my feet.

"Sorry," he said good-naturedly, offering out his hand to help me up. When I shook my head in refusal, he looked a little worried.

"Don't sweat it," I told him with a calm I didn't feel. I jabbed at him a couple of times, and he responded in turn with a couple of his own combinations. Our friendly banter of a few minutes ago was ancient history, and the tension between us was palpable. It was wrong to blame him for what pissed me off but my rage had no sense of direction. I guess it was in me to hide it from Em, but everyone else lately was fair game. Twenty minutes into our session and I'd made it clear that he was out of his depth. We'd passed what could respectively be called sparring long ago. For the most part, Earnshaw just kept his guard up, jabbing at me when he could, while I used him like a human punch bag. He knew what I was doing, and although the look on his face was murderous, he didn't call me out on it.

"If the job is a bit out of your league, Earnshaw, there's no shame in admitting it," I taunted him. I was basically asking him if he'd had enough. Hell, I was practically daring him to quit. I'd smacked him around a fair bit already but he looked me straight in the eye when he told me to go fuck myself.

"If you're too chicken shit to take on major professional fighters, there ain't no shame in that either."

Fuck him. I'd show him exactly how out of his depth he was. Dancing around, I deftly dogged a predictable combination and delivered a right hook with the force of a freight train. The hit connected, and I felt a momentary swell of relief. If I could just do that enough times, maybe I could purge the anger and frustration that stayed with me constantly. I didn't much care about Earnshaw. Not when his eyes snapped shut, not when he flew through the air completely unconscious, and not when he landed with a smack against the canvas. I cared about what happened next.

# CHAPTER 6

"No," cried Em from across the gym. Kieran stood in the doorway behind her. Both of them ran across the room and climbed into the ring, but it was Earnshaw they went to and it fucking burned. Kieran checked his vitals while Em looked at me accusingly.

"What have you done?" she whispered.

"What have I done?" I asked, shocked. Watching Em kneeling next to him felt like betrayal. "He shouldn't be here, Em. If he can't handle a simple sparring session, how's he going to handle world-class title fights?"

"He's not here to fight world-class fucking fighters, he's here to promote your career." The fact that she was shouting at me should have made me pause. Em rarely raised her voice, let alone swore. Unfortunately for me, I was on a roll.

"Nobody made him get in the fucking ring with me. It's not my fault if the stupid bastard doesn't know when to quit."

"Bullshit! You've been spoiling for a fight for ages and you should never have let him get in the ring with you. This is on you, O'Connell, and you don't have the balls to admit it. You don't even give a shit whether he's okay or not."

"Why are you taking his side? I'm a fighter. This is what we do!" I shouted, feeling more and more pissed off by the second.

"It's not about taking sides, you arsehole. It's about right from fucking wrong. And don't you ever call this fighting. Stick any label you want on it but you've just bullied and beaten a guy who's done nothing more than try and impress you. That's not the man I married," she answered, her eyes welling up with tears.

"Maybe this is exactly the man you married," I said quietly and turned my back on all of them.

\* \* \*

"Well, you properly fucked that up didn't you," Kieran said smugly as he sat his arse down on the bench next to me.

"You're not supposed to swear in church," I answered softly.

"I drop a quid in the collection box for every time I swear. Me and God have an agreement about it," Kieran replied. I chuckled because I was pretty sure he was serious.

"How did you know where I was?" I asked him.

"After Em's kidnapping I figured that this was probably your bolt-hole for when things go to shit." He waited patiently for me to get my shit together and talk to him.

"How's Earnshaw?" I asked, scared now to know the answer.

"He's gonna have a headache tomorrow, but he's fine. You knocked him old cold but he came round a few minutes after you left."

"Em still pissed at me?" I asked with my head in my hands.

"She loves you, Con. Of course she's still pissed at you."

"I fucked up big didn't I?" I asked him.

"It was a fuck up of epic proportions. Seriously, I think this might be it for the both of you. Don't sweat it. Romeo and Juliet weren't meant to be either."

"You're an arsehole," I told him, "and you're enjoying this."

"I'm not the one who knocked out his manager and yelled at his wife. I'm pretty sure the arsehole of the year trophy belongs to you. And, yes, I'm enjoying this immensely. You making Em curse was entertainment value enough."

"What am I going to do?" I asked him.

Surprising the fuck out of me, he answered me seriously.

"Think about what she said. This shit with Frank has been fucking with your head since Em was kidnapped. You need to talk to her about it. Get it off your chest and tell her everything. Stop acting like a hard arse and let her in. You're gonna lose her if you don't."

I nodded, as I thought about what he said.

"Do you think I should crash at yours tonight? Give her some space and speak to her in the morning?"

He laughed in my face. "I know fuck all about marriage, Con, but common fucking sense tells me that you not going home to her tonight is the worst idea ever. Man up and go make nice with your wife. And whenever the urge strikes you to argue back with her, bite your fucking tongue. Unless you're saying sorry or I love you, you're basically just ringing the bell for round two."

\* \* \*

Everything I meant to say went straight out of my head when I walked through the door.

"Arsehole," was the first thing Em said as she smacked me on the chest, then surprising the fuck out of me, threw her arms around me.

"I'm sorry, baby. I'm so fucking sorry," I blurted out, as I wrapped my arms around her, holding her as tightly to me as I could.

"What's going on, O'Connell?" she mumbled into my chest.

I took a deep breath, knowing that she needed to know where my head was at. But it went against the grain to do anything but protect her and make her feel safe.

"I'm scared, Em," I told her.

"Of what?" she asked.

"Of losing you. I promised I'd protect you and I couldn't have fucked that up more royally if I tried. Now I'm doing it again. Frank's finding ways to get to you that I can't stop. I'm pissed off and frustrated and I'm hurting anyone in my line of fire because I can't hurt Frank."

Bone-wearily tired I sat down on the sofa and pulled Em to sit down in my lap. If she forgave me enough to hold me, then I wasn't letting her go.

"Why the fuck didn't you just talk to me about it," she said.

"I think you've sworn more today than any day since I met you," I answered.

"Stop changing the subject," she replied.

"Because husbands are supposed to protect their wives. It's my job to deal with my shit, not drag you down with me," I said.

"I didn't marry you for protection. I married you because I love you. If there's stuff worrying you, then I'm the one you talk to about it. Because this marriage isn't going to work if you try and keep me in the dark about important stuff. I get that you want to take care of me, I really do. But don't you think it worries me more to see you go off the deep end like this?"

"I'm sorry," I repeated, but I really did mean it. There weren't enough apologies in the world for the way I'd been acting.

"Don't be sorry, O'Connell. Do something about it. You promised me once that you'd be a better man. Well then be one. You can't solve every problem with your fist. This shit has to end now or you're going to end up in prison one day, and I really do not want to be visiting there."

"And if Frank gets to you again?" I asked her.

"Then I'll fight him off again and stay alive until you rescue me. I've lived my life in fear once before, O'Connell. I won't do it again. You can't worry about everything. Just take things a day at a time, and what will be will be. And when you get angry, hit punch bags, not people," she ordered me.

"I can do that," I agreed. I was so relieved that she hadn't just up and left me after knocking Earnshaw out that I'm pretty sure I would have agreed to anything. In all honesty, it felt like a weight had been lifted off me just by sharing with her.

I'm not the only one you need to apologize to either," she reminded me.

"I know, Sunshine," I agreed, as I rested my forehead against hers. "I'm just really not looking forward to it."

\* \* \*

The next day, I sat at the bar of the Royal Oak sipping my orange juice and lemonade. The barman had sniggered when I'd ordered it until I gave him the death stare. I was trying to be a better man but that didn't mean I still couldn't fuck with people from time to time. Any man who mocked another for drinking a non-alcoholic drink deserved to be fucked with anyway. Earnshaw sat down on the stool next to me sporting a killer black eye and looking like someone had stolen the jam out of his doughnut.

"A pint of lager please," he mumbled to the barman.

He nodded and we sat in silence as the barman poured him his drink. He reached for his wallet until I held my hand up.

"I've got this," I told him, sliding a fiver across the bar. "Do you regret coming to London?" I asked.

"I don't regret following my sister. She needed me even if she didn't know it. But yeah, I'm kind of regretting taking a

job with Danny," Earnshaw told me miserably, still not looking at me.

"Danny's the best. I know he comes over as a bit of a
hard arse but what he doesn't know about boxing ain't worth
knowing," I told him.

"It's not Danny that I regret working with. You're a lot
more of a dick than I thought you'd be." Fair play to the man,
he had a pair of balls on him. I'd knocked him into the middle of next week, and here he sat calling me a dick to my
face. Oddly, it made me like him a little bit more.

"Yeah, well, I'm genetically predisposed to be a dick.
You'll learn to get used to it," I told him, which was pretty
much my version of an apology.

"I'm not sure there's any point in sticking around to find
out," he admitted. "I'll be honest, when I came here I had
a real dream about what I wanted to achieve. Emily's Jerry
Maguire call wasn't that far off the mark. I wanted to be part
of something special. When I met Danny and found out he
was looking for the same thing, I figured this was my opportunity. You resenting my help didn't factor into my plans."

Earnshaw took a sip of his pint while I thought about
what I was going to say. Letting him in and trusting him
wasn't going to be easy but he had a right to it. Hell, after the
stunt I pulled, he could have gone to the police and probably had me charged with assault. At this point, I don't even
think he'd told Danny what had gone down.

"Do you know what happened to Em?" I asked him.

"No," he replied and turned sharply to look at me.

"Before we met she lived with her mum and stepfather.

He beat her pretty much daily. She came to university to study for her mathematics degree and changed her name but he found her. We were already married when he kidnapped and tortured her. In a few weeks, he's up for trial. He did all that to my wife, and I've never laid a finger on him. The day I acted like a fucking imbecile was the day he'd written to her from prison. It made me a little crazy, and I took it out on you." I left out the fact that she'd been raped. My baby girl wouldn't want him knowing that. But his face was ashen anyway.

"Shit, man. I'm so sorry. I had no idea."

"Are you kidding me? You have nothing to apologize for. I was out of order in the worst way, and I'm sorry. If you'll stay, I'd like to give this manager thing a go."

"That absolutely killed you to say, didn't it?" he said with a grin.

"Yeah, so make the most of it. I can't promise not to be a dick again but being a dick also means that I don't apologize often."

"How does Em put up with your moody ass?" he commented.

"Fuck knows. She owns the balls of every man at Driscoll's so be warned she'll own yours by the end of the week," I warned him.

"I've already got one sister, and she's enough of a handful. I'm not sure I could handle another," he said with a grimace.

"Em is gentle and kind. She doesn't shout or even raise her voice much. She doesn't bark orders or ask for anything but she is the strongest woman you'll ever meet. If Danny's the backbone of our family, then Em's the heart. That's why she'll own your balls like she owns ours. You'll love her and won't be able to help it."

He nodded thoughtfully as he stared into his pint.

"She's your voice of reason then?" he asked curiously.

"That and my moral compass," I agreed. "But I have a short fuse when it comes to people flirting or fucking with her. I'll work on reining that in, but our relationship will be easier if you bear that in mind."

"I don't have any interest in her other than being friends, so you have no worries on that score. She's important enough to you that I'll take her advice and consult with her a fair bit of the time but consider this my word that I won't be messing with your head that way."

"I appreciate it," I told him honestly.

"Look, if you're serious and you can get a handle on your anger management, then I think I can help you. But you need to listen and take my advice. You do that and fight like you've been fighting, and I'll take you to the top."

"Done," I agreed with a rare smile.

# CHAPTER 7

I loved to watch Em sleep. It was the most peaceful thing in the world to watch her pulse tick gently at her throat while her chest moved slowly up and down. Every protective instinct in me flared to life, like my body knew she was at her most vulnerable and it was my job to protect her.

Usually I could watch her sleep for hours. Usually. Today I paced back and forth in front of the bed waiting for her to open her eyes. I'd already been for a five-mile run to burn off some excess energy but it hadn't worked. What if she didn't like it? Today was her twenty-first birthday. I'd spent my twenty-first in a series of bars and fuck knows where after that. I had no memory after the first ten pints. Sunshine's birthday was going to be different though. With everything that had gone down this year, she needed a day filled with happiness, and I was going to give it to her. Her flushed, warm cheeks dimpled as she grinned, amused by my excitement.

"Happy birthday, baby," I whispered.

"Best birthday ever," she replied.

"How do you know? You've only just woken up," I asked.

"Because it's the first birthday I've ever woken up with you," she told me.

God, sometimes it's like she reached into my chest and held my heart in her hand, just to remind me why it belonged to her.

Her answer was rewarded with another lingering kiss before I bounded from the bed to the kitchenette, full of excitement and restless energy. I opened the oven and put the pastries I had warming on a plate, then placed them on the tray next to the expensive coffee I prayed was still hot. Frowning down, I figured the tray needed something fancy like a flower or something. Grabbing a couple of paper towels off the countertop, I folded them origami style into a sailboat and placed it next to the pastries. Placing the folded tea towel over my arm in my best imitation of a butler, I turned to look at her.

"Ma'am, breakfast is served."

I'd like to say I walked the tray through to the breakfast room but our flat was so tiny that you were literally in the bedroom/living room if you turned around in the kitchenette.

Giggling in delight she sat up against the pillows and groaned sexily when she poured the coffee.

"This is wonderful. I can't believe you did this," she squealed in delight.

"I'll be back in a minute, love," I told her. Placing a kiss on her forehead, I disappeared to get everything ready. When I came back breakfast was over, and she was in the kitchenette washing dishes.

"Hey! None of that. It's your birthday. No one washes dishes on their birthday."

"It's just another day, O'Connell." She laughed and I growled at her for not wanting more for herself today. I love that, even growling I didn't intimidate her. Mostly my acting tough just made her giggle or roll her eyes. We'd come a long way since our spectacular showdown and were closer for it. I sat down on the bed and pulled her by her wrist to sit down on my lap. Pulling a box from behind my back, I placed it in her hands. Her eyes instantly welled up, and all my fears evaporated. It didn't matter what was in the box. She'd love it anyway. She was tracing her fingers over the ribbon reverently.

"Are you going to open that or stare at it all day?" I asked, amused.

She wound her hand around the base of my neck and kissed me gently, then carefully peeled away the ribbon and tape. I swear to God, I was about to rip open the damn thing myself if she took much longer. Finally she slid off the lid to reveal a silver locket.

"Oh, O'Connell. It's breathtaking." She sighed wondrously.

"Open it up," I told her. Inside was a tiny, perfectly sized picture. Danny was in the center looking pretty pissed off, Liam was smirking, Kieran was grinning, Tommy was pulling a face, and I was smiling as I thought about what my girl would think when she saw this. To get all of us in the locket picture, we had to squeeze around Danny. We looked like a scary arse version of the Brady Bunch. Em burst out laughing when she saw it.

"This is wonderful," she told me. "How on earth did you get them all to sit for it?"

"I asked Danny to do it, and he told me to fuck off. Pleading and begging didn't work, and finally Kieran asked him what he had bought you for your birthday. Danny went a bit green and told me he'd sit for one picture and give me fifty pounds if I let him say it was a joint present."

"I would have loved to be a fly on the wall when it was being taken. I really can't imagine Danny doing this, even for me," she said with a laugh.

"Kieran and Tommy fucked about so much, Danny was just about hoarse from telling them off when the picture was taken. He told the photographer he'd stay for one shot, after that Kieran and Tommy wouldn't have been in it anyway because he would have murdered them. That was the picture, and the photo people sized it down enough to fit in your locket."

"Thank you so much, love. I'll treasure it. But you shouldn't have spent so much money on me."

"I spent exactly the limit we set for birthdays. The boys all chipped in so I even managed to get a couple of odds and ends in." She stared at it, running her finger gently across the picture. "It's a Celtic family locket. You got us in one picture, and I've left the other one blank. You know. In case we ever have kids."

She bit her lip, and her eyes teared up. She handed me the locket as she lifted her hair and secured it around her neck. Grabbing her hand, I pulled her to her feet and toward the bathroom.

"Time to get dressed. There's one more thing you need to see," I told her and with a quick kiss and a tap on the arse, I left her to get ready.

* * *

"Okay. Open your eyes. What do you think?" I took my hands away and let her look. This was almost as nerve-wracking as asking her to marry me. Back then I was asking her to forget all the crap surrounding me and imagine a better version who'd made something of himself. I was asking her to take a chance on me. Now I was doing the same with this house. Tommy was right. It was a shithole. But when I was done, it would be a palace. A home for the two of us no one could ever take away. I stared at her expression, looking for any sign at all about how she felt.

"I love it," she whispered, looking up at it in awe. I let out a deep breath I hadn't realized I'd been holding.

"I know it doesn't look like much now, but imagine if I cleared out and repaired the front garden, put in new windows and new fencing. Liam and I have gone over this place inch by inch, and the roof is sound. With a bit of hard work, it'll look great."

I was rambling now. She'd already agreed to it, so I have no idea why I was giving her the hard sell.

"Can we afford it?" she asked, her eyes full of wonder.

"It'd take all our money and then some. But I've worked

out a loan with Danny for what we need, and we can pay him back with the rent money we'll save on our flat. We'll have to fix it up on a budget but the boys have offered to help with the labor."

With a squeal she threw her arms around my neck and kissed me loudly. "I can't believe you found this place. It's going to be amazing! I know I can't do any building work but I can clean, strip wallpaper, and paint," she babbled excitedly. "Ooow, we could go and get some paint samples today," she suggested.

"We haven't even had an offer accepted yet," I pointed out with a chuckle.

"I know, but there's nothing wrong with planning ahead. Can we look inside?"

"Sure. The agent is meeting us in a few minutes to show us around. It's pretty rough inside, but the rooms are a nice size. You just have to use your imagination."

"I can do that," she whispered as she smiled at me adoringly. Her eyes were full of everything I'd felt when I'd first seen the place, and I knew she was imagining our future in a real home of our own. My heart was so full I felt invincible. The way she was looking at me, you'd think I'd built this place brick by brick myself. I'd spend the rest of the day trailing after her doing whatever she liked just to keep that look. With another squeal she covered my face in tiny kisses, making me laugh, until a discreet cough sounded behind us.

"Are you here for the viewing?" a skinny kid who looked about my age asked.

"Yes, please," Em answered. She was lit up inside and

practically radiated happiness. People couldn't help but be charmed by her natural warmth, and he was no exception. He smiled broadly at her and with a wink said, "Let's go and check it out." My crossed arms and fierce glare told him that I wouldn't tolerate another wink, and he got the message as he messed around with the keys nervously. Rolling her eyes Em pulled on my arms until I uncrossed them and clasped her fingers between mine. She was used to me getting territorial around her but she really had no idea how many hungry looks followed her around. The agent used his shoulder to push open the front door, past a mountain of junk mail, then fussed about brushing the dirt and paint chips off his suit. The previous owner really had gone to town with a baseball bat, and literally everything would need replacing but it didn't matter. The more we looked, the more Em fell in love. By the time we were done, there were stars in her eyes. Having realized that flirting with Em was hazardous to his health, the agent couldn't get out of there quick enough. He told us to call the office if we wanted to make an offer. "I'll be in touch," I promised him menacingly, mostly just to fuck with him, but he practically wet himself as he hightailed it back to his car. Em was so caught up in the house she didn't notice. It was going to be a hell of a day.

* * *

"Can we stop by the gym on the way home?" I asked her. "I forgot to grab my dirty kit, and my wraps need washing and drying by tomorrow."

"Sure" she replied, happily. I looked at my watch and slowed my steps a little. Kieran was expecting us at five o'clock, and I didn't want to mess up the surprise by getting there too early. From a distance I could see Tommy standing sentry at the door, though Em was too busy chatting about paint colors to notice him. He lifted his hand in a wave to me then hurried inside. I opened the door of the gym and stood behind her as she climbed up the stairs. She still didn't notice that anything was amiss until the boys shouted "surprise." Kieran yanked on a rope, pulling back the net they'd tacked to the ceiling and dozens of colorful balloons rained down on us. I'd warned Tommy and Kieran both that I'd kick their arses if this surprise had turned out to be shite. I seriously owed them one for the fantastic job they'd done, though it probably hadn't hurt that Tommy's ma, Mary, had been on hand to oversee the proceedings. The room fell silent as everyone looked to Em who burst into big, fat, ugly tears.

"Shit, I knew she wouldn't like it," Tommy said.

"Well, it ain't my fault. I told Con we should 'ave got her one of them sexy male strippers like in *Magic Mike*," Kieran replied.

"*Magic Mike*," breathed Mary wistfully, looking a bit flushed. I bit back a smile as Tommy and Kieran grimaced at Mary, horrified at the thought of one of their ma's getting horny over Channing Tatum.

Rubbing Em's back as she buried her face into my chest, I knew these were happy tears. As usual Mary was the first to barrel over with a hug.

"Come on now, lovely girl. No more tears on your birthday," Mary admonished as she peeled Em off me and stole her for a hug.

"Thank you all so much," Em told everyone, smiling through the tears. "I can't believe you all did this!"

"We did the balloons," Tommy said, indicating himself and Kieran with a big grin.

"That right?" Liam asked him, and Tommy's dad didn't look too happy at being left out either.

Rolling his eyes, Tommy mumbled, "We may 'ave had help."

"You've all done a wonderful job. I love it," she praised them, giving each of them a hug and a big kiss. For the first time, possibly ever, I didn't get territorial about her showing affection to the lads. Happiness practically radiated from her, and I knew, watching her work her way around the gym, that she wouldn't be back by my side until she'd said hello and thanked everyone in the room.

A few hours later and I collared Kieran as he was wrestling with Tommy over the last chocolate cupcake. He had Tommy in a headlock as I reminded him we were meeting in Brady's at ten o'clock. "No problem. I'm sharing a taxi with the guys so we'll meet you in the downstairs bar," he told me.

"Earnshaw still coming?" I asked, still feeling guilty about acting like a complete eejit toward him.

"Yeah, but he's bringing his kid sister so he'll meet us there."

"Seriously, arsehole, you're cutting off the blood supply

to my brain," complained Tommy as he tried to get enough leverage to punch Kieran in the kidney.

"How'll you know if it does any damage?" Kier taunted back.

"Fuck you! Let go, and you can have the last fucking cake, lard arse," Tommy said.

"You snooze, you lose ladies," Liam muttered as he reached behind them both for the cake and devoured it in two bites.

"Motherfucker," Kieran exclaimed, slack-jawed at Liam's audacity. He let Tom go and they both scowled at Liam before pouncing on him. Liam was a big fucker, and instead of taking him down as they intended, he just dragged them both across the floor. Rolling my eyes at the losers, I said my good-byes and grabbed my girl.

"Wait!" Kieran yelled as Em was kissing Mary good-bye. Most people had gone, and I frowned trying to work out what he wanted with Em. Liam reached under the table to grab a box. It looked like a toddler had gotten hold of paper and tape and had decided to cover the whole thing as much as they could before it ran out.

"This is from all of us at Driscoll's," Liam told her. Em bit her lip and said nothing and I knew she was trying not to cry again. She handled the parcel reverently as she searched for a gap in the tape. Seeing there wasn't one, she reached into her pocket for her keychain with the fold-out scissors.

"You are seriously the most organized woman I've ever met," Kieran joked.

"Come on, Em. Hurry up," Tommy grumbled.

"Why are you rushing her? You already know what's in there," Kieran retorted.

"I wanna know if she likes it," Tommy argued.

"Why wouldn't she like it? It's a brilliant idea."

"Oh my God," Em whispered. I was so focused on the two arsehats arguing that I hadn't realized that she'd already opened it. Peering over her shoulder, I saw her pull out the emerald green robe that matched my own. The words "Mrs. The Hurricane" were emblazoned on the back in thick black letters.

"It's silk, mind, so you'll have to be careful not to get stains on it," Tommy informed her matter-of-factly, watching her cheeks color.

"Way to fuck up a really good present," Liam chimed in, smacking Tommy on the arm.

"Oww! That really hurt," Tommy moaned.

"Man up," Liam said with a chuckle.

"Thank you so much guys. I love it," she told them and, handing me the box, wrapped her tiny arms around all three of them.

"Well, you know," Kieran said with a shrug, as they all hugged her back, "you're our girl. Happy birthday, Sunshine."

# CHAPTER 8

I couldn't keep my eyes off her. I hadn't been able to all night. Nikki's gift to Em had been a fitted black dress and black heels. If Nikki hadn't gotten ready at our place, making sure Em was halfway tipsy before we got out the door, I don't think she'd have worn it. I'm so fucking glad she did. It was definitely the most revealing thing she'd ever worn, and I loved it. My cock, which had been semihard since she walked out our bedroom door, loved it as well.

"I'm having such an amazing night," she shouted at me. If she was tipsy when she left, she was definitely well on her way to being hammered now.

"Me too, baby," I replied.

"You know, O'Connell, you've been talking to my boobs all night," she replied.

"I know, Sunshine, but we're married now. It means I'm

legally entitled to stare at your tits every time you wear something hot and not get punished for it."

She thought about this really hard for a moment. "I don't recall that being in the small print of our marriage certificate but I'll take your word for it."

I patted my knee, and she sat down in my lap with a thump, making me smile. Damn she was cute when she'd been drinking.

"Great, the one place I go to kick back on my only night off, and you're here."

We both turned our heads to see that bitch Em waitressed with.

"Seriously, Katrina, what is your problem with me?" Em confronted her, and I knew she'd never have been in her face if she'd been sober.

"What's my problem? Where do I start? How about the fact that you looked me up and down the first day you started and pinned me as a slut without knowing a thing about me. Do you even know how you look at any sexually confident girl?"

"So the fact that you're always late, if you turn up to work at all, isn't enough reason to dislike you? You know, it's me who covers when that happens or when you're not doing your job properly," Em retorted but without much conviction.

"If I'm even less than one hundred percent, it's usually because I'm exhausted, and in case you haven't wondered why I've never been fired for taking time off at short notice, it's because Rhona and Mike are good people who took the trouble to get to know me before judging me."

"Look, I don't know what's been going on with you, but you're not the only one with problems."

I honestly never thought about how Em saw other women, didn't really give a shit either to be honest, but there was no way this girl was fucking up my wife's birthday, if she hadn't already. "Look, whatever you have to say to Em can wait until another day. Her twenty-first fucking birthday ain't the time to do it."

"No, it's okay, O'Connell," Em said looking pretty white and seeming a lot more sober than she had a few minutes ago. "Baby, would you go and get us some drinks?" she asked me.

"Uh, no," I replied. "Darlin', I ain't leaving you alone for some bitch to rip into you as soon as I'm gone."

Rolling her eyes at my stubbornness, she asked the girl to join us. Looking suspicious and a little less pissed off, Katrina sat down.

"I'm sorry if I ever made you feel that way, and you're absolutely right. I have been judging you. Thing is, O'Connell was my first but I was beaten and called a slut every day for as far back as I can remember for doing things like wearing strappy tops with no sleeves or leaving my underwear on the dryer. When that's your benchmark for slutiness, I guess it's easy to judge. I should have taken the time to get to know you. I'm sorry."

"Shit. Are you always this fucking nice? You apologizing never occurred to me so now I'm pissed off with nothing to do about it."

"Welcome to my world," I chuckled humorously and

sipped on my beer. Em smiled tightly at Katrina but I had a feeling she was beating herself up over what this girl had said.

"If it makes you feel any better, I was lying when I said you'd smell your husband's aftershave on me if you ever let him out of your sight. I was just trying to get a rise out of you. I don't mess with married men," she admitted to Em, and I was horrified. I don't care how badly Em had judged this girl in the past, but making a wife think her husband is going to fool around behind her back is a low blow.

"Thanks," Em replied with a half-smile, "but that didn't really bother me that much. My husband wouldn't cheat on me. But it's nice of you to say so."

"Are you for real? I thought judgy Emily was bad. I'm not drunk enough to deal with sorry, sweet, sugary Em. Let's just agree that we're not gonna be best friends any time soon. I'll stop being bitchy if you stop being disapproving, and we'll see if we can go a whole shift at least pretending to be nice."

Man, this girl sucked at being nice almost as much as I did. She seriously needed to spend more time with Em. No doubt Em was racked with guilt for misjudging this girl.

"Okay," Em said, still looking tortured.

"I'll see you at Daisy's then," she said standing up from the table, "and happy twenty-first."

She walked away, and Em sighed deeply.

"Hey, no browbeating today. It's your birthday so let's dance."

Lifting her off my lap, I let her guide me through the throng of people to the dance floor, my hands resting on the gentle curve of her hips to make sure I didn't lose her. I felt her tighten up as we moved our way through everyone. Even drunk she struggled to fight being a natural introvert. A lifetime of trying to blend into the background didn't change just because she'd become my wife. Staying behind her, I stoked my hands up and down her hips, moving us to the beat as I nuzzled my nose gently against her neck and she shivered. It was too loud to talk without shouting but I didn't need words. The scent of vanilla had me captivated, and I couldn't have gotten closer to her if I tried.

"What's up, bitches?" Tommy shouted as he parted the crowd like Moses at the Red Sea. There aren't words to describe what he did on the dance floor. The cheesier the song, the more outlandishly he danced, and the girls loved him for it. Only when he was creeping out of their bed the next morning did they realize what kind of a player he really was.

Watching Nikki, Albie, Ryan, and the others flood the dance floor was my first warning that I was about to lose my excuse to hold Em close. When the opening bars of "We Are Family" by Sister Sledge sounded, the DJ took to the mike. "Yo, ladies and gentlemen. Let's give it up for Em out celebrating her twenty-first birthday." We whooped and hollered as Em reddened like a tomato. "Join her and her friends on the dance floor, and if you've got it, shake it."

The music blared, and I rolled my eyes knowing that this was Kieran's doing. Usually when Tom got going, I ran for cover, but as I watched Em's face light up with happiness, I figured if you can't beat 'em, join 'em, and shook my arse so bad I gave even Tommy a run for his money. By the time the song ended, we were all hot, sweaty, and laughing our arses off. One song morphed into another but no one was in a hurry to leave. Tommy had already caught the eye of some girl, and by the way he danced, with her between his legs and pressed up against his chest, it wasn't hard to imagine how the night would end for both of them.

"What the fuck . . . ?" said a voice to my left. I turned to see Earnshaw staring daggers at Tom.

"She your girl?" I asked.

"My sister," he answered through clenched teeth. Kieran, who'd been eavesdropping on our conversation, sniggered while I winced. Monday morning at the gym was going to be pretty interesting if Tom humped and dumped Earnshaw's sister. Kier and I both turned to look at her. She was quite pretty, really. Long, tanned legs, nice, curvy figure, and straight brown hair. Em would probably call it some weird shade but as far as I was concerned, women's hair came in six colors: black, brown, blond, red, white, and gray. Hers was brown.

"Amy, can we have a word please?" Earnshaw asked, and it amused me to see the tick in the side of his jaw. Fair play to the bloke. If Tom was rubbing up like that against my sister, I'd smack him first and ask questions later. His sister looked pissed to be pulled away from Tom's wandering hands, but to her credit, she did what he asked without making a fuss. Me and Kier were like old women when it came to gossip, so we were all ears when he pulled her to the side of us.

"Look, Amy, I'm really pleased you decided to come out

but I have to work with these guys so I don't want one of them hooking up with my sister," he reasoned.

"Jesus, you worry far too much. We're all adults here. Who's going to be bothered if Tommy and I have a little fun?" she answered.

"I'll be fucking bothered!" he told her, losing his temper. "You don't think I won't get a detailed and graphic account of what you two did?"

"Don't be such a fucking drama queen. If you had your way, I'd never date anyone," she complained.

"Dating, yes! Dry humping on the dance floor with people I work with, no!"

Amy crossed her arms and stared at him. I half expected one of them to start growling. It was Earnshaw who broke the standoff first, his frown morphing into a mischievous smile.

"Fine. Dry hump away, but if you leave the club with anyone but me, I'm phoning Dad to tell him that you've gone off with a man you've just met."

"You'd slut shame me?" she shrieked.

"In a heartbeat," he answered, grinning away like he knew he'd won.

"You really are a dick, you know that?" she told him.

"Yeah, but I'm a dick who loves you."

She elbowed him in the stomach on her way back to Tommy, which made him grunt. She went straight back to dancing up close and personal with our very own slut bag. Shit, if they got any closer, she'd be pregnant by osmosis. Amy was obviously showing her brother she wouldn't be pushed around, but I'd bet good money she'd be sleeping alone tonight.

"I'm so fecking glad I don't have a sister," Kieran said to us both. Earnshaw's once smug face now looked ashen as he loitered awkwardly, not dancing but trying hard to look anywhere but at his sister. Taking pity on him, I nudged his shoulder to get his attention.

"Come on. I'll buy you a pint while your sister lets off some steam." He nodded gratefully, and I turned toward Em who was still kicking it with Nikki.

"If you're going to the bar, can you get me a lemonade?" she asked, "I'm going to stay and dance."

"You had enough to drink, baby?" I asked.

"Yeah, I'm happy to stick to soft drinks now that I've danced all the tequila out of me."

Leaving her with Nikki, Earnshaw, Kieran, and I headed to the bar. The barman slid three pints and a lemonade across on a tray and I handed him a note.

Walking back toward Em, Earnshaw frowned, looking confused. "We're going back on the dance floor?" he asked Kieran. I placed our drinks down at a tall table that overlooked the lower dance floor.

"Em's been drinking, so we stand somewhere he can keep watch over her," Kieran explained. Earnshaw looked at me like I was some kind of freak with three heads, which made me laugh.

I nodded toward the girls. "See Em, cutting loose and having a good time?" He nodded in response. "It's taken a long time for her to feel that comfortable in her own skin. Even with her stepdad behind bars, she's confident and carefree because she knows that she can have a drink and I've got her back. And if I haven't, Kieran has or Tommy has. So as long as she's there, we stay here." I figured that I'd done a pretty good job of explaining how me and Em worked but he still looked at me like I was some kind of possessive Neanderthal. Whatever. I gave it a week before he watched over Sunshine as much as the rest of us.

We shot the breeze about boxing mostly while Earnshaw tried hard not to look at his sister and I tried hard to peel my eyes away from Em. Watching her dance in that figure-hugging black dress with those long, gorgeous legs that I'd had wrapped around my waist was making my cock twitch. If I had my way, she'd finish off her birthday clutching the sheets and screaming my name. A couple of the lads joined us, and Liam, who I hadn't seen much of all night, stood next to me. He shifted from side to side looking pretty uncomfortable.

"Spit it out," I told him finally. "What's on your mind?"

"Just wondering if we're still good. You know. About the other night."

"Why wouldn't we be?" I asked him, confused.

"A lot of people won't be when they find out," he admitted. Liam was usually laidback and steadfast. There was no pressuring or pushing him into doing anything he didn't want to do. He was one of us but he was also his own man, and we respected him for it.

"Look, mate, when the truth comes out, everyone who means anything to you will feel exactly the same. We love you for who you are, not where you stick your dick. Finding someone to love who loves you back is a pretty big achievement in this shitty, little world. So if you get that, be brave, and everything will work itself out in the end."

"Thanks, Con. I appreciate that," he said.

"You know you're going to have to tell the other guys eventually," I pointed out.

"I know," he said looking around wistfully, "just not today."

As our friends trickled slowly from the dance floor to our table, Tommy and Earnshaw's sister joined us. Earnshaw had gone from clenching his teeth to full-on grinding them. I couldn't tell if the look on Tommy's face was because he was really into this girl or because he was yanking Earnshaw's chain. When a beautiful redhead walked past our table and Tommy stared at her adoringly like she hung the moon, I had my answer.

"Hey, Evelyn," Liam said to her. "You seen your brother round lately? I don't have his number, and I was looking for his help with a job."

"I haven't seen him for a couple weeks but I can give you his number, if you like," she replied. They made small talk while she programmed her number into Liam's phone. When she caught sight of Tommy and Amy, she took in their intimate position and her expression became completely stone-faced. By the time anything resembling hello came out of Tommy's mouth, she was gone. When he realized that she'd seen him with his arms around another girl, Tommy looked devastated.

"Hello, love," Em said, bouncing toward me.

"Still think it's the best birthday ever?" I asked.

"Absolutely," she agreed. "I can think of something that would make it even better though," she said with a cheeky grin, then leaned over to whisper something erotic in my ear. I had us both in a cab home less than ten minutes later.

# CHAPTER 9

Slumped in the chair, I folded my arms and tried not to laugh as the newest member of Danny's dream team got comfortable.

"Can I help you, Father Pat?" I asked him as he messed around with a load of papers.

"Well, now that you mention it, Cormac, I could use a nice cup of tea," he replied as he unloaded his old leather satchel while he searched for whatever it was he was looking for. By the time I placed his tea down in front of him, he was ready.

"Now, did Danny explain why I'm here?" he asked me.

"Not really," I answered.

"Well, Danny is concerned about your difficulty controlling your temper in certain situations, so I'm here to help you talk through those issues."

"Kind of like a therapist," I clarified.

"Exactly!" he said, as he smiled broadly.

"But you're our parish priest. I don't mean to be rude but why does Danny think you can help?" I asked, intrigued and a little shell-shocked about what he might want me to do in this makeshift therapy.

"Well son, let me ask you. Would you ever lose your temper at me?"

"It's doubtful, Father," I responded.

"And if I asked you a question, would you give me an honest answer?"

"Yes," I answered.

"Well, how is it any different from confession then? What you tell me stays between us and God, and you have someone to speak to if you ever want to talk to someone other than Em."

"I don't mean to be rude, Father, but why does Danny think you'll be better than an actual psychologist?" I asked him curiously.

"Because you'll actually talk to me and I'll know when you're lying. With a psychologist, Danny thinks you'd either tell him what you think he needs to hear or not speak to him at all."

"Don't you think being angry is a good thing when you're getting in the ring?" I asked him. He put down his papers and looked at me in a way that made me feel like a clueless little kid.

"Holding on to your anger is like drinking poison and expecting the other person to die," he told me.

"That's a bit deep, isn't it?"

"Well, Buddha knows his stuff."

I let what he'd said sink in for a moment before making my first confession. "I'm not sure I know how to fight without the anger."

"As long as I've known you, it's been a big part of who you are. But you went from a good fighter to a great fighter the day you met Em, and that tells me it's the love that fuels you more than the hate." I never thought of it like that but maybe he had a point.

"Now," he said shuffling his papers as he put on his reading glasses.

"Think about the last time you reacted in an unhealthy or negative way to anger. What happened right before you got angry?" He read the question out slowly like the font was too small to read but he looked up expectantly when he was done.

I glanced down at his lap and there were several pages of questions to answer. "Father, where did you get all these questions from?"

"That Google is brilliant isn't it? Kieran sorted me out with a laptop when he got Danny that satellite TV. I tell you, I have e-mail and Twitter and everything. Absolutely marvelous contraption it is."

"You've got a Twitter account?" I asked skeptically. I didn't even have e-mail, and my parish priest-slash-anger management counsellor had a Twitter account.

"Oh yes. I have over three hundred followers."

"You're kidding?" I was stunned.

"It appears to be mostly ladies following me, which I put down to the picture of me as a younger man wearing my kilt that I tweeted. Fine set of legs I had back then so I can't say I blame them."

"But you're a priest!" I blurted out, horrified at the idea of Father Pat with his harem of Twitter followers.

"Aye," he said as he leaned over to wink at me conspiratorially. "But that's what makes me attractive, you see. I'm unattainable. They all want what they can't have." There were absolutely no words to respond to that.

"Next question. What is the one behavior you most want to avoid when you experience anger?" He read out the question slowly again, and I closed my eyes with a groan knowing that this was going to be very long and painful.

* * *

"Which one of you fuckers shot me?" Tommy whined like a little girl. Kieran sniggered next to me, making me smile. Turns out that my session with Father Pat had made me feel better. Like confession, it was cathartic, and it did me good to off-load. Of course, it wasn't nearly as good therapy as shooting Tommy in the arse with a pink paintball. When Kieran came up with the idea to welcome Earnshaw to the gym, I was skeptical. Now that I'd hit Tommy, I thought it was a brilliant idea. We were split into two teams with me, Kier, and Earnshaw on one side and Liam, Tommy, and John, a friend of Kier's looking to join Driscoll's, on the other.

"What's the plan?" whispered Earnshaw. He held his weapon tightly as he surveyed the forest ahead. You'd think he was in training for the special forces given how seriously he was taking this thing.

"I need to shoot you," I told him, and he scrambled away from me looking alarmed. Kier just about pissed himself laughing. Rolling my eyes, I explained. "The whole way here you've been stressing about how much getting shot hurts. You're so wound up now you're about ready to snap. If I shoot you, you'll know how much pain to expect, and you won't be so upright anymore." I could see by the look on his face that he knew I was right.

"Where are you going to do it?" he asked.

"Pretty much everywhere hurts," I explained. "But it's more painful the closer you get."

"I don't know, back maybe?" he suggested, nervously. Sucking in breath, Kier winced exaggeratedly.

"I wouldn't do that either, my friend. You won't sleep for a week if you can't lie down."

"Chest then?" Earnshaw suggested. I wasn't known for my patience so, while he was making up his mind, I shot him in the thigh.

"Fuck!" he whispered harshly, but to his credit, he didn't scream soprano like Tommy had. "That fucking hurt," he complained.

"Of course it did. You're getting shot. What did you expect?"

"I don't know. It's paint. I didn't expect it to hurt this bad."

"Best try not to get shot again then," Kier told him gravely. His expression neutral, Earnshaw didn't give away anything about what he was going to do next when he shot Kier in the leg.

"Motherfucker," Kier muttered. "What d'you do that for?"

"Fucking hurts, doesn't it?" Earnshaw told him with a smirk. Kier let it go, knowing they were even.

"We're supposed to be on the same team, you know," I pointed out.

"Well you started it," Earnshaw complained. "So what really is the game plan?"

"Draw them out and shoot Tommy as many times as you can," Kier told him.

"Why Tommy?" he asked.

"Because it's fun," Kier and I both said together.

"Besides, Liam and Big Joe don't even flinch when they get shot. Tommy screams," Kieran said. Earnshaw looked a little unsure about the plan so I leaned over to whisper to him. "Your sister get home okay the other night then?" Kier grinned, seeing what I was doing, while Earnshaw grimaced.

"Yes, thanks," he replied through gritted teeth.

"You know I saw him and your sister swapping numbers along with saliva the other night. They could even be dating already," Kieran informed him. Of course it was all total bollocks. As far as I knew, they hadn't spoken since that night when we'd all bumped into Evelyn.

"She only met him five minutes ago, and she needs to be focusing on her new job. They are *not dating*," he informed us emphatically.

"If you say so," Kieran said in a tone suggesting he didn't believe a word of it.

"You know you could do worse for a brother-in-law. I'm sure he'd behave himself if she ever brought him to the US to meet your parents," I added. We could see the wheels in Earnshaw's head turning as he envisioned his sister married to Tommy, and I was surprised he didn't crack the gun because he held onto it so tight.

"How do we flush him out?" he asked us, and I fist-bumped Kieran behind Tom's back. Our work here was done. Tommy was so getting shot in the arse again.

"I'll go round to the left and push him toward you as you come round on the right. He's quick. So once you got a shot, you have to be fast." We nodded and moved stealthily through the woods as we followed Kier's directions. I could just about see the top of Liam's head behind a bush. Knowing him and Big Joe, they were probably waiting for Tommy to get taken out, so we'd expose ourselves before they made their move. Poor Tom was always the bait without even realizing it. As far as he was concerned, the SAS were missing out on his skills big time.

"Tommy?" Kier called out in a singsong voice in the distance. "Come and get me, Tommy. You know you want to shoot me!" Kier taunted him for a few minutes but Tommy wasn't biting.

Finally after a few minutes of quiet, Kieran called out to him again. "Listen Tom. If you've got your hands full now with Earnshaw's sister, you mind if I take Evelyn out on a date? That's one fine-looking Irish woman I wouldn't mind taking home to meet me ma. Shame she doesn't want you now she knows about your STDs."

"Keep your filthy fucking hands off Evelyn, and for the last time, I don't have any fucking STDs!" Tommy shouted indignantly.

"Bingo" I whispered as the three of us opened fire at the bush where Tommy's call had come from. He screamed like he was being murdered, and even getting shot by Liam and Joe was worth it. Today was turning into a good day, even if we'd probably have to carry Tommy home. Maybe I needed to buy one of them guns so every time he flirted with Em I could shoot him in the arse again. The idea was tempting.

# CHAPTER 10

"Look at the state of you!" Em shrieked when she saw Tommy's back. Of course the little fecker had to come into the office without his top on.

"We got shot too!" complained Kieran but Em tutted, knowing Tommy had probably taken most of the hits and why. She fussed over him and mothered him as she made him a cup of tea. Of course Tom really didn't help himself by giving us the finger the minute Em's back was turned.

"Some people never learn," Kier said with a sigh. He was probably dreaming up some more ways he could torture him. Tommy was sitting in Danny's seat again so Kieran and I sat there expectantly, waiting for the fallout as the old man shuffled in through the door. Preempting him, Em handed him a steaming hot cup of coffee, and he graced her with a rare and loving smile, before turning his scowl on the rest of us.

"Heath's got some good news about Con's next fight so I want you all to listen up. Tommy get out of my feckin' seat. Now!" he demanded.

"But, Danny," he whined, "I'm really badly injured!" He turned his downtrodden expression toward Danny, who was the least sympathetic person I had ever met.

"I don't give a feck if you're actually bloody dying. Unless you're planning on donating one of those organs to me, get out of me feckin' chair." Looking like Danny had kicked him, he made it out of the chair to stand next to Kier. Em brought the rest of us cups of tea, and I patted my knee when she was done, loving that all the seats were taken so that she'd sit on my lap. I wrapped my arm around her tiny waist, pulling her in close, and inhaled her vanilla scent. The door opened and closed as an excited Earnshaw bounded in. Heath was cautious, reserved, and stoic most of the time so to see him excited was quite funny.

"I'd just like to announce that I'm an absolute genius," he told us. Danny rolled his eyes and glared at us, like we'd somehow infected Earnshaw with our self-confidence.

"All right, genius, want to tell us why?" I asked.

"I've got you a title fight with Rico Temple."

"The same Rico Temple who kicked Con's arse and swore he'd never give him a title shot?" Tommy asked.

"You know any other Rico Temples?" Earnshaw responded. I grinned at Kieran because this was my chance for redemption. The exhibition against Temple had been an absolute travesty. This time I would show Danny what I was really made of.

"That's good news, Heath," Kier congratulated him. "How d'you get him to agree to it?"

"Pretty much the same way Kieran got us to shoot Tommy," he answered, and he and Kieran smiled conspiratorially. "It's only fair to warn you though, Con," he told me. "You fuck up this fight, and you won't get another chance at Temple. His star is on the rise, and he's telling everyone who'll listen that he's already knocked you out. You were just too stupid to go down."

"That right?" I said smiling. There's nothing like going into a fight as the underdog. Temple thought he knew me, knew my play because he'd seen me on a bad day. I was going to bring his whole world crashing down around him. Danny looked stern and not too happy at all. "What's wrong, Danny?" I asked him.

"Not sure if your head is in the right place yet. Physically you'll be fine but one sort of goes hand in hand with the other."

"We'll make sure he's ready," Kieran reassured him, and it was pretty obvious how much he wanted me to take on this fight.

"When's all this meant to be going down anyway?" Liam asked.

"December tenth," Earnshaw answered, and the whole room went quiet.

"We can't take the fight," I told him, my voice echoing in the silence.

"Why not?" he said, alarmed.

"The trial for Em's stepfather Frank starts a month before," I told him.

"Fuck," Earnshaw muttered. "What're the chances of Temple changing the date?" Kieran asked, knowing there was no way I could do that to Em.

"Zero. This is it. Take it or leave it. You'll get another chance at the title again but you can kiss it good-bye for another three or four years."

"Shit," I added, trying to remember all the stuff that Father Pat had told me as I started losing hold of my temper. Finally, after counting to fifty in my head, I made a decision. "Then we wait three or four years. Nothing is more important than Em."

* * *

Four weeks to the day that we made an offer, the run-down, ramshackle shithole that we'd fallen in love with became officially ours. It had been torn down and beat up but I intended to rebuild it, and Em would give it a soul. The irony that the house mirrored our own situation was not lost on me.

After picking up the keys from the agent we walked toward the house through the park. When we got to the bench, Em tugged on my hand as she sat, pulling me down next to her. Without needing to be asked, she cuddled her body into mine and rested her head on my chest. Watching her as she listened to my heartbeat, I felt safe. Is that odd? For a woman to make a man feel safe?

I don't mean to say that I was afraid of the people around me. I could take care of myself well enough that the prospect of ever getting mugged or jumped didn't bother me. Most of the time my only fear was of losing Em. She was the beating heart of me that walked around outside my body. She was my greatest strength and my Achilles' heel. The only way to hurt me was to hurt her.

"You know you need this fight so why are you procrastinating?" she asked me.

"Procrastinating means putting it off, I take it?" I queried with a raised eyebrow.

"Yes, love," she said with a smile, "That's exactly what it means." She slid her fingers back and forth between mine, and I watched her tiny, pale hands, against the contrast of my own dark, calloused hand. My ring was missing from her finger and she wouldn't let me replace it, but truthfully I'd lost hope of ever getting it back. It amazed me every day that someone so small and fragile could be so strong and brave and I couldn't find the words to explain that I wasn't giving up. I was standing my ground to stay and protect what was mine.

"I know why you don't want to take the fight," she told me. "I know, but you're making the wrong decision. This trial could be adjourned or it could be over in a couple of days, and then what? You've thrown away your shot at the title for nothing."

"And what if the trial goes ahead. What kind of man am I to leave his wife to go through that alone? The fact that I couldn't protect you once is something I have to live with for the rest of my life. But to let you stand there and face him by yourself is something I won't ever do. So please, baby, please don't ask."

"But I'm not alone, O'Connell. Neither of us are. We both have enough family that I'll practically have an army behind me. It doesn't matter what Frank did because I will be in the front of that courtroom making sure that he never gets the chance to do it ever again. And when I'm done, I'm going to be exactly where I should have been last time. In the front row, ringside, watching my husband raise his title belt."

A swell of pride ran through me as I imagined the look on Em's face if I did exactly that. She was asking me to sacrifice my place at her side so that I could stand before her and lay the world at her feet. I didn't like it. Not one little bit, but Em was the smart one. If this was what she wanted, I'd swallow the bitter pill and give it to her.

"Okay, love. You win. I'll fight." She squealed with excitement. "There are rules. Lots and lots of rules," I warned her.

"I wouldn't expect anything less," she said. It humbled me that she was pleased with my decision. Frank terrified her, and she was facing him alone to offer me my dream. If there was ever a bigger gesture of love than that, I couldn't think of one, and I knew I'd change my mind about it if I thought about it long enough.

"I'll train with Kier and Danny alone, *everyone* else goes to court with you." She nodded her head at the most obvious of my conditions. "Every time the court adjourns, you call me. I don't care if it's seventeen times a fucking day. You call me. I need to know you're doing okay or it will fuck with my head." She nodded in agreement. "I want you to sign up for rape counseling. I want to take you between my training sessions. If I can't be with you for the trial, then I can be there for this."

"I don't think I need counseling, O'Connell. I'm coping with everything fine."

"Baby, coping and dealing with it are two different things. The trial is going to bring up some ugly stuff and you need to prepare for that." She snorted through the thick, ugly tears rolling down her face.

"Finally," I said, threading my fingers through her hair and pulling her head gently toward me so that I could look into her eyes. "No matter which way that sick fuck looks at you, no matter what he says, you remember that you're mine. Body and soul, just like I'm yours. I didn't know the girl you were before he did what he did, but I know the woman you are now and I'm proud. Not because I'm a fighter but because my wife was one first and she taught me how. Nothing he can say or do in that courtroom will ever change that. I need you to remember how much I love you. You can't let him inside your head. You survived, and when he goes down, he's going to get in prison everything he gave to you."

"I love you, O'Connell. You know that?" she said to me, blowing her nose.

"I love you too, Mrs. O'Connell," I whispered, kissing the top of her head. The next couple of months would be some of the hardest we'd been through, but once Frank had been put away, I had faith that the worst would definitely be behind us.

\* \* \*

"So we're on? For real?" Kieran asked me.

"I don't like it, but it's what Em wants. So, yeah, we're on." Kieran and Earnshaw fist-bumped each other, and I knew they were excited about making the most of this opportunity. It didn't occur to me to worry about whether or not I could win or how painful the cost would be to achieve that win. My body was conditioned to feel pain for so long that I didn't fear it. I worried about how much Em could endure with this trial and without me, and it bothered me that she had to try.

Earnshaw looked at me and could see my unease. "I think you're making the right decision, but that's easy for me to say because I have nothing to lose. So what do we need to do to get you through this?" he asked. I looked over at Danny, who still looked concerned. He loved Em like a daughter, and he was by her side when Frank stabbed her. But this was a world title fight, which meant he needed to be with me. I wasn't the only one who was struggling, and there was no easy fix.

"You, me, Kier, and Danny will train and everyone else stays with Em. We make ourselves as close and accessible as possible until we fight and she stays with me for every minute she's not in court," I said. Earnshaw ran his hand back and forth through his hair as he contemplated something, and I guessed he did that a lot.

"Here's the thing. Temple has one of the best boxing training facilities in the world, and its public knowledge. They don't want the underdog claiming that Temple's had unfair advantages, so they're offering you a state-of-the-art training camp in the US where you can train for the fight and acclimatize."

"We're not going," I told him. "It's bad enough we're missing the trial. I won't miss having her by my side every night," I explained.

"We're not set up here to train for this kind of fight, Con," Kier reasoned with me, but I wasn't hearing it.

"Years ago, there was none of these state-of-the-art fancy gyms. We ain't from money, and we don't need it to get where we're going. If we're doing this, then we're doing it old school," barked Danny, which was pretty much the first contribution he'd made to this discussion, and the last word on the subject.

# CHAPTER 11

We stood in what once passed as a kitchen. The sink had been taken out, and the plumbing capped. The floor was torn up, and the concrete exposed, and there wasn't a single door on the filth-laden cabinets at our backs.

"Right, lads," I said, raising my bottle of beer in the air. "Here's to one last weekend, for me at least, of beer, marital relations, and unhealthy eating before I hand Danny my balls and get training. I know you could be doing anything you want this weekend, and I thank you for spending it helping me fix up our place."

"Sláinte," I toasted, tapping my bottles against theirs.

"Any idea where to start?" asked Tommy, as he kicked at a loose floor tile.

I tipped my bottle toward Liam. "You're the expert. What do you think?"

"We've got two Dumpsters out front. Let's gut and clean

this place to give us our blank canvas. Then next week when you're training, Tommy and his dad can start the plumbing and Big Joe can take a look at the electric. I'm a fair hand at plastering, so I can get cracking when they finish. By the time the fight's done, you should be ready for carpentry and decorating so you can take over." Liam laid it all out, but a part of me worried that this whole thing would stand still while I was training but Liam caught my eye, pulling me out of my own head.

"Listen, Con, I can see you stressing already, and we ain't even started. Me and the lads, we got your back. You gotta job to do, and that job is to put Rico Temple on his arse and win us some money."

"Huh?" I grunted stupidly. From his back pocket, Liam pulled out a betting slip. "Soon as news of the fight went live, bookies started posting odds, and we all went down." Looking around, they all pulled out their betting slips.

"No pressure then," I said, touched that they believed in me enough to risk what little money they had.

"No pressure at all," said Liam with a grin. "We all bet on the other guy so we couldn't give a shit whether you train or sit around for three months getting fat. In fact we're actively encouraging Em with her baking."

"Fuck off," I told him playfully. "You guys can sit back and become fat arses. I've got work to do."

"Of course we bet on you, brother," said Kieran. "But you're not doing this for us, or for Danny or Em. You do this for yourself."

He was right but that didn't change the fact that I wouldn't be standing here on the brink of a life-changing opportunity without them.

"Of course that don't mean we're not gonna make the most of it when you do win. Ringside seats in Vegas with a hot girl on each arm sounds like a bloody good plan to me," Tommy chipped in.

"Shouldn't you be getting those STDs cleared up before you go on the hunt for more hotties?" warned Kieran.

"Fuck you and your fucking STDs," grumbled Tommy.

"Take your frustration out on the house, my little friend," Kier teased Tommy as he patted him condescendingly. "You can roll around with me when you're feeling better," he told him.

"I'd like to beat the shit out of you," Tommy told him.

"Beat the shit out of, roll around, it's the same difference. You wanna get hot and sweaty and jump all over me. I'm not gay but I understand your feelings. It's just the effect I have on people. You're not made of wood," Kieran told him matter-of-factly.

"Whatever arse munch. I've got a sledgehammer and I'm going upstairs so you'd best stay out of my way," he warned Kier.

"Trust me, little man, I have no interest in coming upstairs to see your big hammer," Kier retorted.

"You need help," grumbled Tommy, as he walked away and we fell about pissing ourselves laughing.

I glanced quickly at Liam to see if their gay references had made him feel uncomfortable but he looked as bemused as ever with them both. Mentally I chastised myself for thinking he'd be any different. The lads wouldn't change who they were or how they acted because he was gay, and he wouldn't want or expect them to. In fact, he'd probably kick their arses if they did. My only concern for him was that he was still keeping it a secret. I know he worried the news would spread when it got out, but he needed his friends around him. His parents were staunch Catholics, and as much as they loved him, when they found out there'd be fucking hell to pay.

* * *

The steam rose up from the hot bath in waves and rolled decadently up to the ceiling. The slight ache in the muscles I didn't train regularly felt good. For the first time ever, I felt like I was building something. For a guy who hadn't achieved a whole lot up until this point, a couple of days hard graft on our first real home gave me a hunter-gatherer feeling that was pretty heady.

"How's it coming on?" Em asked from the doorway.

"Looks beautiful, darlin'," I told her, watching the steam making her hair curl even tighter.

"In one weekend, you made our house a palace?" she teased.

"I wasn't talking about the house," I said. Beckoning her over, I waited until she was almost beside me before hauling her by the hips and pulling her over the edge of the tub into my lap.

"Woman, you've got curves that would tempt the angels

themselves," I told her as I ran my thumb under the elastic of her panties. She'd shrieked when I'd grabbed her but, dressed in only panties and a tank top, I didn't think she'd be too mad about the wet clothes. She moaned slightly as I gently grazed her clit, and my cock grew even harder beneath her.

"Baby, flattery really does get you everywhere," she replied breathlessly.

Jesus, I was a lucky man. Some men marry young and quickly regret their decision even faster. What was that saying again, "marry in haste, repent at leisure"? Most men don't know what the fuck they're doing but I did. I may not be a smart man, but it didn't take a fancy degree to understand that marrying Em was the best thing I'd ever done. She was strong, smart, sexy, and funny. The most intelligent woman I've ever met. There hasn't been a single moment since the day I met her where I've waivered in my belief that she was the woman for me. Convincing her that I was the man for her had been another matter.

"We have to get out," she whispered, "If we get any more water on the floor, it's going to leak through to the flat below."

"Fuck the guy downstairs. He's a dick who plays music far too fucking loud. With a bit of luck, the leak will fry the stereo equipment and the whole building will love us." She giggled until I touched my lips to hers. With kissing and coaxing, she opened her mouth slightly as she brushed her tongue against mine. Darts of pleasure went straight to my dick which was practically impaling her.

Getting her into the bath was one thing, getting her underwear off was another. Soaking wet, they weren't coming off easily and there was only one thing for it.

"Don't even think about it, O'Connell," she warned me, with the wagging finger and everything. Grinning playfully, I nipped the finger gently between my teeth, then sucked on the end to salve the skin.

"I have no idea what you're talking about," I retorted, looking like the cat that got the cream.

"We can't afford to rip off underwear every five minutes and replace it with expensive lingerie. Besides, I bought these panties in a six-pack with my first-ever wage packet from Daisy's. They have sentimental value." Maneuvering herself carefully, she somehow found a small space in the tub to place her feet and stood. Her crotch was perfectly positioned in line with my face, and the green-, purple-, and pink-striped panties suddenly became my new favorites.

Looking at me seductively, she bit her lip, hooked her thumbs inside her underwear, and peeled them down achingly, painfully slowly. Unhooking them from around her feet, I threw them into the sink just as she reached up to peel away her top. A pair of pale, perfectly formed, and glorious tits fell loose, and my willpower to resist them evaporated. Cupping both tits between my hands, I sucked and teased them until Em cried out in ecstasy. Dropping suddenly to her knees, she repositioned my cock and sank down on it, almost effortlessly.

"Jesus, baby," I cautioned as I held on to her hips to steady her. I fucking loved that she was as ferocious as I was when it came to making love. I was possessive, bossy, and probably annoying most of the time, but in bed, she fucking owned me. Who was I kidding? She was the love of my life. She always fucking owned me.

Leaning forward, she captured my bottom lip between her teeth, drawing me in for a kiss. Moving to lean back against the tub, I looked up at her blissful expression, and I hardened even more inside her. She'd found a slow, steady rhythm that was making me crazy, and I watched a bead of perspiration roll slowly down her chest until I captured it with my thumb, massaging it into her nipple. Lifting her slightly, I pistoned my hips against hers, making her cry out.

"O'Connell, I'm so close," she whispered. My own orgasm was clawing down on me like a hungry animal, willing me to set it free. I held it back, wanting Em to come first and take me with her. With one hand, I rubbed small circles over her clit, and with the other hand, I did the same to her nipple. The combination had her clenching and tightening around me until she screamed my name and milked my cock, hard. I came at the sight of her, back arched in ecstasy and hair cascading down behind her. This woman was mine, and I'd never felt more fucking possessive than when my cock was buried deep inside of her, staking my claim and making her a part of me. Making me feel like a fucking lion.

"I can't believe that was the last time we get to do that for months," Em said.

"Last time, what do you mean?"

"Isn't this the last night before the sex ban is imposed?" she asked.

"Uh-huh, last night. Not last time." I answered. "It's only eight o'clock," I reasoned. "We have until midnight before the sex bans starts and I'm about sixty seconds from going at it again." On cue, I hardened inside her again, and I wasn't anywhere near done by the time the Chinese takeaway arrived. Donning some jeans so that I didn't scare the delivery guy, I shoved the money at him, left the food in the kitchenette, and joined a damp Em in bed with a running jump.

"Again?" she asked with a laugh. "Until the clock strikes twelve, baby," I answered with a kiss.

* * *

The breeze blew in through the window, caressing us both, and it wouldn't be long before autumn became winter. I lay with my head in Em's lap as she ran her fingers lazily through my hair.

"I could stay like this forever," I told her.

"I wish we could, but your favorite alarm is on his way over."

"Who?" I asked.

"Tommy. He's coming over to talk to me about something," Em told me.

"That sounds interesting," I said, trying not to sound pissed that he was about to shatter my peace. Maybe it was for the best. I had to be at the gym soon and having Em all soft and warm in my arms wasn't exactly motivating me to get up. We moved around each other to brush our teeth, sneaking little kisses as we went. By the time Tommy arrived, I was dressed in my training gear and ready to go. I let Tommy in as I was making a quick breakfast of porridge. Without asking, I fixed him a bowl as well, knowing he'd only be poking around the kitchen looking for food otherwise.

"Thanks, Con," he said. He looked serious, which was kind of worrying in itself. Tommy was never serious. We watched the news in silence as we ate.

"Cup of tea, Tommy?" she asked him and he nodded glumly. She set about making him a cuppa, then settled in next to me as I finished. She knew better than to offer me a hot drink. There was absolutely no caffeine for me now until the fight was over.

"What's up, lovely?" Em asked him.

"Do you know what I've always wanted to be, ever since I was a little kid?" Tommy asked me.

"Taller?" I responded, laughing at my own joke. Tom gave me an evil look, and Em smacked my arm.

"A fireman," Em told me.

"No shit really? How do you know that?" I asked her.

"Because he told me," she explained patiently.

"Well, since you've taken up the boxing full-time and you and Kier stopped the partying and shit, I decided to take a chance and fill out a fire service application," he said.

"Is that why you're looking so glum then? Because you didn't get through? Don't beat yourself up over it. I hear they have thousands of applications for every place," I consoled him.

"That's just it," he said, still looking a little stunned. "Out of all those applications, they've picked mine to go through to the next round, but look at me, they're never gonna let someone like me be a firefighter. Somehow being one step closer to getting what I always wanted is worse than never having a chance at all. Em, I need your help!"

# CHAPTER 12

"I'd love to help Tommy but I don't know how I can," Em admitted.

"The next stage of the process is an exam which is kind of like a psychometric test. I managed to get some past papers off the Internet, and it's frying my brain. I was shit in school, and I'm shit at all this book-learning stuff, but I know I'd make a fucking amazing firefighter." I don't remember Tom ever mentioning anything to do with the fire service to me. I honestly thought he was happy ticking along as a plumber like his old man. That he had the motivation to fill out a fire service application stunned me, and I realized how badly I'd underestimated him. I wondered if Kier knew anything about this.

"Of course I can help," Sunshine told him, looking at the fire service letter he'd handed her and over all the past test papers.

"A lot of these questions are just a matter of common sense. You have to get used to reading the questions quickly and accurately, making a decision about your answer, and moving on to the next one without panicking. There's also a technique in working out how much time you can afford to spend on any one question. We can go over some papers until you feel comfortable with your answers, then we'll have a go at them under test conditions."

Tommy smiled, looking like a weight had been lifted off his shoulders. "I knew you'd know what to do," he told her, making her blush. Even from someone she knew as well as Tommy, she still wasn't good at accepting compliments.

"Why don't we get started tomorrow?" Em suggested. "I've got classes until five p.m., but if you can meet me later in the evening, we can make a start."

"I should be able to meet you by five fifteen. We can do it in the library by your school, can't we? Or will they kick people like me out?" he asked seriously, making Em giggle.

"I don't know what you mean by 'people like you' but no, they won't kick you out. Education is for everyone with a thirst for knowledge, Tommy."

"I just figured, you know, with the tattoos and all, that I wouldn't be welcome in a place like that."

"Dr. Matt Taylor led the Rosetta project to land a probe on a comet for the first time, and he's covered in tattoos. If the European Space Agency will let him do that, I'm pretty sure the maths department at UCL can handle you using the library to study."

"No shit, really?" he said, pulling out his phone. No doubt

to see if Em was right about this doctor guy. I didn't know his name but I was pretty sure Sunshine was right. I wouldn't put it past her to make up shite to help Tommy feel better, but she made me watch the news now—something I never did before—and I do remember her getting excited about the Rosetta thing and the bloke with all the tats. The enormous, shitty-looking clock on the wall of our kitchenette counted down the minutes before I had to leave for the gym. Both of us hated the clock but it hid a patch of mold on the wall that we hated even more. A part of me was itching to get between the ropes but the other part of me knew what this fight meant. It was the fight of my career, and it meant relentless, backbreaking training that would take me away from my girl every day for months. Sunshine made me soft, and I couldn't afford soft. Today was the day I went to work. Em looked at the clock the same time I did and knew what it meant.

"It's not forever you know," she told me, holding the door open for me to leave.

"Hold up, I'll walk with you," Tommy told me as he gathered up his stuff. Reaching for her, I threaded my fingers through her silky soft hair and pulled her toward me for a kiss.

"I just want to make sure you're okay," I admitted to her.

"I'm fine," she reassured me. "I'll get to come and watch you train when I'm not in class, and I'll miss you over the next few months, baby, but this is life-changing. You've got an opportunity to show what I, Danny, and every one of your brothers know. That you are the best fighter this country has ever seen. And when you're done, I'll still be here. The woman you get to grow old with when all the fight is gone."

"I'm Irish, love. That fight will never be gone, but I promised myself once that I would conquer the world for you, and that's what I'm gonna do. I'm gonna be a legend, and when they ask me how I did it, I'm gonna tell them it was all you."

"I love you," she told me with tears in her eyes.

"Love you too, Mrs. O'Connell."

"For fuck's sake. You love him. He loves you. We all love each other. Can we go now? We're only going to the fucking gym, you know. He'll be back tonight." Em rolled her eyes at Tommy's interruption but I knew why he'd done it. I ragged on Tommy a whole lot, but he worshipped my wife. Loved her like family and would lay down his life for her. He knew that no matter how much she put a brave face on it, the next few months would be hard on her, on all of us. I needed Tom to keep her safe, to keep her cheerful, to be her friend.

"Come on then, arsewipe. Let's see how fucking fast and cocky you are tomorrow after a few rounds with me."

"Done," he agreed, and after kissing Em on the cheek and reminding her about tomorrow, he was bounding down the stairs next to me.

"Thanks for that, Tom. I really don't know how this shit with Frank is going to go down, but I need you by Em's side through this. It's the only way my head's gonna be in any place good for the fight."

"That missus of yours is stronger than people give her

credit for. She may well be the strongest one of us all," he told me gravely.

"She has to be," I told him.

"Listen, you do what you have to do, and I'll take care of your girl. Ma knows what's going down. Da's giving me a couple of weeks off when the trial is on so I can go with her, and Ma and the family will most likely be there too. Being alone ain't something Em's gotta worry about."

"I owe you big, I know that. Not just for this but for last time as well."

"There's no debt. You're like my brother, but I ain't doing this for you. I'm doing this for her." He pressed my buttons and deliberately wound me up, but when it came to taking care of my wife, there was no better man I could have picked than Tommy. I knew then that I'd let him get at least one hit in when we were sparring. No more than that though. When he got one in, he usually didn't shut up about it for days. Walking through the heavy oak doors of Danny's gym, I breathed in the smell of home and smiled. This place was my sanctuary, my haven, and my church. Every good thing that ever happened to me, I could attribute to these brick walls. In the corner, past all the kids knocking about on bags and doing their circuits, sat the old, weathered boxing ring in all her majesty. Before this thing was over, she would bring me to my knees and remind me that, no matter how much I thought I knew about fighting, she would always show me I had more to learn. Walking over there, I placed my bag down on the floor and ran my hand across the canvas reverently.

"You ready for this, son?" Danny asked, coming out of nowhere.

"I think so," I told him.

"There's no 'think' about it. If you're ready—be ready. I'm gonna take you to the limit of what you know your body can do and keep going. When I'm done, Thor himself would crap lightning bolts at the thought of getting in the ring with you. That boy, he beat you once. No doubt about it. But a good fighter knows when to quit. A great fighter doesn't know what the word means. When you're seconds from the bell, you keep fighting. When you can't see out of either eye cause they're busted up so bad, you keep fighting. If you can do that, if you can give me that, I'll make you world champion. Now I'll ask you again, son. You ready?"

"Yes, sir," I answered with a big fuckin' grin. As his speech went on, one by one the guys moved to the edge of the ring to hear what he was saying.

"Well, then," said Danny.

"Let's get to work."

"I got something for you that's gonna help," Tommy chipped in. Jumping down from the edge of the canvas where he'd been sitting he ran flat out to the office and back again. "Here," he said, handing me a clear case with "Con" scribbled in black marker across the front.

"What's this?" I asked.

"I made you a CD. It's like the *Rocky* theme and a load of other songs to train to."

I grinned broadly at him. "You made me a mixtape. Does that mean we're going steady?" I said, making Kieran laugh.

"Fuck you!" he said. "I try and do something nice and this is the fucking thanks I get."

"No this is great, really. Thanks, Tom," I told him sincerely.

No longer caring, he walked toward the changing room, flipping me the backward bird. "Whatever, loser," he shouted back.

"Let's get this show on the road," said Kieran, grabbing the CD off me. We changed quickly and walked back into the gym just as the opening bars to the *Rocky* theme song sounded through the gym speakers.

"It might be cheesy, but it definitely pumps you up," Liam pointed out.

"Fucking told you bitch, didn't I?" said Tommy, smirking. Kieran grinned at me, and I gave him a rare grin back. We all felt it. We were the underdogs, the misfits, the castoffs who wouldn't amount to anything. Temple had state-of-the-art training facilities, and we had the *Rocky* soundtrack and a beat-up old gym. But we had each other. We had the fire and the drive to win, to succeed. I wasn't alone in this. We were brothers, and we were bringing it to the fucking table.

* * *

The first day of serious training is always the worst. I was always in good shape but a few weeks of eating takeaway food and Em's baking had taken its toll. The six-pack never went anywhere but my body knew the difference. My diet was so strictly regimented I didn't dare even open one of the tins at home for fear I'd be licking cake crumbs out of desperation. I was up at 5 a.m. and running by 5:30. A five-mile jog started off the day, followed by bag work, circuits, core training, sparring, and more running. I landed more punches an hour than I cared to count. Danny pushed me to the absolute limit of what I ever imagined my body could do.

The worst part was the mental game. Every day he waited for me to quit, to tell him that I'd had enough and needed to rest, and every day I took pleasure in disappointing him. I came pretty close a few times to caving. There were days when my arms hurt so much that I could barely lift them. I had enough energy at the end of the day to stand under the blissfully hot spray of the shower, and I let water and gravity do the rest. There were times when Em came into the shower with me. These were painful and pleasurable in equal measure. She'd massage her fingers gently into my scalp, making me groan. Despite the fact that I could barely stand some days, my cock apparently hadn't received the memo that energy was in short supply. Every single time she stood in the shower next to me, water beading down those beautiful pale tits of hers, my cock was rock hard. After staring hard at her gorgeous body, I succumbed once and sucked one of her pert, pink nipples into my mouth and hated myself for it. I was seconds away from sinking my dick inside her and damning the consequences when, with a moan of complaint, she reminded me of the sex ban.

This time Danny had imposed it from the first day of training, and I swear to God, he knew when I'd so much as thought about sex. The day after I'd copped a feel with Em, he pushed me harder than ever before, scowling the whole time. I swear to Christ he acted as though Sunshine really was his daughter. I tried really, really hard not to be naked with Em again or to watch her bend over or brush her hair or laugh or do any one of a million fucking things that turned me on when it came to my wife.

When it came to my training, Em was as fierce as Danny. Maybe more so. He'd created a monster. Although she'd been back at school for a while now, there were often days where her classes would finish at three or four and she'd head straight for the gym just in time to see me hit the mental wall of pain that every athlete hits at some point in his training. That point where you feel like everything is about to shut down and you just can't go on. Around four o'clock every day was that time for me. And my cure? The one thing that got me past the pain barrier? Sunshine.

"Forty-three, forty-four, forty-five..." Earnshaw called out the numbers as I repeated each hanging sit-up. My legs hooked over the back of the crossbar and my hands behind my head meant that I was completely upside down between each sit-up. I'd done fifty this morning at the start of training, no problem. Now I felt like puking.

"Forty-six, forty-seven..." That quiet, gentle voice I'd know anywhere took over the count and I no longer thought about the pain. I thought about impressing my wife. What was she wearing? How had her day been?

"Forty-eight, forty-nine..." With me still upside down, she gently held my head and kissed me deeply. With Em there, everything was instantly better. Unhooking myself from the bar, I dropped down and kissed her hard, telling her without words just how much I missed her. Once upon a time, Danny had frowned on having Em in the gym. Once he realized how much of a motivator she was, she became a permanent fixture. Now it was an unspoken rule that I had five minutes alone with my wife when she arrived. It was precious little of the day to be spending together but I'd take whatever I could get when it came to Em.

"Hey, Sunshine. How was your day?"

"Really good. I've been doing a couple of hours with Nikki, and she's totally getting a hang of the module now," she told me gleefully. My wife was a fucking genius when it came to math. Well, when it came to most things actually. I loved seeing that dreamy, spaced-out look she'd get when she was trying to work out some freaky-hard equations. How one girl could have the same look reading a romance novel as she did doing math baffled me. But I didn't need to work out what made her tick, or understand any of the shit she was talking about when it came to her degree. I just loved her, and that was all that mattered. I didn't give a shit that she was smarter than me; most people were. She was the brains and the beauty, and if I was the brawn in our little family, I was happy with that. As long as she was happy too, that's all I cared about.

"You ready for tomorrow?" I asked.

"As ready as I'll ever be. They'll be digging over all that shit in court soon anyway so I guess it's better to go over it first with someone who's on my side at least." Tomorrow was her first rape counseling session, and Danny was ending training at five o'clock so I could take her. It still stuck in my gut that I couldn't be with her in court and as much as I burned to fight Rico Temple again, I suspected that this was something else I'd have to learn to live with. I tilted her face up to look at me.

"We're gonna get through this, baby. Whatever happens, whatever shit goes down, it's me and you forever now."

# CHAPTER 13

As I sat in the cheap plastic chair, I imagined that this was how families of patients in the hospital felt. My girl was next door crying over shit I didn't think I could stand to hear and tearing open old wounds I had no way of healing. She'd had a nightmare last night, and it was fucking brutal. I felt like I was standing in the corner of the room as Frank raped her. Fucking unable to do anything other than to listen to her endure it. If there was anything more emasculating than experiencing that, I didn't want to know what it was.

The counselor was one set up by the Crown Prosecution Service. Apparently they weren't just there to help Em deal with what had happened, but to support her through the trial. Given the brutality of what Frank had done, they'd offered her the option of giving evidence by video. I wished desperately that she'd chosen that option, but I should have known better. As terrified as she was, my girl was too strong for that. She'd read somewhere that juries were more supportive of a victim when evidence was given in person. Something about seeing and hearing their emotional responses humanized them.

Everything that was going down now terrified me and pissed me off in equal measure. Here in this plastic chair I might as well have been back in the changing room at the fight, unable to process any of this shit. The only thing inside stronger than hate and rage was my love for Em and the overwhelming and fundamental need to protect her. So instead of beating the crap out of someone, I sat here in this shitty plastic chair watching the clock tick by painfully slowly. Waiting for my wife. I ran through everything Father Pat had told me about how to control my temper. The things he taught me didn't change who I was or what I felt but they helped me pretend to be a better man, so by the time the door in front of me opened, I was ready to deal with whatever condition I found Em in on the other side. Her face was a mess, and it looked like she'd spent the whole hour crying. She blew her nose loudly into her tissue as she walked out followed by her counselor. The second I saw her, she was in my arms, her face buried in my chest.

"You must be Cormac. I'm Nora," she said to me smiling warmly. She was an older lady, maybe me ma's age, only unlike me ma, she wore very little makeup and had a kindly look about her.

"Nice to meet you," I told her without offering her my hand. They were wrapped firmly around my girl and weren't going anywhere.

"Will you be bringing her back on Wednesday?"

"As long as she wants to come, I'll be here," I told her.

"Well, I'll see you both then. Have a safe journey home."

"Thank you, for everything," Em told her, twisting in my arms.

"You're welcome," she said with a smile.

"See you soon." I tucked Em into my side and held her tightly all the way down the stairs.

"How was it?" I asked.

"Brutal, like I expected," she admitted. "But good too. Cathartic, I think. I thought it would hurt to talk about it, and it did, but it also felt like I was taking some of the power away from him by telling someone what he was really like."

I swallowed hard and squeezed her arm in support as she blew her nose again. I was right about it being hard to hear. Em was dealing a lot better than I was. We walked outside, and I automatically scanned the road for a taxi. There was no way I was letting her get on a bus like this. When Em elbowed me, I realized I didn't need to bother. Across the road from us, Liam and Kieran leaned against Liam's truck chatting. We hurried across the road to meet them.

"What are you doing here?" Em asked, throwing herself in Kieran's arms, then Liam's for a hug. I knew exactly why they were here. Giving Kieran a fist bump and back slap, I spoke quietly to him while Em spoke to Liam.

"Thanks, Kier."

"No problem, Con. There's no way we were letting you make your own way home after this. I'm on strict instructions to update Danny once we get you home as well. So how's she doing?"

"You know how she is. On the outside, she's amazing but sleep tonight's gonna be fucking brutal."

"Anything we can do?" he asked.

"I wish there was, but I've got no fucking clue what I'm doing. I guess I've just gotta be here for her while she processes everything."

"No man. I meant is there anything I can do for you? You need to go a few rounds in the morning, let off some steam?"

"I could use a hug," I told him straight-faced. Anyone else and they'd have told me to fuck off, and even though I really was taking the piss, Kier hugged me.

\* \* \*

Listening to my girl sobbing in her sleep in the dead of night, was fucking heartbreaking. Last week I came home to find her crying over a chick flick about some guy who couldn't find a way to tell his girl that he loved her until he'd nearly lost her. I didn't get it. If you love someone, you don't sit there fucking moaning about it. You get your arse up and make her see you're the only man for her. Or kidnap her until she sees sense. If you don't love something enough to fight for it, you don't really love it at all. Still Em had cried like it was the end of the world. A big hug, cup of tea, and a bar of chocolate, and she was all good. But this was not good. It was so fucking far from good I didn't know where to begin.

"No, no, no," she moaned quietly into her pillow. Her body was curled up in the fetal position in the middle of the bed, her frowning face tortured in sleep.

"Mum, help me!" she cried into the dark. Lying on my back, my arms out at my sides, I tried to let her cries pass over me, not through me. My fists were clenched so tight I thought the knuckles would burst through the skin any minute. I hoped for it. The pain would give me something else to focus on.

"Mum, please help me, please, please." That was it. I seriously couldn't take this anymore. I tried to wake her up when she first had them but she'd start hyperventilating and it took me ages to calm her down. Her therapist told us that as long as the dreams weren't chronic or violent, I should let her sleep. That it was her brain's way of working though shit. Until recently, she hadn't had one since we first met. It was like Frank got locked up, and bam, no more dreams. Some days now, she'd wake up and not remember she'd been dreaming. I learned not to bring it up after she'd kissed me good morning once and I'd asked how she slept after her nightmare. The look of pure joy drained out of her and what was left was fear.

Now with the training, I wasn't there when she woke. So I went back to the notes. Every morning, whether she'd been dreaming or not, I'd leave a note for her. I would always be the dragon she woke up to whether in person or on paper. I'd even leave a doodle on some of them to make her smile, and I can't draw for shit. Love makes us do stupid things.

"Please, Frank. Don't do this." To my shame, I sat up and ran my fingers through my hair, and with one last, painful look at Em I walked to the bathroom, shut the door, and sank to the floor, resting my head in my hands. Banging my head against the door, I crossed my hands over my knees, and I looked up at the water-stained ceiling. How do you fight an enemy you can't see? Frank's arse was in jail, and even if I could beat the ever-loving shit out of him, it wouldn't help Em.

A soft groan sounded from behind the door, and a new wave of shame washed over me. I wanted to hurt someone, but there was no one to hurt. No one that would make me feel any better anyway. I wanted to rage at someone, but there was nothing I could shout that could take back what was done. In the end I realized that there was only one way left to fight. And that was by my girl's side.

Growing a pair of balls, I dragged my sorry arse off the floor and back to bed. Wrapping my arms around her, I pulled her into my side. She burrowed in subconsciously, looking for my body heat. For more than a year, she'd been my sunshine in a dark place. Now it was my turn to be hers. So when I left for training the next morning, I made sure she knew I was still with her. Even with my scrawl, it was still pretty legible with no lines through it or spelling mistakes, which was a big fucking achievement for me. In fact, I was pretty pleased until I decided to doodle a teddy bear on the front, which ended up looking more like a Chucky doll. Still, I'd bet she'd keep it with all the others.

*Hey Sunshine,*

*I hope you slept well. By the time you read this, I'll probably be running. But I just wanted to let you know I'm with you at school or court. I'm with you. Always. One lifetime will never be enough, baby.*

*I love you,*
*OC xxx*

*PS. Sleeping in sexy red panties is banned for the foreseeable fucking future. I can't go running with a hard-on anymore. It's getting embarrassing!*

\* \* \*

"What the fuck?" I said as Kieran, Tommy, and I walked in through the door of our flat to the sight of Nikki holding a giant purple dildo.

"Hey guys" she greeted us with a smile. "How's the training going?" The three of us stood there with our mouths open like goldfish. All of us were distracted by the hypnotic, therapeutic buzz of the dildo as it vibrated in her hands.

"Tell me I've died and gone to porn heaven," Tommy mumbled as he stood incredulously beside me.

"You have any thoughts about my wife that even feature a dildo, you're gonna wish you were dead," I responded.

"Okay. No dildo," he said, still looking pretty happy with himself.

"Just to be clear. No sexual fantasies about my wife whatsoever. In fact, the only time you need to be thinking about my wife is when you're where her husband is. And more importantly where his fist is in relation to your face."

"You suck all the fun out of life," Tommy said.

Our tiny flat was full of women passing around lingerie and sex toys. I coughed to clear my throat as I locked eyes on my wife.

"So what's going on, Sunshine?" I asked, trying to sound casual. She was holding a black lace bra up against herself and talking to Nikki's housemate.

"Sorry, love. I didn't know you'd be home this early. Nikki's friend Helen is helping us host an Ann Summers party."

"I thought it would take her mind off tomorrow," Nikki told me.

"Good call," I said with a smile.

"I'm gonna head over to Kieran's and grab some dinner. Give you ladies some peace and quiet."

"Sorry. I feel like I'm pushing you out. I forgot to mention that the girls were coming by," Em said as she squeezed past the women, who were mainly sprawled over the bed comparing toys.

"It's fine, baby. Go and have a good time, and I'll see you later."

"I won't spend too much money, I promise!" I looked down again at that black lace underwear and imagined Em wearing it.

"Spend as much as you like," I told her. My voice full of conviction.

"Mine's bigger and a prettier color. Do you want to see?" Em and I both turned around just in time to catch Tommy's generous offer to the ladies. Most of them giggled and looked at Tom lovingly. How the fuck did he do that? He said something crude or danced like a woman, and girls thought he was cute. But if Kier or I ever did it, we'd just come off as being dicks.

"They think he's gay," Kier said, reading my mind, "that's why they think he's cute."

"No they don't," Tommy called back. "I'm not saying men don't want me," he told Nikki matter-of-factly, "but there's not enough of me to share with the ladies as it is."

"You know it really is purple," I told the girls, as I nodded my head toward Tommy's junk.

"STDs," Kieran whispered conspiratorially to a captive audience.

"Jealousy is an ugly thing, my friend," Tommy said to Kieran, as he tried to rise above all Kieran's insults.

"I'm not jealous of your STDs," Kieran said.

"You're such a dick," Tommy told him.

"Do you want to hold my dick?" Nikki offered to Tommy as Em laughed. I spotted a bottle of white wine on the table and figured they'd all had a few drinks to unwind.

"It's a mood cock," Nikki told him. "It vibrates and changes color depending on your mood."

"Okay," he agreed without hesitation.

"Go, Tommy!" Em encouraged him.

"It's all right," he said. "I'm man enough to hold a fucking dildo."

Nikki handed it to him and he held it out like it was plutonium. Within seconds it turned blue. Sunshine was holding her side from laughing so hard. After last night, I'd be happy to stay here all night listening to Tommy talk up a storm just to see her smile.

"Seriously, ladies! How can you possibly think this could replace the real thing?" Tom asked curiously.

"Do you think you could get yours to vibrate and change color?" Nikki asked him through her laughter. Tommy looked her up and down suggestively.

"For you Nik, I could make it stand at attention and dance to the national anthem." The women erupted as they considered what Tommy's dancing cock looked like.

Hauling my girl in for a hug. I called over to Kieran. "I think that's our cue to leave," I told him. He didn't hear me. Smiles all gone, he'd locked eyes on the girl who'd just walked out of the bathroom.

"Hey, Marie," he said softly. "It's good to see you again."

"It's good to see you too," she replied.

I looked from one to the other and felt like I was missing something. She was the girl who'd designed Em's wedding dress, and since the wedding she, Em, Nikki, and a few of their university and waitressing friends had spent a lot more time together. Sunshine had been denied friendship for most of her life by that evil fuck Frank so I loved that she was building her own circle of friends, especially with me out training so much.

Then I spotted someone I never expected to see in our flat. "What's Katrina doing here?" I asked Em. I spoke quietly but Katrina obviously overheard me as she turned to see me looking at her.

"We're friends now, remember," Em told me.

"No, we're not," Katrina replied. "We just don't hate each other anymore. Apparently your wife has a bit of a guilt complex about how things went down between us and making me shop for sex toys and drink wine with her is going to make us BFFs," she told me sarcastically.

"Making you?" I asked her.

"Have you ever said no to your wife when she's made up her mind about something? She's being nice to me now, and it's even more fucking annoying than when she hated me," Katrina said grumpily. Em turned to me with a grin, and I knew Katrina had a point. My girl had a real bee in her bonnet about her relationship with this chick. She wanted to make things right between them, and she was more stubborn than I was when she got it in her head to do something.

"Well, have fun," I told them all and bent to kiss Sunshine on the lips.

"Especially you," I whispered.

Turning to leave, I bumped Kieran to get his attention but what I found made me pause. His eyes followed Marie, who'd gone back into the fray, and I realized that I'd seen the look on his face in the mirror over a year ago. Kieran Doherty, joker, pussy magnet, corner man, and friend, had found his girl.

# CHAPTER 14

For the first three days of Frank's trial, it rained endlessly. It was winter in London so it rained pretty much every day. Those three days were different though. The black clouds were foreboding, like the bad weather was an omen for things to come. I was dog tired from training and worried sick the whole time about what was happening in that courtroom. The more of each day that passed, the worse I trained. My feet were slow and sluggish on the bounce, and my punches were hitting the mark but that was probably the best you could say about them.

"What the fuck, Con," Danny said, throwing the towel into the ring. Kieran and I had been trading punches for an hour. He might as well have been trading fists with Danny for all the fucking good it was doing. The wall that I usually hit around four had struck me the minute I left Em this morning. She was facing Frank without me. The hustle and bustle of the gym, that felt so much like home, was gone because everyone else was either at work or with my girl. Until this trial was over and Frank was behind bars, my Sunshine was gone. Without Em by my side, nothing made sense. Not even in the ring.

"Jesus Christ, Cormac. In weeks, you're fighting the goddamn world champion, and you're not ready. You're nowhere near ready because you can't get your head on straight."

"And you can?" I shouted at him. Kieran walked away and left us to it. I never raised my voice at Danny, no one did. But he needed to hear this. "I know this fight is important, and I know it's what Em wants. Shit, it's what I want too. But I feel like we're throwing her to the fucking wolves not being there."

"I understand that. I really do. But you get a once-in-a-lifetime chance. It may never come around again, and if it does, who's to say if it's gonna be any good for you. In three or four years, you could be injured, maybe even retired. You're in peak physical condition now, and if you don't take this opportunity, there are plenty more who will. Men with fire in their heart and hunger in their gut who'd kill just for the opportunity to get toe to toe with Temple. Men who'd sacrifice anything to get that one chance that you're pissing away."

"Then maybe I ain't meant to be world champion. Because it doesn't mean the whole fucking world to me. I want that title so bad I can taste it, but what fucking good is it to me? What kind of man am I to be chasing my dream instead of protecting my wife? What kind of man has titles but can't protect his own family?" All of a sudden, the fight just seemed to leave Danny. He sat down on the old wooden stool by the side of the ring, and I slumped down on the floor next to him.

"You know, son, sometimes there ain't no right and wrong choice to make. Life ain't black and white. Sometimes there's just shitty choices, and you have to make the best of them."

"Danny, I ain't never had anything except shitty choices until Em came along. She went through worse shit than I ever did, and she came out of it pure and loving and kind. But now she can't see any of that. It doesn't matter what she says to my face. I know she's in a bad fucking place right now, and I can't help feeling that this choice is the worse one."

"So you tell me, kid, what d'you wanna do?"

"Keep her here with me so she never has to see that fucker again, win the world title, then accidentally bump into Frank in a dark alley where I can introduce all of his vital organs to my fist."

"Shit, you really do have a big Christmas list, don't you?" said Danny as he lit up a cigarette.

"I may be able to help with the keeping Em here part," added Kieran as he jogged over.

"What do you mean?" I asked him.

"Liam just called. Something big went down in court today. They cleared out the jury and then adjourned because some kind of mini evidence trial is going on tomorrow and needed to be settled. The lawyers were arguing about whether or not stuff was admissible. The Crown Prosecution

Service barrister told Em she wouldn't be needed tomorrow but she has to be back the day after. Liam's gonna go there anyway and find out what's happening."

"We bring her here tomorrow then. If she's not in court, I want her with me all day."

Danny nodded. "I agree. I don't want her on her own but I need a full day's training from you tomorrow. This trial shit's like a fucking circus. You need to get focused."

"No problem, Danny. I understand," I told him. With Em here, tomorrow everything would be better. But I didn't like the sound of what was going down in court. Those black clouds were definitely rolling in.

Two hours later, Liam walked in through the door, and I looked straight past him.

"Well, hello to you too!" he said to me.

"Where's Em? I thought you were taking care of her today?" I barked at him. I didn't mean to get shitty. It'd been a rough day all around.

"She's fine. Her mum was waiting outside the courtroom for her. They've gone for a coffee."

"You let that bitch get near her?" I said. "You know what she's capable of."

"Con, this woman is fucking tiny. There's no way she could hurt her if she tried."

"It's not the physical abuse I'm worried about. This woman was the reason Em endured abuse for six years without telling anyone. I don't even want to know what kind of shit she's filling Em's head with."

"Shit, I'm so sorry."

"No, I'm sorry. Looking after her is my job. You're helping me out. I shouldn't get up in your face about it."

"Looking after her isn't a job. She's like our sister, and there ain't nothing we wouldn't do for her. Keeping her safe ain't solely on you. Con. It never has been." I acknowledged him with a nod. He and the guys all felt the same way, and I knew that. It still didn't stop me feeling the way I did though.

"Come on," he told me.

"You can spar with me for an hour until she gets here. That should keep your mind off things for a bit." I snorted at him. In good form, I could put Liam down inside of two rounds. Like this, he'd probably put me on my arse in one. Still, good as his word, he changed quickly and climbed into the ring.

"Danny says you're fighting like shit. He's wrong is he?" he taunted me.

"Fuck you. You'd be the same if it was your girl." He looked at me funny until I got it.

"Fine. If it was your guy." I looked around as we bounced about the canvas but no one was listening to us.

"You told anyone else yet?" I asked.

"No," he replied.

"The guy I'm seeing hasn't really come to terms with everything yet. I mean it's pretty new for both of us. We're both gonna face a boatload of grief when people do find out. Guess we just want to see where this is going before we have to face that."

"Makes sense. You know I'm here for you when that time comes though."

"I know, and I appreciate that. It's just gonna be a fucking shit storm when it does happen." I nodded and threw a combination at him to stop him thinking too hard. But he wasn't wrong. The fallout with his Irish Catholic family would be fucking huge. All I could do was stand by him.

"So you gonna tell me who they guy is?" I asked him. He grinned that same smile that had been plastered all over my face since I first kissed Em. Whoever he was, Liam had fallen hard.

"I can't. He doesn't want people knowing, and I respect that. He's fucking hot though."

"Well, that narrows it down. We're all fucking hot."

"I've been looking at your ugly mugs every day since I was about twelve so I don't see you that way. None of you," he said, then paused. "And even if I did, you still wouldn't be as hot as my guy."

I rolled my eyes. Was I really that fucking cheesy about Em?

"You realize that Tommy is gonna claim that he's the reason you turned."

Liam shuddered before replying "I didn't turn. I was born this way, and if I had 'turned,' Tom would be a pretty good reason to turn back."

"I hear you," I said with a chuckle.

"Earnshaw's gunning for Tommy since he hooked up with his sister. I'll piss myself laughing if he ends up trying it on with your man just to prove he's still got it."

"Tom ain't gay," Liam replied with a scowl.

"I don't think that matters...he'd flirt with your guy just

to fuck with you. He does it to me all the time." Liam didn't like the sound of that at all. Good. Maybe he wouldn't find it so funny anymore when Tom was pressing my buttons. Apparently I'd pressed a wrong one of Liam's. His jabs became heavier, and I could tell by the look on his face that he was gonna give me a pounding while he worked shit out in his head.

I moved my head from side to side and bounced as I shook out the tension. Bring it on. He wasn't the only one who needed to dump shit in the ring. If I was ever in need of any therapy, this square of canvas gave it to me.

\* \* \*

I stood in front of my locker, searching through hundreds of cans of deodorant to find that one that wasn't empty, when my girl's hands wrapped themselves around my damp, over-heated body.

"You'll get yourself all wet," I warned, pulling her hands around tighter so that her front was flush against my back.

"That's pretty much a given whenever you're standing in front of me wearing only a towel," she said quietly into my ear before nibbling lightly on the lobe. Instantly I was hard and desperately fighting the urge to turn her around, slam her against the lockers, and wrap those gorgeous legs of hers around my waist. I sang quietly to myself.

"What are you doing, O'Connell?" she asked me, and I could hear the confusion in her voice.

"I'm singing the Irish National Anthem."

"Yes, I can hear that," she replied, and I could hear the humor in her voice. "What I meant was, why?"

"I'm trying to get rid of my hard-on because I'm a stone's throw away from fucking you against my locker. Or on my bench. Or in the shower. Shit," I said and stopped talking to start singing again. After a moment of standing really still against me, she said, "Maybe you should teach me the words too."

Half an hour later, I at least had a barrier of clothes between us as we walked, hand in hand together, back to the flat.

"How did it go with your mum today?" I asked, trying to sound more casual than I actually felt.

"My bodyguard told you about that, did he?" she asked with a smile that told me she wasn't bothered.

"Like you keep any secrets from me anyway," I snorted.

"It was okay," she said with a sigh that told me it absolutely wasn't okay.

"It's just she's this person I don't really know at all. She comes by the café now and then, and sometimes when I'm busy she just drinks her tea and leaves without even speaking to me. Lately she's more like the person she was before dad died, but I'm not the little girl I was back then so she doesn't get to be the mum she was either. I worry that I'm making a horrible mistake letting her back into my life."

I held back on saying exactly what I thought of her mother and recited the national anthem in my head for different reasons. Turns out it kind of worked as a filter between my shitty temper and my big mouth. "Did she say why she acted the way she did for all those years?" I asked. In my mind, there was no reason on earth she could have for doing what she did to Em.

"She said that when Dad died, Frank was a shoulder to cry on. When she couldn't find a way back from the depression he gave her something to take. Instantly it made everything, all the pain and grief, go away until she felt nothing at all. I guess eventually she became dependent on whatever he was supplying to keep her like a zombie. Once she was hooked, he convinced her to give up work and live off Dad's life insurance money, and he moved in. The rest is history."

"So Frank's wife thinks, by telling you this, all will be forgiven, and she gets to be a mother again. I must have missed the part of that story which didn't make her sound like a selfish bitch." Shit. I needed to start singing the fucking national anthem again. My brain to mouth filter was broken. She shrugged, and I knew she was fighting the urge to defend her mum. It's what I always did whenever anyone attacked her. Even if they were right.

"I didn't know what to say to her either. She's told me that she's clean of whatever Frank was giving her now."

"Put her in a room with my ma," I told her. "They can have a pity party together."

"It is true that we are the awesome product of really shitty stock. Well, half shitty. My dad was pretty amazing. He'd have loved you!"

"Really?" I asked sarcastically. "I hate to break it to you, Sunshine, because I know you love your dad. But I reckon

I'm pretty much the embodiment of every father's worst nightmare."

She stopped dead in the street, across the road from the block of flats, and turned to me. "You saw me when very few people in this world did. You took care of me, protected me, and made me happy. You waited until I was ready for you. Well sort of, and you never pushed me into being something I'm not. You love me more than anyone else in the world, and you became a better man for it. What more could any man ever want for his daughter? I love you. Dad would have loved you, and if you ever think anything else, you're an idiot."

I smiled from ear to ear. This girl saw me with blinkers on her eyes. She was totally blind to the fact that any father would look at my tattoos, listen to me speak, and hear what I did for a living and wonder what he'd done that was so wrong that his daughter would pick this loser. It didn't matter if that's exactly what he would have thought though because she would have picked me anyway. Sunshine loved me forever and, whether or not I deserved that love, I never doubted it.

"Love, I'm your husband which pretty much means that the need to protect you is programmed into my DNA. Your mum hurt you badly, so it's only natural that I want to protect you from that. But that don't necessarily mean I'm right. If you think that building a relationship with your ma will make you happy, then I'll be right behind you. I won't be fucking happy if she hurts you again, but I'll support you in whatever you decide. I'll even try and be nice to her if you want me to."

"Really?" she asked, her eyebrow raised in surprise.

"Hey, I can do nice!" I said, with a mock wounded expression. "And if I can't be nice, I'll be quiet," I added as an afterthought.

"You don't think there's any chance of making up with your mum then? Even if she quits drinking," she asked.

"Baby, that ship sailed the minute she tried to turn you against me. It's nothing to do with the drinking. I've lost track of the number of treatment programs and detox centers that I've gotten her into and she never saw them through, even when she showed up at all. You can't help someone who doesn't want to be helped. She's an addict, but that didn't change the fact that she's me ma and I loved her. But when she tried to take you from me, I knew for sure that she never loved me back.

"And you're okay with that?" she asked.

"I found someone who puts me first and loves me with all her heart. I gained more than I lost," I replied. "Sylvia only wanted to be a part of my life as long as she had something to gain from it. Your ma is telling you that she just wants to get to know you. Give it some time. She'll either prove herself or condemn herself. Either way, you'll never look back and wonder 'what if.'"

\* \* \*

Closing the door behind me, I turned her shoulders and walked her toward the bathroom.

"Come on. I'll run you a nice, hot bath. With candles and

that foamy shit you like." She nodded and gave me a small, sad smile.

"You okay? I haven't really asked how you're doing with all this court stuff."

"It's been a rough couple of days. The court stuff's been mostly procedural so far. It's going to get rough when it comes to giving evidence because the defense will get to cross-examine me."

Hearing shit like that made it hard for me not to punch a hole through the middle of the plasterboard.

"Seeing him though was the worst. I know he's trying to catch my eye in the courtroom. I sit in the stalls with the guys around me and look anywhere but at him. I don't want to give him any more power over me, you know?"

My fists clenched and released as I tried to let go of the stranglehold on my temple. Father Pat told me to make lists in my head, to focus on one thing, then move on to the next. Put the plug in the bath, add the foamy shit, turn on the taps.

Em stood before me, slowly getting undressed. Instead of thinking about how angry I was, I focused on how to take that sad look from her face. As the tiny room started filling up with the steam of the hot water, I grabbed her waist. Gently moving her body between my legs I swirled my tongue around that pink, teasing little nub. One hand drifted to massage the neglected breast, as the steam wound around us like a blanket.

She gasped as my tongue swirled around her nipple then flicked it back and forth. I knew by the spasm in her body that pleasure was going straight to her core. Swapping hands, I released one breast only to feast on the other.

I fucking burned to be inside her so bad. But this wasn't about me. It was about taking Em away from that dark place and reminding her that she wasn't alone. Rising up, I lifted her to sit on the sink. Her hands gripped it to brace herself, and her feet rested on either side of me on the edge of the tub. That was a testament to how small the bathroom was. I sat back down and kissed my way from her ankle all the way to her clit. Swirling around it with my tongue, I teased and teased her closer and closer to the edge of orgasm then brought her back down again. When I knew that every bit of her undivided attention was focused on me, I slid one finger gently inside her warm, wet pussy and carried on licking.

"Jesus, O'Connell. Don't stop please," she begged me. My answer was to slide a second digit into her tight little hole. She moaned as my momentum increased. Thrusting her pelvis toward me, I could feel from the slight tightening and tremor around my fingers just how close she was to coming. When she was almost there, I scissored my fingers gently inside her, took her clit between my lips and sucked. Arching her spine she threw her head back in overwhelming pleasure. The sight of her coming, clenching and tightening around my fingers as she tried to milk a cock that wasn't there, blew me away. This wasn't just sex, it was making love. Both of us knew the difference.

"I think I broke my spine," she told me with a slight giggle. I lifted her off the sink onto wobbly legs.

"How d'you feel?" I asked, before nibbling gently on her ear.

"Loved up. Very, very, very loved up," she told me, kissing her way across my jaw until finally pressing a kiss to my lips. Grabbing her head, I kissed her harder, pulling her warm, naked body hard against my clothed one. My dick pressed painfully against her but I ignored it. She needed that to get rid of the stress and relieve some pressure, and I made sure my girl got what she needed. I always would.

"I'm desperate to return the favor, you know that, right?" she asked.

"I know, Sunshine. But with blue balls is my favorite way to train," I assured her with a wink. Yanking my T-shirt over the top of my head, I pulled the warm fabric down over her. It swamped her as always but I took comfort seeing her wrapped in something of mine and covered in my scent. As I carried her to bed, I thought about all the dark shit behind us and everything we had yet to face but then I focused on the fact that Em would spend the whole of the next day with me. When you find yourself fighting a battle that might consume you, you have to take the small victories where you find them.

\* \* \*

Pounding the London streets at 6 a.m. on a dark winter's morning would seem like most people's idea of hell. I loved it. There was an energy about this city, kind of like an electric pulse that made everything feel alive and connected. But I fucking loved Ireland too. Killarney was maybe the most beautiful place I'd ever seen, but this city had been my home for most of my life. As I thumped one heavy foot in front of the other, I realized that I loved it because London at this hour of the day was so very different to the one people thought they knew. Shopkeepers, bakers, and tradesmen that I passed on my daily route waved and called out words of encouragement. There was a camaraderie among the morning crowd that made me feel like I belonged.

I pulled open the door of the gym just as a light rain started to fall. No matter how early I arrived, Danny was always there first. He was just putting on his coat when I arrived. Sometimes I wondered if he slept here.

"You off for breakfast?" I asked him.

"Same as I do every morning." He huffed at the stupid question it was. Danny was a man of routine.

"Take an umbrella," I warned him. "It's just starting to rain."

"Do I look like I own a feckin' umbrella?" he barked, tucking his scarf into his long coat and donning his flat cap.

"What's got into you today?" I asked him. Danny was the crankiest fucker I ever met but he was in a special mood today.

"Did you see that sky this morning? Red sky at night, shepherd's delight. Red sky in the morning, shepherd's warning. That sky was redder than I've ever seen it until those black clouds rolled it. It's gonna be a bad feckin' day. I feel it in my bones," he informed me, lighting up his cigarette and shivering a little.

"Don't be so superstitious. It's gonna be a great day," I answered him with a grin. My girl was going to be by my side all day today. When we were together, everything was good.

"Pisses me off when you're feckin' cheerful at this hour of the mornin'. At least before you got married, you were too hungover to get on my nerves." I laughed at that.

"Yeah, 'cause me showing up half-baked for training cheered you up no end."

After a pause he looked at me. "You're right. You've always pissed me off in the mornings. Maybe by this afternoon, I'll warm up to you. Now you know the routine. All circuits, no bag work until I get back. Most of the guys are working today so Earnshaw's on point. Don't give him shit 'cause I ain't in the mood."

"Don't stress it," I reassured him. "Didn't you hear? We're friends now."

"That mean you're not going to knock him out again?"

"Maybe," I answered with a grin, which at least got a chuckle out of him.

"Get to work you, cheeky fecker," he told me, still smiling.

He let the heavy door close behind him, and I looked around the empty room. Like London first thing in the morning, this place had its own special energy at this time of day. Since I met Em and quit drinking, it became the best time to work things through.

It was crazy how excited I was having Sunshine with me for the whole day. Some arsehole told me once that the bloom would fade from the rose soon enough, and after a couple of years of marriage, we wouldn't be able to stand each other. Kieran convinced me not to smack him, because the man was in seventies and Em wouldn't like it. Also he'd be dead soon anyway.

I think the fundamental problem was that people didn't understand Em and me. They saw two horny, impetuous kids with no money who'd rushed into marriage and who'd regret it later. Fuck most people. We'd been through more shit than most people went through in their whole life. There was a billion-to-one chance of us finding each other, and now that we had, there was no fucker on this earth who was separating us. Let them try.

Old men in pubs sounding off about how love fades don't know shit. The bloom fades because you fucking let it. You take your woman for granted, you become complacent with your lot in life, and that's when you stand to lose the best thing you never knew you had. My wife was the center of my fucking universe. If that ever changed, I deserved to lose her.

Only I knew better. That would never change. When Em finally met her maker, I'd be right behind her, scorching the earth behind me. We were for life. As I contemplated this, she walked through the door carrying coffee and a box of pastries and wearing one of my hoodies. That right there made my morning. "Hey, baby, how's the training going?"

"Better now you're here," I called out.

"How many you up to?" she asked about the number of press-ups I'd done.

"I don't keep count," I told her. "Only Danny does that. I just keeping going until I can't lift my arms." Flipping onto my back, I beckoned her over for a kiss then swapped the press-ups for sit-ups. The view was better. Earnshaw chose that moment to walk in through the door.

"Hey, part-timer"

"Fuck you. It's still the arsecrack of dawn as far as I'm concerned, and the States are five hours behind us. So when you're at home with your feet up, I'm making magic happen."

Shit, I really didn't have any idea what he did or how much work it took. I was just glad I only had to put on the gloves. "Fair enough," I told him.

"You got one of those things for me?" he asked.

"Sure," Em said. "I always get extra in case some of the guys are around. Kieran literally hoovers these things."

He sat down close to her on the edge of the ring and reached into the box to grab one of her pastries. It was halfway to his mouth when I stopped mid-sit-up and growled. Pausing, his arm still in the air, he stood up and put about two feet between him and Em before sitting back down on the ring. Satisfied that he'd gotten my message, I carried on, and he got his breakfast.

"You know, you'll never get abs like mine you keep eating that shit," I told him.

"I think I'm okay," he replied, lifting his shirt with the hand that wasn't stuffing his face. Em took a sneak peek at the six-pack on show, giggling when I growled again. I still wasn't entirely comfortable with her being around Earnshaw, mainly because I was a possessive, jealous arsehole, but I'd put up with almost anything to hear the beautiful sound of her happiness, however fleeting it was.

"You ready for some real work then?"

"Bring it on," I dared him as I switched to one-handed push-ups. "Let's see what you've got."

# CHAPTER 15

"Kier!" I shouted across the gym.

"What?" he called back.

"Come and rescue me from the American before I punch him in the face," I answered him.

"You can punch me if you can catch me. But you can't because you're not fight-ready and you're slow as shit." Earnshaw danced around the ring like he was Muhammad Ali.

I'd been training since before dawn, I was dog tired, and getting fucking sick of making him look bad in front of my wife. I rolled my head around my shoulders and bounced a while to loosen up.

"You know the great thing about having lifelong friends who'd do anything for you," I said quietly, so that only he could hear. "There's always someone around to hold you down," I told him without waiting for his answer. I looked behind him, and he followed my gaze, expecting to see my guys jump him. When he turned back after realizing that no one was there, I punched him in the face and knocked him out.

"Con, you're gonna give that kid brain damage."

"Danny, he left a good job in America to come and work for you and get in the ring with me. I think he was a little bit brain-damaged anyway."

"Did you angry knock him out?" he asked me.

"I'm not mad. He was just annoying me," I answered him truthfully.

"I'd give you a feckin' bollocking but his constant yammering's been gettin' on my feckin' nerves for the last half an hour."

"Is he all right?" Em asked me. She always got worried when one of us was knocked out. Well, one of *them*. I never got knocked out. I can't imagine how ape shit she'd go if I was. I checked him over, not wanting her to worry. I knew he'd be okay. Already he was starting to come round.

"Can you please stop knocking me out?" he asked me as he pushed himself up to sit against the ropes.

"Can you please stop pushing my buttons in front of Em? As long as she's here, motivation isn't a problem. But you telling her I'm slow or that I'm not ready, it pisses me off but it upsets her. Makes her worry. I can't have that." I nodded in her direction as I spoke, and she gave me a small, nervous smile.

"I hear you," he said as Em handed him a mug.

"Cup of tea," she replied, as she climbed out of the ring.

"I don't drink tea," he whispered to me, and he got points from me for not offending her.

"If it's going spare, I'll take that," Kieran told him as he climbed in the ring after Em.

"Don't worry about it," I told Earnshaw. "It's sort of what Em does when someone needs comfort. She either drinks tea or makes it for someone else. We'll break it to her that you only like coffee when you haven't just been knocked out." The three of us sat propped up against the ropes, Kieran drinking his tea, Earnshaw trying to focus his vision, and me waiting for Danny to come out of the office and bawl me out for taking a break.

"What the feckin' hell is this?" I heard, and we all smiled. "Deaf, dumb, and blind, the three feckin' stupid monkeys. You wanna sit round like a bunch of old ladies, fuck off down the Salvation Army café. They're having tea and biscuits with the pensioners today. They invited me but I told them I couldn't take all the excitement. Watching you three train is much more relaxing. It shouldn't be. Now move!" he barked across the ring, and we jumped to attention.

Earnshaw got up too quick, got dizzy, and fell back down, which made Danny roll his eyes and walk toward the storage cupboard, muttering all the while about the travesty that was our generation. He came back with three skipping ropes and chucked them at us. Climbing out of the ring, I nudged Earnshaw. "Change out of your trainers and put some boxing shoes on. Danny keeps a couple of spare pairs in the cupboard."

"I've got my own. I've just never used them for jumping rope before."

"In this country, mate, it's called skipping," Kieran told him.

"Skipping is for little girls. Jumping rope is for fighters," he replied.

"Well us 'little girls' are gonna kick your arse."

"Con, maybe," Earnshaw retorted, "but not you."

"We'll see," said Kieran, grinning cockily. "Danny makes every fighter, from the juniors to us, skip for hours. It teaches you how to transfer weight from foot to foot quickly and builds solid muscle."

"Why not focus on squats like most trainers do?" he asked curiously.

"Because squats ain't nowhere near fast enough. You need hundreds of repetitions for hours to get the sort of muscle development I'm looking for. These boys ain't been training like this for the last few months. They've been training like this since the day they first walked through the doors," Kieran said, adding his opinion into the mix.

"But squats combined with circuits and running will give you that," Earnshaw argued. Kieran and I smirked at each other. No one argued with Danny's training schedule.

"Skipping is fast and constant. You don't just need strength in a fight, you need speed and efficiency. There's a technique to skipping that will teach you to jump and bounce for hours without getting tired. You need proof, then let's give it a go. Both my boys will outlast you skipping any day of the week," Kieran said.

"You're on," he agreed, and Danny laughed. Two hours later, Earnshaw was in the bathroom, puking his guts up, when Liam called Kieran's phone.

"Shit, man, is that serious? What does it mean for the rest

of the trial? No fucking way...Shit! Yeah, just get back here as soon as you can, okay. The shit's gonna hit the fan, and I'm gonna need your help keeping it together." By the end of the conversation, Kier had turned his back on us and was talking quietly into his phone.

"Okay, bye," he said, disconnecting the call.

"Where's Em?" he asked me, turning around.

"In the office making coffee. What's going on?" He ignored me and jogged over to Danny.

"Go in the office with Em, turn the music up higher on the gym speakers, close the door, and keep her busy." Danny looked at Kieran's mobile and then at me.

"How long d'you need?"

"An hour," he said. "Liam will be here by then. Either we'll have it under control or we'll get him out of here."

My heart was beating nearly out of my chest with anxiety, trying to imagine what was going on that was so bad they'd separate me and Sunshine. Danny walked toward the office and shut the door behind him. Seconds later, the music went higher as Kieran had instructed.

"What the fuck is going on?" I asked. Sitting in front of the ring, he ran his hand down his face. The look of utter fucking devastation scared me.

"The judge ruled Em's rape kit inadmissible as evidence."

"I don't understand, why?"

"The police officer who arrested Frank went to the hospital to check on Em. While he was there, he offered to transport the rape kit to the lab. He thought he was doing a good thing. Thought it would speed up the charges. Anyway,

Frank's solicitor claimed that his involvement after Frank's arrest contaminated the rape kit. Judge ruled in his favor today. The jury won't get to know the results of the kit. It's Frank's word against Em's now."

"Motherfucker," I screamed and grabbed the nearest thing I could find. The stool splintered and fell apart as it crashed into the wall. This wasn't anger...this was blind fucking rage. The motherfucker was gonna get away with it. Em deserved to have people know the results of that kit. It shouldn't have to be his word against hers. The kit was supposed to convict him, and now it was all on Em's testimony.

I stood with my hands behind my head as I tried to rein it in but it was no good. There was no rationality, just the blind, fucking inescapable urge to rip something apart. This would destroy Sunshine, and I couldn't see that look on her face when she found out. I stared at the door of the office and was torn between embracing my rage and needing to protect her.

"Ring. Now," Kieran demanded, and I followed his lead. Whipping his T-shirt over his head, he chucked it to the floor and gave me a right hook to the face. His fists weren't wrapped, and his knuckles split on impact. It was all I needed to trip the switch. My own hands were wrapped, which meant I could go for hours before my hands gave out. Jab, jab, hook. Jab, jab uppercut. I pounded on him with no technique. No grace. Just anger and pain.

When I'd given him a pretty decent going-over, he dropped his guard and bounced around the ring returning what I'd delivered. His hits weren't as heavy as mine but they still hurt. With every hit my anger drained away and Kier stopped punching as soon as I dropped to my knees.

"Shit, Kier, I'm so sorry."

"Don't worry, Con. You'd do the same thing for me. God willing, you'll never have to."

"What am I going to do?" I asked him.

"There's nothing you can do. Calm down, shower, and change, and we'll sit down and tell her together," said Kier.

"No," I told them, swallowing hard. "She won't want to talk to you about this. Just keep her company long enough for me to shower and I'll break it to her myself. She has another counseling session tonight so we'll go straight there after we leave. It might do her some good."

Kier bent down and wrapped his arm around my neck, pulling my head down to rest on his shoulder. "It's gonna be all right. I don't know how things are going to go from here but I do know that everything will work itself out in the end."

I showered and changed quickly while Liam sat with Em. I was fucking devastated about what I was about to do to Em. Everything was falling apart, including me, and I had no clue how to keep it all together. If there was a way of getting out of this dark hole without Em suffering even more, I couldn't see it. As soon as I opened the door to the office, she knew that something was wrong.

"What's happened?" she asked me softly. Looking around the room, I could see the devastation on the guy's faces and the worried look on Danny's. Saying nothing, I held out my hand to her, and she took it. I closed the door behind us, leaving Kier to tell Danny. Sitting up against the ropes seems to have been where I spent most of the day so that's where I told her.

When it was done, she put her head in my lap, curled up into the fetal position, and sobbed. Her anguished cries racked her body, and I did nothing but hold her tight and stroke her hair. I didn't tell her everything would be all right, or that Frank would get sent down. I'd only made one promise to her as she wept, I made another to myself. My promise to her was that he would never get to touch her ever again. My promise to myself was that justice would be served. Either in the courtroom or out of it. If he went down, I'd let it go. If he went free, vengeance would have its day.

* * *

It wasn't a huge surprise to find the motley crew of both our sets of friends standing around in suits on the steep steps of the law courts.

"You look like the cast of *Ocean's Eleven*," I told them.

"I'm Brad Pitt," Kieran called out.

"I'm George Clooney," Liam said.

"I should be Brad Pitt," Tommy grumbled.

"Nah, you'd be one of the stupid brothers," Kieran told him.

"Do I get to be one?" Earnshaw asked.

"Depends," Tommy answered. "Who d'you wanna be?"

"How 'bout Don Cheadle?" he said.

"You know you're not black, don't you?" Tommy asked him seriously.

"Don't be racist," Kieran told him.

"I'm not being fuckin' racist. I'm just asking if he knows." Kieran turned to me and Em. "You ever hear that saying, 'sometimes I listen to you speak and I wonder who ties your shoelaces.'"

We all turned to Tommy, and Kieran winked as Em giggled.

\* \* \*

For an hour, we stood on those steps shivering so Em felt like she could breathe. Even Danny sat out there with us.

Finally she turned to me. "You know how much I love you," she told me quietly.

"I know. Why?" I asked warily, knowing that I wouldn't like the sound of what was coming next.

"I don't want you to come in with me," she told me.

"Why?" I asked through clenched teeth.

"It's enough for me knowing that you're on the other side of the door. It's enough for me to get through this. But I can't go through every detail of what happened, knowing that you're listening. I'd try and make it sound better than it was because I don't want to hurt you. And when I'm cross-examined, I'll be worried about you losing your temper at the barrister. If I know that you're just a door away, I can do what I need to, and I can do it honestly," she explained.

"Emily O'Connell," the clerk called out in a clear voice, and we all stood.

"I don't fuckin' like this, Em; you're my wife. You shouldn't have to face Frank alone. I should be with you."

"You will be," she said and kissed me.

# CHAPTER 16

Apart from the hour they had for lunch, during which neither of them really spoke, Em and Danny were both in that courtroom all day. When they came out, Danny looked devastated, and Em just looked vacant. If it had gone badly, I expected tears or at least a boatload of hugs. But it was like she'd completely shut down.

"How did it go?" I asked.

"Oh, fine," she said. I went to pull her in for a hug. Fuck knows I needed it but she moved out of the way, telling me she needed the bathroom. Once she'd gone, I turned to Danny.

"What the fuck is going on?" I asked him. Looking every single one of his years, he sat dejectedly on the bench in the foyer.

"It was an absolute bloodbath. She did amazing giving her evidence. Held it all together. When the defense examined her, they tore her apart though. I think that, with the rape kit, they would have gone easier, maybe tried to paint Frank in a different light. Without it, it's his word against theirs so they're basically calling Em a liar. A trouble-making teenager who saw this as an opportunity to split up her parents. Their version of events is that she was raped at a house party where she dressed provocatively, and that she tried to pin it on Frank. She answered all their questions but the defense painted a pretty graphic picture of what they think happened."

"Fuck!" Kieran muttered but I was still in shock that it could have gone down that way.

"Didn't the judge step in?" I asked.

"Not his place to. Defense has a right to cross-examine," he countered.

"What about your evidence? What about the kidnapping?" He held his flat cap tightly between his hands and looked down at the floor.

"They still don't know the address of the flat he took her to. It's probably where he left her rings. The only physical evidence tying him to the kidnapping are the prints on the knife in her chest. He claims he was on a fishing trip when she was taken, Em's mum eventually got hold of him, explained what happened, and he came straight to the gym to see if he could help. He told police that, when he arrived, she was already on the floor with the knife in her chest. He touched it and her as he assessed her wounds, then ran off to get help, which is when he says he was picked up. I know Em said he made some calls from the flat but it was probably on a prepaid burner phone. Either it's at the flat or he dumped it before he got picked up."

"What about your testimony?" Liam asked him.

"They did the same to me that they did to her. They must 'ave done a background check on me. Me da was a nasty drunk who killed me sister. He ran off when she died and he was never caught. Lawyers brought it up and my relationship with Em, saying I wasn't above lying for Em to get the justice for her that my sister never had. By the time they were done, I didn't sound like a very credible witness."

"What does that mean? Does he get away with this?" Tommy asked, clearly as pissed off as we all were.

"I think it's all gonna come down to her ma's evidence to-morrow. Our barrister says if she tells the jury what she told Em, we got a chance at a conviction. If she sides with Frank over her own daughter, the barrister thinks he'll walk."

I ran my hands through my hair wildly as my thoughts crashed together in my head. What would I do to Frank if he got out? How would Em ever move forward from this if he was loose? How much time would I go down for making him a fucking cripple?

Kieran grabbed me roughly and pulled me to one side. "No! You don't get to fucking do this! You had your moment of meltdown. Now you have to pull your shit together and get your head out of your arse. Sunshine needs you now more than ever. This ain't about you, it's about her. He gets off, we'll deal with it but not now."

He looked around to see Em heading back. I nodded to

indicate that I was keeping it together, and he squeezed my shoulder before letting go. We walked the short distance to all the cars, the tension so thick you could cut it with a knife. Em's little hand trembled in mine, and I didn't know how someone so tiny, who'd been through so much, could be so strong. She made me seem like a fucking pussy.

"Liam," I spoke to him from the back of the car, "could you take us to our house?"

"That's where I'm going," he replied in confusion.

"Not the flat. Our house." Understanding dawned on him, and he nodded his head as he made the detour. Sunshine continued to stare out of the window like she hadn't heard a word I said. When we arrived, she followed me out of the car on autopilot, stopping only when we reached the front door. Coming around from wherever her head had been, she looked at me funny.

"What are we doing here?" she asked.

"Just checking out the place, seeing how the work is going," I answered.

The others had all headed home except for Liam and Kieran who sat up in the front of Liam's truck. I knew they weren't going anywhere until we were ready to leave. I opened the door and sidestepped past the tools so Em could follow. Even from a quick glance around, you could see that Liam had been busy. Once we'd gutted it, the place was a blank canvas. Now pretty much all the trades were hard at work. Wires hung loose ready to be connected to light fittings, gas pipes stuck out from the walls ready to connect to radiators. The house was a mess, but definitely a work in progress. Em stayed silent as we walked from room to room. When we got to the smallest bedroom, I recognized a couple of Liam's toolboxes and, sitting down on one, pulled her hand to sit down opposite me.

"Danny tell you what happened?" she asked me.

I nodded in reply. "I'm so sorry, love," I said. "I don't know what to say."

"I know you want to make this right. You want to fix me. I'd want exactly the same for you if our roles were reversed. But I'm not the same person I was a year ago. Being cross-examined was like being raped all over again. Only this time they all know. The science even told them I was telling the truth, and still they don't believe me. I'm different than I was then, though. I feel dirty and abused. I want a shower so hot it'll boil my skin, and when we're curled up in bed later, I'll want a good cry. But when that's all done, I won't run and hide. I won't be the little mouse to his big, fat cat. This time I have you and Danny and the rest of my family. So today is going to be shitty, and tomorrow is probably going to be worse, but we'll get through it."

"And if he gets released?" I asked because I'd seen how fearful she was back then and I didn't want that life for her.

"Then we'll deal with that too. And honestly I don't know what he'll do if he does go free. I'm not alone anymore, and he's been accused once. Even if there isn't enough evidence to convict him, maybe mud will stick," she answered. She still sounded strangely detached, but at least now I had more of an idea where her head was at.

"How do you get to be so strong?" I asked.

"I found myself a family of fighters," she replied with a small smile. It was small but I would take it. "Why did we really come here?" she asked.

"Because I wanted to remind you that Frank is all about your past, but this is our future. For better or worse, once this trial is done, this is the future we have to look forward to together."

"You're a good man, Cormac O'Connell," she replied softly.

"I know, baby," I said on a sigh, like my goodness was more like a burden I had to carry. It was all sarcasm. I wasn't a good man. Given the opportunity, I'd cut Frank's balls off with a rusty bread knife and feed them to him. In my book, rapists deserved nothing less. Em knew that about me and loved me anyway. "Come on, baby. Let's get you home. You get a hot shower and a broad chest to cry on."

She reached over and linked her fingers with mine, and I thanked God for the connection. My Em was buried under a mountain of pain and grief, but she was still there, and I'd keep digging until she was back here with me where she belonged.

\* \* \*

The next day dawned and I can't say I'd had much sleep. I spent nearly the whole night just watching over her. After the stress and worry of having to give evidence, Em seemed exhausted. She'd slept for more than ten hours when I woke her.

"We have to get going soon if we're going to make it to court," I warned her. I'd showered and shaved and was already wearing my suit when I crouched beside her. She turned over in bed and leaned on one arm as she brushed some lint off my shirt with the other.

"I'm not going." Her voice was gravelly, like she'd been crying. I hadn't taken my eyes off her for most of the night but I had the feeling she'd have a good cry the minute she was alone.

"Then I'll stay too," I told her.

"No. I need her to see you in that courtroom. She's talked a lot about wanting to be part of my life again, so let's see if she saves me or throws me to the wolves. Seeing you there will remind her of the choice she's making."

"I'd never make you do anything you didn't want to do but don't you think she'd be more rattled if you were there?"

She fiddled with my tie knot absentmindedly as she chose her words. "When she closed the door and let Frank rape me, a part of me died. I lost my virginity and my mother at the same time. I can't go back there. If she's going to betray me again, I need you to cushion the fall."

I nodded and kissed her forehead. "Try and get some sleep, baby," I told her. "You look exhausted."

"You'll ring me as soon as you know anything?" she asked.

"No. Whatever there is to tell you, I'll say as soon as I get home. That way you won't fear the worst if you don't hear and you won't be waiting on my call."

Sitting up, she hugged me tightly, like it was the last time she'd ever get to do it, and kissed me good-bye. I let Kieran in after a gentle knock sounded at the flat door. The main security door was about as secure as our gym lockers, meaning that none of the guys ever bothered even buzzing anymore.

"Can you give me a sec?" I asked Kieran.

"Sure why?"

"I need to leave Em a note. She's not coming with us. And I need to ask Nikki to come over and sit with her. Can you give her a call for me?" I said.

"No need," he replied. "She got a flat this morning and phoned for a lift. She's downstairs in Tommy's car. I'll go and get her."

"Thanks, Kier," I told him as I grabbed one of Em's lined notebooks and a pen.

*Hey Sunshine,*

*I know you couldn't be here but I don't want you feeling bad about it either. Pretty soon for better or worse, this will all be over and I promise you that happy ever after I've been selling you will be just around the corner. Remember how much I love you and if things get really bad, I've hid an emergency bar of chocolate behind the herbal tea bags in the cupboard.*

*Love you forever*
*OC xxx*

*P.S. Why the fuck do we have herbal tea bags?*

I handed the note to Nikki as she walked through the door in a black suit. "Are you sure you don't mind staying with her?" I asked quietly from the doorway.

"She's my best friend, Con. Of course I don't mind. I've given Tommy my flat keys, which is probably a *really* bad idea, but he's going to go back to my place for a hoodie, my laptop, and some DVDs. He'll probably end up hanging out here with us then if his dad doesn't need him. I'll make him do some practice papers on those psychometric tests."

"He told you about that?" I asked curiously.

"Sure. We butt heads a lot but we're becoming fairly good friends." I raised my eyebrow at her.

"It's not like that! Jesus, I knew your mind would be in the gutter about it."

"Hey, as long as you've had all of your jabs, carry on." She knew I was winding her up so she just rolled her eyes at me.

"See you later," I said, grabbing my wallet and keys as I made my way to the door.

"When should I give it to her?" she asked me, waving the note.

"When you think she needs it most," was my answer.

* * *

I walked up the steps of the law courts, flanked by Liam and Kieran like bodyguards, and met Danny at the top. Surprisingly Earnshaw was with him.

"What are you doing here?" I asked him, and he shrugged.

"It didn't feel right at the gym yesterday. I know I don't know you that well, but I thought I'd show my support."

"Appreciate that," I told him. Looking at him standing there with his hands in his pockets, I was selfishly glad Em had stayed at home. He wore his expensive suit far better than I wore my cheap one.

"Looks like I'm not the only one," Earnshaw said, nodding his head toward the steps. Looking fairly respectable in dark trousers, shirt, white collar, and what looked like a hand-knitted sweater with a small hole at the collar, strode Father Patrick.

"Looking sharp, Father Pat," Kieran said straight-faced.

"Thank you, Kieran. I think this jumper really brings out my eyes."

The jumper was beige. I really had no idea whether he was being serious or not.

"Not that I don't appreciate it. But why are you here as well, Father?" I asked him and he turned to Danny to explain.

"You ever lose your temper in front of Father Pat?" Danny asked.

"No," I responded.

"Then that's why," he explained, lighting up another cigarette only minutes after putting out the last one.

"Jesus, I don't need feckin' babysitters, Danny," I scoffed.

"Can we leave Jesus out of this, son? I have a feeling we'll need him on our side later," Father Pat reprimanded.

"Sorry, Father," I apologized.

"You ever seen Frank?" Danny asked.

"No. You know I haven't," I replied grinding my teeth.

"When you do see that smug, slimy bastard, you're gonna want to vault over the barriers and smash his nose into the back of his skull. I know 'cause I've been feelin' that way since I first saw him. Now I'm old enough and wise enough to know my hip would give out long before I ever made that barrier and that destroying his face might feel good but it ain't what Em needs right now."

"And you don't think I've got it in me to keep my temper in check in a courtroom, especially for something this impor-tant?"

"No, I don't. I just said that, didn't I? You're young and im-petuous, and the idea of anyone hurting your girl is gonna twist you up. When that red mist descends, you won't see nothing but him and the great deal of space between his face and your fist. So to be on the safe side, I'm gonna stand on one side of you and Father Pat will be on the other. Kieran, Heath, and Liam will be the human shield in front of you."

"Gee thanks," Earnshaw said, and Danny frowned at him.

"One in, all in," Danny explained to him.

"Let's get this show on the road then," Kieran told them, and we all headed into court.

"I still think this is overkill," I grumbled.

"Well, feckin' deal with it," he answered, putting out his cigarette at the last possible moment.

We were shown to seats in the viewing gallery by the court clerk who eyeballed me like a troublemaker he needed to keep his eye on. The judge came out of his anteroom and sat down just as Frank was brought up from the cells. The bastard was dressed sharply in a dark suit, and his newly cut hair was styled neatly back. If there was any fucking justice in the world, he'd come up from the cells looking like he'd been run over.

As the judge was getting settled, Frank turned and caught my eye. This guy knew exactly who I was. With a sick smirk, he lifted his cuffed hand and waved. Just long enough for me to see Em's tiny wedding ring glittering from his pinkie finger.

# CHAPTER 17

"Motherfucker," I muttered.

"What is it?" Kieran whispered, turning around to face me.

"Pinkie finger, left hand. He's wearing Em's wedding ring."

"He's got to be working with someone. He wasn't arrested with it, so someone's brought it to him."

"Look, there's nothing we can do about that now, so let's just see how this pans out," Danny said quietly. I caught eyes with Frank and stared intently. I wasn't taking any shit from this prick, so I gave him the same look I gave every opponent. The one that told them, without apology, that they were going down. It was the price you paid for going toe to toe with me. It was the price anyone paid for wronging my wife.

After a bit of preamble, Em's mum was called as a witness. Unlike the woman who first turned up at the café to see Em, she'd cleaned herself up. Her newly cut and colored hair sat in a bob around her chin, and she wore a dark suit with a cream blouse and a small gold cross. Nice touch that. Made her seem like a smart, respectable God-fearing woman. She sat down and placed her hands neatly on her lap. After a quiet word from the court clerk, she was sworn in, and when she was done looked straight at Frank. That's when I knew exactly how this was going to go down. If she was going to do the right thing and give evidence against Frank, she would have avoided his gaze. Losing evidence from the rape kit had killed this case but Em's mum was about to drive the nails into the coffin.

"So, Mrs. Thomas, I understand that prior to the incident in question, Emily lived at home with you and Mr. Thomas."

"That's right," she answered quietly.

"For how long prior to the incident had Mr. Thomas been living with you?" The lawyer questioned. "And in what capacity?"

"I lost my first husband eight years ago in a car accident. Mr. Thomas helped me through that grieving process, and he moved in about six months later. I'm sorry to say that I wasn't a good mother at that time but Mr. Thomas helped me raise my daughter, Emily."

"When Mr. Thomas was, as you say, helping you through the grief of losing your husband, did he at any time offer you any drugs or pills to assist you in dealing with your grief and depression?" She listened to the barrister's question then looked first at me and then toward Frank. "No," she said quietly.

"Let me be clear, are you saying that he never offered you as much as a paracetamol?"

"That's right," she said again, much too quickly.

"I see. And at any point during your relationship did that change?"

"No," she answered and didn't embellish any further. The barrister, seeing that this wasn't going anywhere, changed tack.

"How would you describe yourself or your behavior during those early periods of grief and depression?" he asked her.

"I don't remember it in much detail. I do know that there were some days when the pain of grief was so crippling, it felt like waking up with someone sitting on your chest. I'd wake up and forget that my husband was dead, and when I'd remember, I'd have full-blown panic attacks." The way she described herself left me in no doubt that she was being honest. It was probably the only piece of truth there was to this bitch's story.

"How was your relationship with your daughter during this time?" he said.

After a slight pause she replied, but this time she looked firmly down at her hands the whole time. "It was difficult. I guess part of me blamed her for the fact that she was still alive while my husband was dead. Emily was an accident you see. I wanted an abortion, but my husband begged me to keep her. I guess I resented the fact that he was gone and I'd been left to raise her alone."

"I see. And it was during this time that you met Mr. Thomas?" he added.

"Yes," she added, looking briefly at Frank. "When my

husband was alive, I worked part-time as an administrative assistant in the probationary office, with Frank. We didn't really speak much but then I saw him at a family barbecue. The office staff had organized it for some fundraiser. We got talking and then went for lunch on the next Monday morning. We remained friends until after my husband had passed away."

"And at this family barbecue where he first noticed you, tell me, were your husband and daughter with you?"

"Yes, but they didn't meet Frank. Well, Emily did. She was with me, but my husband was helping out with the barbecue."

"And do you recall whether Frank spoke to Emily during this meeting?"

She looked quickly at Frank. "Yes, but he was very nice to her. He told her that her dress was lovely. That she was very pretty. She liked him. We both did," she added defensively, looking up at the barrister.

"And Emily would have been around nine or ten at the time?"

"Nine," she answered suspiciously. "What are you suggesting?"

The barrister held his chin and shook his head. "I'm merely suggesting that Frank paid very little attention to you before he saw Emily. It may be that he formed an attachment to her and used you as an opportunity to get closer to her."

"Objection!" the defense barrister called out.

"Sustained," the judge answered. "And please do try and refrain from making wild conjectures in my courtroom. Let's try to stick with the facts of the case."

"Yes, your honor," the barrister agreed respectfully.

"How did Emily react to your marrying another man so closely following the death of her father?"

"I don't know. We didn't discuss it," she answered without feeling. "I thought she would be pleased. Frank really did love her. He tried very hard to be a good father."

"In what way?" the barrister asked.

"He was always buying her gifts and lots of pretty dresses. When he wasn't at work he spent every minute he could with her."

"And you were resentful of all the attention and affection that he lavished on her?"

She swallowed and looked down again. "Of course not. She was a young girl without a father. It was only natural that she'd need him as much as I did." It was the most unconvincing answer she'd given so far. We might not have any physical evidence, but the barrister was doing a pretty good job of painting Frank as some sick pedophile who'd targeted her mum as a way to get to Em. It made me sick to my stomach to imagine how it played out.

"And in the years following your marriage to Mr. Thomas, did you ever see him hit or punish your daughter in any way?" She looked down again. Surely I wasn't the only one seeing that this was what she did when she was lying. "He disciplined her. As she grew up, she became more willful and disobedient. I wasn't equipped to deal with a teenager so Frank handled it." Frank's face twisted ever so slightly, and it was clear he wasn't happy with how she'd phrased that.

"In what way did Frank discipline Emily?" The barrister

asked. She swallowed again, and I clenched and unclenched my hands to stop me calling her out on all these fucking lies.

"He would ground her mostly. Confiscate things if she was really bad. Send her to her room. The usual way of punishing teenagers, I guess," she replied so quietly I had trouble hearing her.

"Let me be clear then. You are telling the court that at no point did you ever see or hear Frank strike or beat Emily. I would remind you that you're under oath," he pressed her.

She shook her head.

"Please state your answer to the court," the judge directed her.

"No, I never saw or heard him beat or strike her."

"And the night of the alleged rape. What is your account of what happened?"

She looked briefly toward Frank, and he gave her a tiny nod. You'd miss it if you weren't looking.

"We'd had a disagreement. She wanted to go out to a party. We didn't want her wandering around at that time of night, so Frank offered to drive her there and pick her up. We argued about a curfew. She hadn't even turned eighteen yet, and we felt that midnight was a reasonable hour to be home. She didn't agree and argued with us. I don't remember exactly what was said but eventually she walked out, still in her school uniform, and slammed the door behind her."

"What happened then?"

"Frank wanted to go after her but I convinced him to let her calm down. She came home a couple of hours later, and her uniform was all torn up. Her face was bruised and beaten but she wouldn't tell us what happened. She just kept screaming at Frank that it was all his fault. If he hadn't been laying down the law, it would never have happened. She was yelling that she wanted to go back to when it was just me and her. Frank went over to try and calm her down and she scratched his face like a wildcat. One of the neighbors must have heard her and called the police. When they turned up and saw the state of Frank's face, they took him in for questioning."

"Well, that is a very elaborate story, Mrs. Thomas," the barrister responded. "I understand that following the rape you were estranged from your daughter, is that right?"

"Yes. Not by choice, but yes."

She spoke softly, and it was really beginning to piss me off. If you're going to stab someone in the back, do it with conviction.

"May I ask then how you knew anything about Emily's life after leaving your house?"

"We understood that she wanted some space so we left her alone but my husband hired a private investigator."

"And you didn't think that was a breach of her privacy at all?"

"No. We didn't contact her, we just wanted to know that she was all right."

"And once you had this information, did you dispense with the services of your investigator?"

"Yes," she said glancing up at Frank.

"And when she was kidnapped, how did you find out that she was gone?"

"The police telephoned me to tell me that she'd been taken and to ask if I knew where Frank was."

"Is it true that your husband is a probation officer?" he asked.

"Yes, that's right."

"And before that, what did he do?"

"He was a policeman," she told the court.

"And were you aware of Mr. Thomas retaining any of his contacts or friendships from his time with the police force?"

"I don't know. I don't really keep track of who my husband's friend are."

"I understand, Mrs. Thomas. Finally, I would like to know whether you have ever seen or heard Mr. Thomas touch or speak to Emily in a way that would be considered inappropriate for a father with his biological daughter?" The bitch didn't look at me or Frank once. She looked straight at the barrister and crucified her daughter.

"No, I didn't." The barrister had no further questions, and the judge dismissed us for a break.

"What the fuck?" I said walking over to our barrister.

"Not here," he told us authoritatively. "Not in front of the defense." Following his lead, we went into the foyer where all the guys crowded around him looking pretty pissed off.

"What was that? You gonna just stand there and let her spin her bullshit lies and then just walk off the stand?" I barked at him.

"What would you have me do, Mr. O'Connell? I understand your frustration, but without tangible evidence, I can't accuse a sworn witness of being a liar. I did explain to Mr.

Driscoll that if Mrs. Thomas stuck with her original statement, we'd have no case."

"So what now?" Danny asked him dejectedly. He looked so old and forlorn. This was going to destroy Em, and none of us knew what to do about it.

"I'm not going to call Frank to the stand. He's skilled at manipulating his audience so I don't think it will do our case any good. The prosecution will likely call him, and he'll embellish the story they've cooked up. Then we'll go for summations, and the jury will adjourn to deliberate. In all likelihood, he will be acquitted. There really isn't enough corroborated evidence to make either charge stick. Mr. Thomas has done a thorough job of creating the public facade of an honorable and respected member of society and a loving stepfather. We've challenged his character, but I'm sorry, I really don't think that what we have is enough to satisfy the jury beyond all reasonable doubt."

I sat down hard on the bench and rubbed my face with my hands in despair. How can he rape, kidnap, and torture her and just walk out of the courtroom a free man? As Danny and the guys debated shit with the barrister, my fear turned to anger. It wasn't fair for Em to grow up in a home where she was raped and beaten. It wasn't fair that I had an alcoholic mother who'd made my childhood a living hell. None of it was fair but I had the power to make it right and give my girl the justice she deserved. With my mind made up, I felt calmer and more in control than I had for a long time.

"Shall we go back in?" I said to Kieran and stood up. The guys all stopped talking and turned to stare at me.

"What's going on? We thought we'd have to sit on you after her mother's performance."

"It is what it is. There's nothing I can do about it. Let's just get this over with, shall we." Turning, I buttoned up my suit jacket and walked toward the courtroom. The last thing I saw was the grave look on Kieran's and Danny's faces. They knew me better than anyone in the world, except maybe Em. Aside from babysitting me every minute of every day, there was nothing they could do about my plans, even if they did figure them out. The legal system had its chance. It was going to fail Em, but I wouldn't. Not again.

By tomorrow morning, one way or another, we'd know. Frank had given his testimony, and I hadn't flinched while he did it. The guys kept looking at each other worriedly as they noticed my behavior. I was still because I was focused. Like I did when I fought. I tuned out all the outside shite and thought only about what I needed to. I didn't hear a word Frank said. Didn't matter anyway. The lying sack of shit looked like he was having fun up there in the lime-light.

One hour. That's all it took for both sides to finish with him. But, oh, what I did to him in that hour. Every conceivable means of torture ran through my head. In my mind, Frank died a thousand times but I only needed to pick one way to make it happen for real.

Lifting my hand to put the key in the door, I paused and took a minute to work out what I was going to say. I wanted to shield Sunshine from everything and tell her it was all going to be okay. She wouldn't thank me for it. I'd do whatever

I needed to keep her safe, and I wouldn't apologize for it, but I wouldn't lie to her either.

"How's she been?" I asked Nikki, as I walked into the flat.

"Pretty bad," Nikki replied quietly so Em wouldn't hear. She looked worriedly behind her, and I could see Em was still in bed.

"She says she's all right, just having a bad day. How'd it go in court?"

I shook my head slowly and wiped the friendly smile off her face quickly. "He's getting away with it," I told her.

"They've released the verdict already?" she whispered angrily.

"They will tomorrow but our barrister is sure he's going free."

"This will destroy her," she said sadly, looking Em's way.

"After everything she's been through, people still doubt how strong she is. It's going to hit her hard, but if we stick by her, she will move past this."

Nikki nodded and gathered up her things. "I won't say good night," she told me. "She's been asleep for about half an hour so I want her to get some rest. Tell her I sent my love though."

"Kieran is waiting for you downstairs. He's going to give you a ride home."

"Thanks, Con," she said giving me a hug and a quick kiss on the cheek. "Take care of her," she ordered as she left with a wave.

Locking the door behind me, I walked over to see my girl. She looked deceptively peaceful as she slept, and I needed some of that peace now. Peeling off my suit, I climbed into bed and wrapped my body around her. Thinking back over the day, I knew she needed a man who was gentle and kind to see her through this. I was neither of those things. The fury I was going to unleash would take me to a place darker than I'd ever been. Maybe at the end of it, I'd be dead or behind bars myself. Fuck it. The angel in my arms had given me salvation. If I had to go back into hell to keep her safe, so be it.

# CHAPTER 18

Em's eyes blinked open as she woke and automatically looked for me.

"Hey," she said, and I knew by her gravelly voice that she'd spent a good part of yesterday crying.

"Mornin', love," I answered her.

"You been awake for long?" she asked.

"Not long," I assured her. I'd been awake for two hours, and before that, I hadn't slept much all night. The last time I'd fallen into a fitful sleep, I dreamed that Frank had taken her from outside the courtroom, and that her body had been left on the steps of the gym. I woke as I dreamed of holding her in my arms, her blood pooling beneath me as life drained from her tiny body. The tears I'd cried in sleep were still wet on my cheeks when my eyes opened. I didn't try and sleep again. My eyes were scratchy from staring so hard, like she was some kind of ghost who'd fade and disappear if I turned away, even for a moment.

"What's wrong?" she asked, knowingly.

"Things didn't go so well yesterday," I admitted.

"She sold me out, didn't she?" Em said sadly, and I nodded.

"Tell me everything, O'Connell. I need to know," she pleaded.

"Trust me, love. You really don't. She sided with Frank. That's all you need to know." I replied, desperate to protect her from as much of the fallout as I could. "So fuck the bitch," I told her. "She sold you down the river when she let Frank get away with raping you. I never thought any parent who did that would change, so fuck her. Her and that bastard can rot in hell for I care," I told her venomously.

"She's still my mum though. It still hurts," she admitted.

"I know, love," I told her sadly.

I would make this right for her but she couldn't know that. So for the moment, I'd do my best to help her through this.

"Let's stay here today. We'll take a day off from school and training and court and just spend the day in bed, watching old movies," I suggested, knowing full well that I couldn't afford to take the days off from training I already had, let alone another one to just stay in bed. None of that mattered though. Everything was secondary to taking care of my wife. It always would be.

"I can't think of anything I'd love to do more," she said, and I waited for the "but." I knew it was coming by the look of determination on her face.

"But we're going to court," she told me.

"Why put yourself through it, Sunshine? You know your being there won't make any difference to the verdict."

"I want Frank to know I'm not scared of him anymore and that I'm not alone. He might get away with what he did but I've cried the last tear I'm going to cry over what happened. I have a wonderful life ahead of me, and I want to live it. So let's go to court and show them that we're not afraid, get this thing over with, and get on with our lives."

"It can't possibly be that easy, love," I cautioned her.

"It won't be. Of course it won't be. I have waking night-mares every day when a smell or a sound brings back what happened but you told me once that the good stuff takes up room, so we have to let the bad stuff out to make that happen. That's what the therapy is for. But for now, the only thing we have to fear is fear itself."

"That sounds like another one of them famous quotes," I said.

"Franklin D. Roosevelt in his presidential inauguration speech."

"You are wicked smart, you know?" I told her. "I love that you want to be strong and move on from this, I really do. I mean, watching you cry over what this guy did kills me a lit-tle bit more each time I see it. But I don't think I can let it go that easily. I didn't protect you once, despite my promises, and when he's released I feel like I'd be letting you down a second time."

"You have to try, O'Connell, or he's not only ruined my past. He's ruined my future as well." That was never going to happen. I would take care of that for her, and she'd never have to be afraid of anything else ever again.

We turned up for court at nine, but deliberation took much longer than any of us thought. When the steps became too cold, we moved to the benches in the lobby outside the courtrooms. Eventually, when I didn't think I could wait much longer, the clerk came out of the dark, heavy oak door and told us that a verdict had been reached. We filed silently into the courtroom one by one, with Em sitting in the middle of us.

Without prompting, Danny and I, who were seated either side of her, held each of her hands tightly. Em's mum, who was already seated on the other side of the courtroom, had turned to face us when we filed in. For a brief moment, she caught Em's eye, but Sunshine quickly turned her face away. She was done, and by the wave of regret that washed over her mother's face, her mum knew it too. Like I said before, fuck the bitch.

She turned to watch as Frank was brought up from the cells in cuffs; we all did. The bastard had the brass balls to wink at Em as he was led to his seat, and I wanted to vault over the barrier and remove his kidney. Maybe removing it was ambitious but I was pretty sure I could render it useless for the rest of the cock's miserable life with one good punch.

Sunshine filled me with pride. In a gesture completely un-like her, she lifted her hand and gave him the finger. Frank frowned angrily. This wasn't the same girl he left bleeding on the floor. The courtroom went silent as the judge left his chambers and the clerk said, "All rise." We stood, then sat again as the judge was seated. The clerk moved over to Frank. "The defendant will stand," he called out, and Frank stood up smugly.

"Members of the jury, will your foremen please stand," the clerk said, and an older guy rose from the jury. He had a kind look about him, and I closed my eyes, hoping this guy could deliver me a miracle. Hoping that he would deliver me justice.

"Have you reached a verdict upon which you are all agreed?" he asked, and the man replied, "We have."

"Do you find the defendant Frank Stephen Thomas guilty or not guilty of the charge of rape?" There was the slight pause and then the deep baritone voice sounded clearly across the courtroom. "Not guilty."

"And in the charges of kidnapping and assault with the intent to kill, do you find the defendant guilty or not guilty?" The pause didn't seem as long this time because I knew what was coming. "Not guilty."

"Is this the verdict of you all?" the clerk asked.

"It is," the guy replied. The man who I thought looked kind only a minute ago, now looked like any other fat, middle-aged fuck, judging my girl's word over that rapist and finding her the liar.

"Mr. Thomas," the judge called out clearly, "you are free to go."

"All rise," the clerk called out, and the judge had already fucked off for his afternoon game of golf before anyone realized that Em and I still sat in our seats. I looked over to see the bailiff unlocking Frank's cuffs, and Em's mum looking down into her lap. I hope the bitch was fucking petrified at taking Frank back. She'd brought this on herself. On all of us.

"What now?" I asked Em. I didn't know whether to hold her close or carry out my plan of putting one of Frank's kidneys out of commission. I wanted to do both.

"No hugging or commiserating," she told us all. "I don't want to give Frank the satisfaction."

"Let's just go back to the gym."

"You don't want to go straight home?" I asked her.

"No. There's something I need to do first."

"Okay, love," I told her, "whatever you need." Frank's barrister quickly led him outside and down the steps of the law courts, probably for his own safety. I stared a hole in the back of his head but the fucker, grinning ear to ear and laughing with his barrister, ignored me until he climbed into a cab and then turned and fucking waved at me before driving off.

"You guys okay to stay here, and I'll bring the truck round?" Liam said.

"Sure," Kieran replied. "When you're on your way, I'll drop Nikki home on my bike then grab us all some lunch and meet you back at Danny's." I couldn't think about eating after what had just happened.

"I need the bathroom a minute, love. You okay to wait here with everyone?"

"Sure," she replied looking worn out. After a quick kiss, I raced back up the steps of the courthouse, quickly bypassing the doors to walk around the side of the building. Out of sight, I placed my hands against the cold stone and vomited until there was nothing left. A clean, white handkerchief was held in front of me as I turned to face Danny.

"Well done for not doing it in front of her, son," he told me.

"You don't think I'm a pussy for losing my stomach over a guy I could take out in under one round?"

"Son, I puked when I woke up this mornin'. Does that make me a pussy?"

"I'm pretty sure you're the feckin' hardest man I know," I told him. He just nodded his head and grunted, like that was a given.

"Come on. We'd better get back. Told Em I was emptying my catheter bag. If we take much longer, she's likely to walk into the men's toilet to try and help."

"Is she gonna be okay?" I asked him, and he chuckled.

"She asked me that same question about you not five minutes ago. But that's Sunshine for you. Always worrying about everyone else before herself."

"What do we do now, Danny?" I asked, feeling pissed off, sad, despairing, and vengeful all at the same time.

"We train, Con. It's all we can do. Bad shit happens all the time. You keep moving forward until you find some happiness that makes you glad you kept moving," he told me. It was good advice but I wasn't ready to move forward yet. Not until I could purge all this shit building inside me.

\* \* \*

Danny opened up the gym, and we followed him inside, my hand at the small of Em's back. For the first time in as long as I can remember, this place didn't feel like home. No matter what shit my ma put me through, I could almost always find peace here, and what I found inside those four ropes was justice. That was gone now, and killing Frank was the only way I knew how to get that back. I didn't want to tie him down and slice him up like he'd done to Em. No, I wanted one round with him in the ring. Three minutes with no gloves was all I needed to make everything better again. Taking off the wool coat that was a gift from me, she draped it over one of the folding chairs. Pulling another toward her, she sat down.

"What are you doing?" I asked.

"Waiting for you," she replied. I gave her a funny look as I tried to work out what she was talking about.

"I'm your wife, O'Connell. I know you almost better than anyone else in the world. If we go home now, all that hate is going to eat you up, and you won't sleep any better than you did last night," she said.

"How do you know I didn't sleep last night?" I asked.

"Wife, remember?" she said, holding up her hand and wiggling her ring finger. Knowing she was right, I changed quickly, wrapped my hands, and taking the time to kiss Em gently on the forehead, went to the bag and unleashed hell. I pounded on it relentlessly, not bothering with combinations, just hooking and jabbing repeatedly, with power that came only from hours of discipline and dedication.

At the speed I was punching, there was no way I should

be able to hit the same mark every time but I was, because every spot on the bag I hit was one of Frank's vital organs. In normal training, Danny would time me on each apparatus then move me on. Strengthen my arms and toughen my knuckles but work on my core as well. There was no stopping me now though. I heard Kieran and the other guys talking quietly as they ate their lunch. No one else trained, they just sat and waited with me.

"I can't take this anymore," I heard Kieran say. "I'll go toe to toe with him if that's what he needs."

"Sit down, Kier. Let him work this out himself."

The sun had long set when my punches finally slowed. The once grayish-white wraps were soaked with blood where my knuckles had split, and I could barely lift my arms. Slumping down, I leaned my back against the ring and, raising my knees up, rested my hands over the top as I looked for my girl. Already out of her chair, she knelt down in front of me and started to carefully undo my wraps. When they were off, she kissed the back of each set of bloodied knuckles before cupping my cheek with her tiny hand.

"Let's go home now," she told me. Danny, Kieran, Liam, Tommy, and Earnshaw all sat waiting for me. Not only had they been there today but they waited while I vented my rage in case I needed them. That was family for you.

# CHAPTER 19

Bruises fade, torn skin scabs and heals, but hate festers. When left unchecked, it festers deep in the pit of your soul. My hatred for Frank had been festering for a long fucking time. There are many things in this world I'd do for Em but I didn't think that letting go of that hate would be one of them.

This arsehole had wronged my girl in the worst fucking way. I could maybe have lived with justice. Maybe. But when there was no justice, all I had was fucking vengeance. My brand of vengeance might even kill. Only I wasn't sure that death would be justice either. All I knew was that I had to be the one to deliver it.

For the most part, I pretended that things were going back to normal. Em had gone back to school which I fucking hated. I'd grown used to having her with me when I trained, and like I told her before, I was needy. I trained like an absolute fucking demon. God help Rico Temple if I got to him before Frank because no motherfucker wanted to be the vessel for my rage at the moment.

There wasn't enough training that Danny could throw my way that would curb my appetite for violence. I was hungry for it in the worst possible way. Danny had that look in his eyes that said he was worried I was going into the ring half-cocked again. But this time anger hadn't made me stupid. It motivated me to shape my body into the most lethal killing machine I could so that, when the time was right, I'd be ready. Frank had already sealed his fate. He just didn't know it.

Just over a week since the trial had gone by. I was nine hours into training, when Danny had hung his head in despair and sent me on a run. No matter what he threw at me, it wasn't enough to slow me down. It wasn't so much that I was pushing myself too hard, but what fueled me that pissed him off. Kieran arrived just as I was leaving but Danny barked at him to get his arse into the office before I could do little more than say hi. The only thing I struggled with, the only pull on my conscience, was that voice in the back of my mind telling me that Em wouldn't want me to follow through with this. That voice was probably the reason why I found myself outside St. Paul's. The church was empty but Father Pat was tidying up hymn books as I let the door close behind me with a bang.

"Jesus, Mary, and Joseph, Cormac. Do you have to sneak up on an old man like that?" he said.

"Sorry, Father. D'you have a minute to talk about some stuff?" I asked him.

"Does this talk come before or after you've lost your temper?" he asked.

"Both," I replied immediately.

"Ah. It's permission and forgiveness you'll be wanting then. You best come into the back for a cup of tea. Bolt those doors behind you would you? I thought they were locked already. That's why you scared me." He didn't wait for a reply but shuffled into the vestry to boil the kettle. After bolting the door, I joined him.

"Well then," he said, as I sat down and fiddled with my cross absentmindedly. "What's going on in that head of yours?"

"Did you hear? Frank, Emily's stepfather, got away with everything."

"Aye, I heard. Terrible business it was. How's your lovely lady doing?"

"She's doing her best to move on. The therapy's helping with that. She's a lot sadder than she used to be. More cautious. But every day that goes by, she seems better."

"And you?" he asked me.

"I'm struggling with something, but if I talk to you 'bout it, you can't go to Danny or Em, right?" I asked him.

"Well, technically this isn't confession, son, but if you're telling me in confidence, it stays between us."

Satisfied that it wouldn't go anywhere, I unloaded my dilemma. "I can't let go of what happened. As long as Frank is walking around a free man, Em will never feel safe, and it's eating me up inside when I think of what he did to her. I want to end him. I want to crush the life out of him and make him scream like he did to Em."

"But?" Father Pat said. Honestly I expected more of a reaction when admitting to wanting to kill a man to my parish priest.

"But if I follow through with this, either I get locked up, which takes me away from Em, or I do something she won't be able to live with. So what do you think?" I asked him.

"Romans chapter twelve, verse nineteen," he said, placing mugs of tea in front of us both.

"Huh?"

"'Beloved, never avenge yourselves, but leave it to the wrath of God, for it is written, "Vengeance is mine," I will repay, says the Lord.'" I laughed because I knew his answer would be along those lines.

"Doesn't it also say 'an eye for an eye, a tooth for a tooth'?" I asked him.

"Ohh, I love me a good Bible debate. Custard cream?" he offered, holding out a plate.

"No, thank you," I answered, automatically turning down anything that would have Danny smacking me over the back of my head if he could see.

"Father, I'm pretty sure I've never ever been in a debate with anyone. If I have a disagreement with someone, and they start winning 'cause they're smarter than me, I usually just punch them and end the argument," I told him.

"I see. And that works with your wife, does it?" he asked me, chuckling as he dunked his fourth biscuit in his tea.

"There's never an argument. Em's always right. Even when she's wrong."

"That, my son, is why you will have a long and happy marriage."

"There's no right or wrong answer here, is there?" I asked.

"Of course there is, Con. You just don't want to see it," he replied.

"If I do nothing and he ever touches her again, I couldn't live with myself, and I can't live with her being afraid and always looking over her shoulder either. If I go to prison or she hates me for what I've done, isn't that a price worth paying to keep her safe?"

"Cormac, there comes a time in any man's life where he has to choose what kind of man he will be. When he reaches that line between good and evil. For some men, they cross the line a fraction then make a series of decisions that takes them farther and farther, until one day they are so far from the line they don't even know where it is anymore. For other men, it's one great big jump they knowingly make. One thing I do know though, is that once you cross, it's nearly impossible to cross back."

"But for Em, wouldn't that jump be worth it?" I asked.

"Tell me then, and answer honestly. Would you be doing it for yourself, lad, or for your wee wife? Because I'm pretty sure the Emily O'Connell I know wouldn't want that for you. That she'd happily have Frank Thomas alive, and all the risks that go with his being free, if it meant she got to spend every day for the rest of her life with you. That's how much she loves you. So when you think about it, the question is, would you give up your vengeance for a lifetime with her?"

I thought about what he said, and it occurred to me that

I'd never thought about it like that before. Was I selfishly giving in to my hate instead of letting it go to be with Em? It's what she was trying to do. Forget a lifetime of hell for a future of heaven. I had a lot to think about.

"I'd best get going. Em will be waiting for me. Thank you for the tea, Father," I told him.

"You're very welcome, Cormac. My door is always open."

"Except when it's double bolted," I said smirking.

"Well, those little feckers round the corner thinks it's funny to sneak in when I nip off for a cup of tea and hide the hymn books round the church." I laughed, remembering how we used to do the same thing.

"Now go on with you and be with that pretty wife of yours. It will do you good to remember everything God's given you, rather than focusing on what's been taken away." I passed him my mug, and he walked me back to the church doors.

"If you ever need to talk again Cormac, if you ever feel your temper getting the best of you, you know where I am." I nodded in thanks, then bracing myself against the cold, put my head down and pounded the streets back to my girl, feeling a little lighter than I had in a while.

\* \* \*

There was a fucking eerie feeling in the air when I got back to the gym. Not one person was training, which was unusual because at least a few of the lads came here after school every day. Knowing something was up, I headed to the office.

Danny, Earnshaw, and Liam all stood there with their arms crossed while Kieran knelt with his arm around the shoulders of my wife. Her puffy face was still red from crying and the tracks of her tears still clung to her cheeks.

Kier moved away quickly as I raced around the desk and grabbed her to me fiercely. "What happened love?" I asked her softly.

"I finished up my last class of the day. I needed to speak to one of my tutors so most of the class had already left. As I was leaving, Frank grabbed me from behind and pulled me into one of the empty classrooms. He wanted to know why I'd betrayed him and the family by pressing charges. He told me he'd missed me. He . . . he sniffed my hair and pushed his thigh between my legs when he shoved me against the wall. I froze. I just stood there and couldn't move. Why couldn't I move?" Em asked me. Fear had paralyzed her. Trying to control my blind fucking fury paralyzed me.

"How did you get away, darlin'?" Kieran asked gently.

"The cleaners came in through the back door. Frank must have panicked because he let me go and ran," she answered him.

"Do you think he was trying to kidnap you again?" he asked. A part of me wanted to tell him to leave her alone but every dumb part of my fucking useless brain was fixated on the fight. Where could I find him? How could I get him alone long enough to take my time with him? What method of torture would hurt the most? These were the thoughts that consumed me.

"No, if he was going to take me, he'd have done it quickly

and before I knew what was coming. I've lost any credibility now he's gotten away with it once. People will think I'm crying wolf if it happens again. He's just letting me know he's not finished with me," she responded.

Earnshaw looked stunned. For him, I guess everything that had happened with the trial happened in the abstract. Seeing Sunshine this upset was pretty fucking real. Liam ran his hand through his hair despairingly. "I just don't get what this guy's problem is," he said. "Why's he so fixated on you, Em? I mean, I thought he was just an opportunistic predator, what with you being under the same roof and all. But this shit's personal. The guy's fucking obsessed with you."

Em's shaking grew worse as the truth of Liam's words sank in. Kieran tightened his arm around her shoulders to anchor her and looked up at me. "Con?" he asked questioningly. Looking back, I regret so many things. Not going straight to Em that night and taking her in my arms was top of that fucking list. I should have comforted her and told her that everything would be all right, that I'd take care of her. In reality, I'd done the exact opposite. In the short time this angel had been mine, I'd failed her in so many ways. That moment was probably the worst. I was two steps and two arms away from making everything seem a little better for her, making her a little less scared. Instead I turned and walked away. Becoming the stupid arrogant kid I used to be, I went to find Frank. Going to my locker, I grabbed a hoodie, chucked it over my head, and shoved my wallet and keys into the pocket. Slamming the door, I went outside only to be flanked by Liam and Kieran. "What do you two think you're doing?" I asked them.

"You know we were never going to let you do this on your own, don't you?" Kieran said to me, shivering against the cold.

"You should walk away. I love that you have my back. I really fucking do. But this ain't gonna have a good end. Frank is my problem. I don't want you both getting your hands dirty with this," I said.

"Con, one of us has a problem, it's on all of us to sort it out," Liam told me. "Been that way since we were kids. Ain't nothing changing that now."

"It's gonna get messy," I warned. "I'm not fucking about with this guy. He ain't never letting go of Sunshine."

"Wouldn't have it any other way, so let's get this done," Liam said. We piled into his truck and drove about half a mile before he pulled over.

"Why'd you stop?" I asked him.

"Tommy," Kieran and Liam both answered together. Sure enough the door opened and he climbed in beside me.

"What's up, bitches?" he screeched annoyingly.

"You dragged Tommy into this?" I asked them. Kieran snorted from the front of the truck.

"Do you think we'd ever hear the end of it if we didn't tell him what was going down?" he replied.

"You were gonna leave me out?" Tommy said sadly.

"Jesus, Tom. It ain't like we're going to party the feckin' night away without you. We're gonna take care of Frank. That ain't something you should want to be a part of," I told him.

As seriously as I'd ever seen him, he asked me, "Would

you do the same for me?" I should have told him no. Made him get out of the truck. But these boys were the nearest thing I had to brothers. They'd know if I was lying. Looking him square in the eyes, I nodded.

"Ain't nothing to talk about then, is there?" he asked with a cocky grin.

We drove in silence until we got to the Severn Bridge, and then a thought occurred to me. "How'd you know where we're going?" I asked Liam.

He paused before answering. "Night Em was taken, I heard the address come through the copper's radio before he turned it down."

"And you didn't think to fucking share this bit of information when I was climbing the fucking walls looking for her?" I shouted at them all.

"Don't get mad at them about it," Liam barked at me. "I heard it, and I kept it to meself. The police were heading there anyway to check it out. If you knew the address, you'd have torn that fucking house apart and scared the shit out of her mother. Instead of being there when they found Em, you'd have been behind bars." His tone told me that he wasn't sorry.

"That should 'ave been my decision," I argued with him.

"I did what I thought was right, and I ain't sorry for it. Now stop your feckin' bitchin'. I'm telling you now, ain't I?"

After a few minutes of brooding silence, I'd calmed down enough to acknowledge that he had a point. Besides, after tonight I'd probably be in prison so I needed to build bridges while I could. "Look, I'm sorry, mate. I ain't exactly rational at the moment. I'd probably have done the same thing if I was you." The whole truck went completely silent. "What?" I asked them.

"The great Hurricane O'Connell fucking apologizing," Liam said with a chuckle.

"Yeah, well," I grumbled, "don't get fucking used to it. I ain't wrong often."

The mood became more serious, the farther into Wales we drove. The rain poured heavily on the road ahead of us and reflected my mood. As I watched one lonely drop of water roll down the window, I thought about the rivers my girl cried as she told me what had happened. Already I knew how badly I'd fucked up, just walking out on her like that. I'd been thinking of my own anger instead of her pain. I hoped she'd forgive me. I hoped that this would bring her some peace. I hoped for a million things when it came to Em. Only time would tell whether I got any of them.

# CHAPTER 20

We pulled up outside a tidy, well-looked-after semidetached house on a quiet street. Immediately I knew Liam had been here before. Not once along the way had he checked the address or asked for directions.

"I'll knock on the door. He'll answer it. I'll kick the shit out of him," I told them.

"How do you know he'll answer it?" Tommy asked.

"Because the guy's a fucking control freak," Kieran answered for me. "I'd be very fucking surprised if he lets his missus take a piss without asking for permission." A car was in the drive, and the lights were on but the rain beat down too heavy for me to see much of anything inside the house. None of the guys pushed me or said anything to me when I just sat there watching that house that was so normal-looking and average on the outside. But knowing what had happened inside was the reason Em relived the rape in her dreams over and over, knowing that it was the reason she flinched whenever new people moved too quickly around her, only loosened the rein I had over my temper.

I pictured everything I'd overheard from her nightmare about the rape, and I remembered, with aching heartbreaking clarity, how I felt when he took her and how tiny, beaten, and broken she looked unconscious and bloodied in that hospital bed.

What the fuck was I still doing sitting in this truck? This ended now. I climbed out and slammed the door before any of the guys had a chance to move.

Running across the street, I pounded on the front door, and when Frank opened it with a cocky smirk, I pulled my shoulder back and punched him square in the face. Like the spineless sack of shit that he was, he collapsed to the floor unconscious. I'd knocked him out with one punch, and it felt fucking amazing. He'd collapsed in the doorway but I was nowhere near done. Hell, this wasn't even the end of round one.

I could have picked him up easily but I didn't want to touch him any more than was necessary to cause him some serious pain. So I grabbed him by the back of the collar and pulled him through the corridor. When I reached the living room, I dropped him, letting his head hit the carpeted floor with an audible thud. As I turned to head back to the front door, it closed gently and in walked Kieran. Sitting himself down on the sofa, he waited for my cue.

"Tommy and Liam?" I asked him.

"Keeping watch," he murmured. Frank started to come

around, and I willed it so I could knock him out again. I wanted to keep doing it until his head was so fucked up he didn't even know his own name. When he came to, the fucker had the audacity to look up at me and laugh.

"This is priceless," he joked. "After this, you'll be looking at a stretch behind bars, and as far as Emily is concerned, I'll make you feel like a distant memory."

"You don't get to fucking say her name. Not to me. Not ever," I warned him, giving him a swift kick to the ribs, which made him wheeze and cough. "What's wrong, old man?" I barked at him. "Not so much fun when you're on the other end of the boot, is it?"

"Fuck you," he wheezed, dragging himself up onto the seat. I let him but only because it put his face at fist height.

"Fuck me?" I shouted at him. "One punch and a kick to the gut is my way of slow dancing up to the arse kicking I'm about to deliver. When I'm fucking finished with you, your own mother won't even recognize your fuck-ugly face." The fucker smiled at me, and without hesitation, I punched him in the face again. Blood streamed from his nose and a cut at the corner of his eye, and he spat more blood onto the floor, not caring that it was his own fucking carpet he was messing up.

"What made you think you had the right to go anywhere near her?" I asked, punching him again.

"You don't touch her, you don't even think about her, or I will fucking end you!"

"Do you know what she sees in you? Absolutely nothing. I gave her a lesson she didn't like, and she ran straight into the arms of the first boy she came across. You knew, from the minute you saw her, she was out of your league, and you've done nothing but try and drag her down to your level ever since."

I hit him in the ribs, winding him enough to shut him up. I hit him for being right. I never was good enough for Sunshine, and maybe I was on borrowed time, but he was wrong about her not seeing anything in me. Her love for me was imprinted in every single cell of my body. I'd give anything to keep her safe and happy. I'd leave this life knowing what it feels like to belong to another person. To belong to her.

"What is this sick, fucking obsession you have with her?" Kieran asked, finally breaking his silence.

"You know nothing about my family," he snarled.

"Well, she certainly ain't your fucking daughter, so what is she to you?" Kieran shouted. He was losing his shit as much as I was. Em was my girl but she was near enough his sister.

"She's mine!" Frank screamed. "She's been mine since she was nine years old. I waited all this time, and now she's coming back where she belongs."

"What did you just say?" I asked him.

"Don't look at me like that! I never fucking touched her. Marrying her whiney, miserable bitch of a mother was the only way to keep Emily close, make sure she was safe."

"But you beat her black and fucking blue. You raped her!" I yelled at him.

"I kept her good and pure. Without my lessons, she would have run wild. Everything I did, I did for her. And I didn't rape her. She wanted it! She wanted it so bad. Every day she did things to show me how much she wanted me to touch her. Always trying to tempt me, and I held out. I resisted her until she was almost eighteen. After that, she'd be an adult. I could have gotten rid of her mother, and it would have just been the two of us. Everything would have been fine. It was fine until you got your grubby little paws on her."

"You're a filthy fucking pedophile!" Kier shouted at him.

"I never touched her when she was a kid!" he defended himself.

"The fact that you even looked at a nine-year-old that way, that you made plans to involve yourself in her life, whether you touched her or not that makes you a pedophile," Kieran threw back at him.

But Frank just smiled, and I knew then why Em had been so scared. Frank would just keep going and going until he had Em again. This fixation would never end. Leaving him there, I went into a couple rooms before I found the kitchen. After rummaging through a few drawers, I found what I was looking for. The kitchen knife in my hand was probably clumsier and less sophisticated than the one he'd used on Em, but I bet the pain would still feel the same. I imagined Em as a little girl standing in this kitchen, never feeling safe. Always afraid. I'd tear this fucking world apart to take that pain away from her but I couldn't, and it was all this sick fuck's fault.

He laughed as I walked back into the room with it in my hand. "You haven't got the balls to stab me," he taunted.

"You just keep talking," I told him.

"And even if you did, I'd die a happy man knowing that you won't get her anyway. You're too fuckin' stupid to get away with murder. Emily is mine. You're going to rot in prison with your own kind, and she'll be with me and under me long before you even get to trial. By the time you get out I might even have a kid in her belly—" He didn't get to finish that sentence before I had the knife to his throat.

"Con, no!" Kieran called out. "We'll take her and go back to Ireland or to train in America. Anywhere away from here and him."

If I'd carried on punching Frank, I'd probably have killed him by now. My mistake was in getting the knife. It wasn't comfortable in my hand. I was weapon enough. I'd never needed anything else.

"No. Fucking. Balls," he taunted me when I paused.

"O'Connell, don't. Please, baby, that's enough. Come home now." I swear to God I could hear Em's voice as loud and as clear as if she was right here with me. For a second, just one second, I caught the faint smell of vanilla. It was enough to make me think of what she'd say if she was here now. I wanted to end his life so fucking badly. Not because I wanted the stain of his passing on my soul, but to give Em peace. Maybe the first peace she'd had since she was nine years old.

But I'd be taking away her future. Our future. Our home, our children, all those plans we made together would all be gone the minute I slit his throat. I didn't want that for her or me. Our future was more important than her past.

If she was here right now, she'd hold my face, look at me

with those beautiful eyes, and tell me she didn't want this. I'd fought so hard to get here, to win her heart when all the odds were stacked against us. I wasn't blowing it now. She needed a better man, so I'd be a better man.

"We ain't going to Ireland or to America. We're staying in Canning Town, and I suggest you keep your arse this side of the bridge and a long way from London. I'm assuming though, that at some point, you'll decide that stupidity over-rules reason, and you'll come looking for her again. When that happens, we'll be waiting, and Em won't be alone. You won't be reporting our little 'visit' to the police because if you do, we'll be reporting your altercation at the univer-sity. I'm sure the university campus will have footage of you on camera. We'll get a restraining order against you and then document you breaking it time and time again until the courts start taking this a little more seriously. How long be-fore this shit bleeds into your job and you lose that? Then what? Your house, your car? How long you wanna keep play-ing this game for?"

"You have no fucking clue who you're dealing with! A few quid to the right police contact and that security footage goes the same way as the rape kit."

"How could you possibly have anything to do with the rape kit?" Kieran asked.

"The kid who arrested me was a newbie. They're all gung-ho, but know hardly anything about evidence collection or procedure. All I needed to do was have a word with a few good friends at the station, grease a few palms, and one of them calls him and asks him to be messenger for the rape kit. Stupid kid thinks he's helping out, and as soon as he touches that box, the case is dead."

"Sooner or later, those contacts will run dry," I warned him.

"You have no idea how far my reach goes. By the time I retire from that piece of shit job, Emily and I will be set for life."

"You weaselly little fucker. What scam have you and your dirty copper friends got going then?" Kieran asked him.

"It doesn't matter, Kier," I told him standing up. "This guy's done. Whoever he's working with ain't got no fucking loyalty if they can be bought. They'll sell out sooner or later, and when that day comes, Frank, you're history," I told him.

"You have no idea what loyalty is. Your own family sold you out for peanuts." The smug smirk on his fuck-ugly, bloodied face made me want to smack the piece of shit again but I held back, letting him say his piece. My family was solid. There's not a single one of my brothers who could be bought. I didn't have to ask him what he was talking about before Kieran muttered "Sylvia" to himself.

"So the penny drops," Frank said sarcastically. "Took me all of five minutes to realize how useful she could be. I walked into the arena the night I came for Emily and offered her fifty quid to separate dipshit over here from her. Fifty quid and she was all alone. So don't preach to me. There isn't a drop of blood in that filthy, inked-up body of yours that's faithful. All the more reason she belongs with me. Twelve years I've been waiting for her. That's devotion."

I waited for the stab of pain that came with Ma's betrayal

but there was none. There wasn't even fucking surprise. "Sylvia ain't family," I told him.

"I give this knife to Kieran and ask him to gut you, tell him this is what our family needs—he'd do it. Just like I would for him. There's no blood or money between any of us. There's just loyalty. That's what makes us family. And our family is a fucking army. You ain't getting to a single one of us without the whole fucker army following. You think about that next time you decide to pay us a visit."

I handed the knife to Kieran. "Find something to clean the prints off this and stick it in the second drawer down in the kitchen. Best wipe the prints off the drawer handles too."

"Your prints are all over this place," he told me.

"I can explain away all the prints except the knife and the drawer." Kieran nodded and went off to do as I asked.

"This isn't over," Frank told me with a sneer.

"The fuck it ain't," I told him. "You come after Em or any other member of my family, and I'll be waiting." Just for good measure, I threw him a right jab to the face and knocked the fucker back out.

"We done here?" Kier asked me.

"We're done," I answered. As we walked to the front door, Em's mum hovered in the doorway of one of the rooms, sporting a killer black eye.

"Did you kill him?" she asked me quietly, her head bent low. I waited until she looked me in the eyes.

"No, I didn't. But let me tell you this. You've fucked me and my wife over for the last time. You betrayed her, and there ain't nothing worse than being betrayed by someone you love. You tore a hole in her heart that can't ever be fixed. Now you need to leave her alone so I can try." She nodded her head solemnly.

There was nothing more to say. Kieran walked through the front door, and I followed, closing it behind me. The rain hammered down harder than I'd ever seen it. In seconds, we were soaked, but I stood there taking a moment to let it cleanse me of Frank's stench. As the rain washed away the shit of my past, I felt redemption.

"Not that I want to interrupt, because I can see you're having a moment there, but can we go home, please? 'Cause I'm freezing my feckin' arse off out here, and by my reckoning, you've got a fair amount of making up to do with your woman," Kieran informed me.

"Fine," I said with a sigh. "Don't get your knickers in a knot. God forbid you'd have to ride home in wet underwear." He rolled his eyes and jogged over to the truck.

"Kier, thanks for having my back," I said to him, and he gave me his usual happy smile.

"Anytime, fuck nuts. Now come on. I really am freezing my bollocks off."

We climbed into the truck and brought Liam and Tommy up to speed about what went down as we put Wales in the rearview mirror. I didn't look back once. The past was behind me, and all I cared about now was the future.

# CHAPTER 21

The block of flats was in darkness when Liam dropped me off. He idled by the curb with the engine running, and I looked at him funny wondering why he hadn't driven away.

"There's no way one of the boys isn't sitting with her. After what happened tonight, Danny wouldn't let her go home alone. Might as well give the poor bugger a lift rather than let him walk home in the rain for his trouble," he explained.

"You're a good man, Liam," I said, and meaning it, as I reached into the window to shake his hand. With a nod of thanks to the other guys, I left them with Kieran, who was still bitching about his wet clothes and walked up to our place. Twisting my key gently in the lock so's not to wake Em if she was sleeping, I walked in to find Earnshaw sitting in the chair reading one of Em's books. She was curled up in the middle of the bed wearing one of my hoodies, her hair fanned out in a golden halo behind her.

"How's she been?" I asked him.

"Not good," he replied. "She stayed at the gym for a few hours but eventually Danny wanted to lock up and I offered to walk her home. She's barely said two words all night," he told me. I nodded my head, acknowledging that I'd fucked up much worse than I thought by leaving her.

"Liam's downstairs. He's gonna give you a lift home, and thanks for staying with her. I appreciate that," I said.

"No problem," he said as he put on his jacket.

"So do I still have a job or have you killed Frank?" he asked me.

"Unfortunately he's alive and well, so it's back to work tomorrow."

"Not that I have anything but disgust for the fucker, but I'm glad to hear it."

"See you tomorrow then," I said.

"I'll be there," he replied. Looking briefly in Em's direction, he added, "I hope she's okay."

My stomach turned over slightly at the thought she might not be. "Me too," I replied, knowing I couldn't promise anything else.

When he'd gone, I locked up, took a quick shower, and after grabbing some clean boxer shorts, walked over to the bed. She looked like a goddamn angel lying there, and I wanted to wrap my body around her, protecting her in the most basic of ways, so I did.

She stirred, her behind brushing against my cock, and immediately I was rock hard. I twisted slightly so she didn't feel it, knowing that she didn't need that shit from me after what she'd been through tonight. She turned over restlessly to face me, and I felt a pang of guilt at disturbing her. A part of me willed her to wake up because I was fucking needy enough to want to know whether I had her forgiveness. I held my breath as her eyes fluttered open.

"Are you all right?" It was the first thing to come out of her beautiful mouth. Frank had attacked her again, and it's me that she was worried for. Lifting up one of her tiny hands, I ran her fingers through mine, playing with them. "I know I've made you some promises that I've done a piss poor job of keeping, but that don't mean I ain't gonna keep trying for the rest of my life. So don't give up on me okay?"

"What happened?" she asked, her body tense as she waited for my confession.

"We went to his house, and I roughed him up. He pushed me into losing my temper and I held a knife to his throat."

"You didn't . . . " She sobbed, grabbing me tightly, like she was afraid I was gonna be dragged away from her. "I wanted to, so fucking badly. It would be over then, and you wouldn't be afraid anymore. But you'd lose me too, and I couldn't have that. So I didn't. We're gonna get a restraining order, and I've warned him what will happen if he comes back. Don't think he'll listen, but if he likes being my punching bag, then I'm happy to keep my fist well exercised."

She closed her eyes, rested her head against my biceps, and sobbed some more.

Grabbing her, I hauled her into my chest, wrapping my arms around her. "Shit, I'm sorry, baby. I'm so fucking sorry. Sorry for leaving you when you needed me, sorry for not being there in the first place. I didn't think you'd want me to kill Frank but I can't have you living in fear. Tell me if I did the wrong thing?" I begged earnestly. She was my fucking compass, and I needed to know what she was thinking. When she finally stopped crying, she wiped away her tears and held my face between her damp hands.

"You're a good man, O'Connell. Don't ever let anyone make you feel any different. You did the right thing not killing him. I don't want that. I don't care about Frank. I care about you, and I don't want you to have to live with that. But I don't want any life that doesn't have you in it either. One day he's going to mess up and land himself back in prison. But from now on, we put all this shit behind us. We have an amazing life ahead of us, and I want to start living it. Okay?" she told me.

"Okay, baby. We'll be careful. I need to make sure you're protected, but we look forward and not back."

She gave me a wobbly smile as she turned her back on the last few shit-filled months. Looking at that gorgeous face, her cheeks soft from the tears, I couldn't help moving in for a kiss. I should have known that once would never be enough. Her lips parted slightly on a gasp and I thrust my tongue into her mouth, her sweet taste making me even harder.

Weeks of not being able to make love to her came crashing over me. I wanted her everywhere. In me, over me, under me. I wanted her so fucking badly I could barely see straight. Running my hands up her silky thighs, I could feel the heat of her core long before my fingers reached their destination. I pulled one leg to wrap around my waist, leaving a gap in her shorts just big enough for me to slide my big fingers through her crease into her core. She cried out, her spine rigid, as she clenched and tightened around me. Needing both my hands I stripped her to expose her fucking gorgeous breasts. Her nipples puckered expectantly, and I lifted one breast to my mouth, sucking at the nub as she twisted and moaned at my touch.

"No, we can't," she groaned as she arched her back to bring her body closer to my mouth. "The ban," she said on an exhale.

"Fuck the ban," I told her. I focused my attention on her neglected breast while moving my finger up inside her. She struggled to talk, and I knew she wanted to argue with me so I moved it in and out of her slowly. Her body knew what it needed, and her hips moved to ride me. I want to be buried deep inside her so fucking badly but patience and discipline made me wait. After all the shit I'd put her through, I needed to make her feel good before I came.

"No, really. We can't. You have the biggest fight of your career in a few weeks. I can't jinx it," she protested, pulling away from my kiss. I moved my hand away from her again and gripped her hips tightly as I bent to rest my forehead between her breasts. Danny had made her so fucking superstitious about this stupid sex ban. It was all bullshit, of course. She was all the motivation I needed to beat this guy, but if there was one thing I knew about Em, it was how stubborn she was when she made up her mind about something.

"You're going to fucking kill me. You know that, right?" I told her.

"I'm pretty sure that no one ever died from blue balls," she giggled.

"They have. It's just that the victims' families' are ashamed of it so they tell people it was a 'heart attack' or some shit like that."

"Well, if you do die of blue balls in the night, I promise I'll tell people the truth, maybe set up a blue balls support group," she joked.

"I can show you lots of ways to support my blue balls," I told her as I nibbled at the corner of her mouth. Working my way down her jaw, I buried my head into the crook of her neck and inhaled, the scent of vanilla making me even harder. A thought occurred to me, and I braced myself up on my forearms to look into her eyes.

"Is this really about the fight? Because if you need some time after what Frank did, then that's fine, Sunshine. You just tell me, and we can wait until you're ready," I reassured her.

"It's not, O'Connell, believe me. I want nothing more now than for you to bury your cock deep inside me and let me ride it until Christmas," she said. "But Danny believes that the ban helps you fight better, and I believe in Danny." I dropped my head back into her neck with a groan.

"What?" she asked.

"Two things. One, don't say 'cock' anymore. My dick twitches every time that word comes out of your pretty pink lips. And two, please don't mention Danny in the same sentence as my cock. You can't know how fucking wrong it feels to have that old codger's face pop into my head when I'm hard as a fucking diamond."

She collapsed against me in a fit of giggles, and I laid my head on her chest as she played absentmindedly with my hair, letting the sound of her laughter seep into my soul. However much I might regret not taking Frank out, I know I would never have this amount of peace with Em in my arms if I had.

That alone made it the right decision. I was a violent man. Throwing punches and taking hits would always be part of who I was. But for her, I had to choose a different path. Because at the end of the day, I'd be walking toward Sunshine. And that was a journey always worth taking.

* * *

We slept late into the next morning, and nobody came to wake us. If Frank had given me up, the police would have been beating down the door long ago.

"Shouldn't you be at the gym?" mumbled Em, her hair sticking up all over the place adorably.

"I think we should call off the Temple fight," I told her.

"Why?" she asked sitting bolt upright in bed.

"I'm fighting in a matter of weeks, and I'm nowhere near ready. Plus Frank isn't going anywhere, and I know we agreed to move forward from that," I said putting my hands up in surrender. "But I still need to keep you safe and I can't do that from the other side of the world."

"No," she said decisively, climbing out of bed.

"What do you mean, no?" I asked, pulling my T-shirt over my head.

"I meant exactly what I said. You are not calling off this fight. This will make your career, and if you drop out at the last minute, you'll destroy it."

"That's exaggerating a bit..." I was six feet five inches but she stopped me in my tracks as she looked at me, stark naked with her hands on her little hips and one eyebrow raised. She didn't say anything, but knowing she'd made her point, she carried on walking to the bathroom. Jeez, my stubborn woman made me all kinds of fucking hot.

"Fine! So my career would take a hit, but what do you propose we do about Frank? I leave for training camp in the US in a couple of weeks. You've got exams in two. How am I supposed to fight when I'm worrying about you here all alone?" She turned on the shower, drowning out my voice.

"Emmm...?" I pleaded, and she kissed me then climbed into the shower.

"Trust me, I've got an enormous brain. I'll think of something. Now get dressed. You've got a lot of work to do, and I need to have a word with Danny."

Rolling my eyes, I did as I was told. Despite all my protests, I knew she was right. Em wanted me to fight, and I wanted to win. Having made my peace with the part of myself that needed revenge, I was ready to show the rest of the world what I was made of.

* * *

The guys were all congregated in the office eating bacon sandwiches when we arrived.

"Here you go, darlin'. I saved you one," Danny said, handing Em a wrapped sandwich.

"Where's mine?" I asked.

"You're in training," Earnshaw pointed out, "or are you?"

"I am," I replied with a smile.

"So what's the plan?" Kieran asked with a mouth full of food.

Em took charge. "O'Connell's fighting this guy, and he's going to win. For the next couple of weeks, he lives here unless he's sleeping, and the same goes for me. I've got exams in two weeks, and I've missed a lot of school lately. So if it's okay with you, Danny, I'm going to use the office to study while O'Connell's training. Heath, do you think you'll be able to pick me up in the mornings on the way in? I know O'Connell won't want me walking in alone, and I don't fancy coming in at the crack of dawn with him," she said.

"Happy to," he answered, licking sauce from his fingers as the soggy meal started disintegrating into his hands.

"What about your shifts at Daisy's?" I asked her.

"I'm going to ask Mike and Rhona to share my shifts between the other waitresses until the fight is over," she answered.

"Honey, he wins this fight, you won't ever need to waitress again. You could be a kept woman," Earnshaw said. He grinned, oblivious to the slashing across the throat gestures Kieran and Tommy were making, telling him to quit it.

My little hellion turned to him, her hands on those cute-arse hips of hers and informed him, quite matter-of-factly, that she had no interest in being any such thing. "Besides, we don't abandon out friends. Mike and Rhona have been good to me. I'll keep waitressing as long as it takes them to find a replacement, even if we don't need the money."

Em never thought too seriously about what I could potentially earn in the future. We never had anything, and we were doing just fine. If Earnshaw made a little money for us from sponsorship, so much the better. But it wouldn't change who we were, and I fucking loved that.

"What do we do about Frank?" Tommy asked. "He ain't just gonna disappear 'cause Con gave him a scare."

"Keep your eyes peeled," Danny replied. "If you see him, take a picture on your phone, or make a note of the date and time. I called the copper this morning who helped us find Em. He's one of the good guys and would love to nail Frank to the wall. Don't think he's a big lover of dirty coppers either. So as of now, he's putting together a harassment case so we can try and get a restraining order. Everything goes to him." We nodded in agreement, the boys too busy stuffing their faces to say much.

"Well if that's decided, then you'd best get your lazy arses out into that gym and do some work. Con, you're a feckin' long way from where you need to be, and we've practically no time to get you there. So what are you waiting for, feckin' Christmas? Get to work," Danny barked. Leaning around him to give Em a quick kiss before he slapped me, I legged it to get changed. I was hungry like I'd never been hungry before, and today was a brand-new day.

# CHAPTER 22

I was doing one-handed press-ups when the iconic trumpets sounded from the speakers of the gym. Some of the other kids had stopped at the music, but hearing what it was, they laughed and carried on training, only harder. I smiled at them. You couldn't help it. "Flying High Now" was fucking electric because it made you root for the underdog. Made you think you could do just about anything if you worked hard and were focused enough.

Danny rolled his eyes and took a deep drag on his cigarette before barking out my numbers, "Seventy-eight, seventy-nine, eighty." When I got to one hundred, I switched arms. Danny was working me harder than I'd ever been worked in my entire life, and I loved it. My body loved it. My days ended with a sparring session with Earnshaw. Fucker was getting quicker, but honestly? He couldn't touch me now. I was the wind. Faster than anyone would believe in a guy my size. I was Ali, I was Tyson, I was Foreman. I was all of the greats, and it made me invincible. There was no one who stood a chance in the ring with me, not even Kieran who was the best sparring partner I'd ever had.

Danny had taken training back to basics, and it was working. Balaam Leisure Center got wind of the fight, and they let me use the pool for an hour every day between their swimming classes. The only condition was that the local kids, although they weren't allowed in the pool with me, got to watch me do laps. I fucking loved that part of my day. I might have been Irish but I was local and doing something to better myself, and that made me their hero. Those kids worked me harder than Danny ever did. Eventually he gave up giving me orders and let the kids do it. They'd shout at me to go faster for just one more lap. Afterward I ran back to the gym through Canning Town Recreation Ground, and they almost always followed me. A few on the first day and more and more with each day that passed. The older ones ran but the younger ones came on their bikes. Rico Temple couldn't possibly have anything near the fuckin' buzz those kids gave me. And people got behind it. The shopkeepers and street cleaners just opening up and doing their jobs knew me from my morning run. Commuters using the railway bridge began to say hello to me on their way home from work. Even the kids from the pool attracted other kids and they hung around outside the gym, often watching me run. Canning Town was a community, and I was their adopted son.

In the afternoons came more bag and leg work. Technique, core training, they were all things we worked on, but in very different ways. While Temple would have used complicated machines, I bench-pressed Em again, which the lads at the gym always seemed to enjoy, and when Danny was grilling me pretty hard about not lifting fast enough, I put her down and used Danny instead, which had the boys in hysterics.

"Put me down, you feckin' eejit. Right Feckin' now!" he screamed at me. After two presses, I did as he asked, then legged it around the gym as he chased me. For an old fucker, he sure was fast. I felt powerful and motivated in the same way I had after I'd walked Em home that first night. Like I could take on the world. Knowing that she was in the office next to me was like always training with your talisman. She worked so fucking hard. Harder than I ever could with all that book-learning stuff. Danny even let Nikki, Ryan, and Albie use the office to study instead of the library. Kieran lent her his laptop as well. Everything the guys could do to make her comfortable, they did. Mary even caught wind of what we were all doing and kept the baked goods in steady supply.

Every day I trained longer, harder, and faster. Tommy got us a tractor tire, fuck knows from where, and once the fight was over, I was gonna fucking burn it. For hours, Danny had me turning that thing over and over, up and down the lane behind the gym. When he'd finished torturing me with that, he had me pounding on it over and over and over with a sledgehammer. Every obstacle was a machine, every movement an exercise. Even the foot bridge up and over the railway track, which had a steep staircase on either side, became our training ground. I lost count of the number of times he's made me run up and over that bridge. Thousands and thousands of tiny steps and every one of 'em counted.

It was a heady feeling to be a part of something so great. Things were going so well that I didn't want to leave for the US, and I sure as shit didn't want to leave Em behind. I was doing hanging sit-ups when she came to find me on our last day together. Just as she walked out of the office, a fresh mug of coffee in her hand, Tommy came running in, grabbed Em by her cheeks, and kissed her loudly on the lips.

"What the fuck..." I said, nearly breaking my leg in my haste to climb down and smack Tommy for getting fresh with my wife. At least that was the plan until he came running over and did exactly the same thing to me. He kissed me. On the motherfucking lips. I should 'ave hit him but I was too bloody shocked to do anything other than stand there. Em giggled happily, probably at the look on my face.

Tommy was like a kid at Christmas, bouncing up and down so much he could barely get his news out. "I did it. I fucking did it," he screamed, pulling a letter out of his back pocket and waving it at us.

"What is it?" Em asked him.

"I passed the psychometric exams for the fire service. Thick as shit Tommy Rierdan passed the exams!" I couldn't be more proud of the little fucker.

"That's so fantastic! Well done, love. I'm so proud of you," Em told him. I hugged him and squeezed his shoulder as Em jumped on him and hugged him even harder than I had.

Danny and Earnshaw walked out of the office together, and even Danny raised a half smile, half smirk when Tommy told him the news. "You did good, kid. You did real good." Tommy looked at Danny like he hung the moon. Danny didn't give praise very often. So when he did, he fucking meant it.

"What does it mean now?" Em asked him.

"It means I get through to the interview stage next. It's like a tier system, I guess. They start off with thousands of applications, and at each stage, they get rid of a load. If you can make it through the interview, the next stage is the medical and optical. If you can pass those, you've got the job."

"Firefighter Rierdan. Who'd have thought?" I said to no one in particular.

"Don't jinx me," he warned me. "There's a long way to go so I ain't getting my hopes up yet."

"Probably sensible," I told him, as though we hadn't just seen him jumping around with excitement and screaming like a girl. Earnshaw congratulated Tommy and asked all the right questions about his future with the fire service. By the time he left to share the news with Mary and his da, he looked like he was king of the world.

"Now he's gone, I can show you this," said Earnshaw excitedly, pulling his own piece of paper from out of his pocket.

"Why d'you need to wait for Tommy to leave before sharing it?" I asked suspiciously, my tone making him pause.

"Because it's good news and I didn't want to steal his thunder," he answered. That shit right there had my respect.

"What is it?" I asked.

"You've got ESPN talking about you. Dan Rafael's written an article about how you're going back to basics for the Temple fight." He read it to us excitedly.

I admit it was pretty cool to hear my name in the same article as so many of my boxing heroes but I did frown as a thought occurred to me. "How does Rafael know about my training techniques all the way from the US?" I asked.

"Because I told him," Earnshaw said. "It will do Temple's camp some good to worry about just how serious a contender you are. And if I want to start securing you sponsorship deals, then it's not a bad thing to get you on ESPN's radar."

Danny didn't give a shit about any of this stuff but he knew it was important, which is why he'd hired Earnshaw in the first place. As they got into a lively debate about who was the all-time heavyweight great, I used the opportunity to snag my girl and drag her back into the office. Shutting the door gently behind me, I whipped her around and had her back against it as she wrapped her legs tightly around my waist. Hiking her cute little arse higher so that my hard cock was pressed tightly up against her core, I kissed her hard and groaned as her sweet little tongue touched tentatively against mine, instantly sending darts of pleasure straight to my dick.

"I'm gonna miss you so badly," I confessed, as I stopped kissing to rest my forehead against hers.

"Me too," she replied breathlessly.

"You okay to stay with Nikki while I'm gone?" I asked, still really reluctant to leave her behind, despite my precautions and her constant reassurances that she'd be fine.

"I'm good, baby. Her roommate Lauren is practically living with her boyfriend anyway so I'm going to have her bed and study with Nikki until the exams are over. Between Nikki, Albie, Ryan, and Max I'll never need to go anywhere alone, and we'll see each other again before you know it. Besides I know you'll be calling me every day," she reasoned.

"That reminds me, I've got something for you," I told her. Letting her down gently, I reached behind the filing cabinet and pulled out a box I'd wrapped in red paper. Well mostly; wrapping wasn't really my thing.

"What is it?" she asked.

"Open it," I urged her. She drove me nuts when she opened gifts. The delicate gentle way she teased it open showed just how few gifts she'd ever had. She almost dropped it, covering her mouth in shock when she realized what was inside. Smoothing her hand over the box of the laptop reverently, she whispered "We can't afford this."

"Listen, I know we used most of our savings on the house, and because we borrowed that money from Danny, I checked this was okay with him, but we need this. You know I fucking hate talking on the phone. If I'm gonna talk to you, I need to see you and see that you're safe and doing okay. I can borrow Kier's laptop while we're away, and he says we can Skype each other if you've got one too. Nikki said she had Wi-Fi and we can get it installed at the house when it's done so we can always see each other when I have to go away."

"Thank you so much," she said, still stroking it as her eyes began to well up with tears.

"No, baby, don't cry. It kills me when you cry. This was supposed to be a good surprise."

"It was, O'Connell. It really was. I'm just a bit run-down and emotional with the exams coming up, and the thought of you being half a world away tomorrow is hard."

"I know, baby. But next time I have to go for a fight, I promise you'll be with me the whole time."

She'd be graduating next summer, and we hadn't discussed what she wanted to do after. I didn't put any pressure on her because, with how hard she worked, I wanted her to know she could do anything she wanted. After one last big hug, she told me to get my arse back to training so she could study, and I left, knowing that leaving her behind would always be the hardest thing I ever had to do.

# CHAPTER 23

Leaving to get on that flight was the worst fucking feeling ever. Em clung to me like I was never going to see her again, and I could barely breathe thinking that I was trusting her safekeeping in someone else's hands. We stood in Nikki's doorway for at least five minutes, our arms wrapped around each other, while I memorized everything that was already imprinted on my heart. The smell of her skin, the hitch in her breath as she tried not to cry, the way her tiny body curled into mine, even the way she held on with a grip stronger than steel. The back of my throat burned as I swallowed hard and pulled away from her. Water pooled in those big eyes of hers, and she looked so beautiful and heartbreakingly vulnerable that my chest hurt at the idea of leaving her behind.

"You're going to miss your flight," she told me.

"I don't want to go," I admitted.

"And I don't want to stay," she replied.

I closed my eyes, touched my forehead to hers, and held my breath one last time. Opening up my backpack, I handed her a letter and kissed her gently on the lips.

"Love you, Mrs. O'Connell," I told her.

"Love you too, Mr. O'Connell," she replied and clutched the letter to her as I left. Waving Nikki good-bye on my way out, I climbed into Liam's truck, and we drove away. She couldn't see me looking back so I didn't. "Here, I forgot to give you this. Some guy from Balaam Leisure Center dropped it off for you, said the kids made it," Kieran said. Liam had picked him and Tommy up on the way to mine. I opened up the large white envelope and smiled broadly. Each kid had drawn a picture of themselves and cut them out to place around a hand-drawn picture of a boxing ring. Inside I was fighting Temple. I could tell which one was me because of the shorts, though Temple appeared to be a dwarf in the picture.

Inside they had written: "Good luck, Hurricane! We hope you knock his block off. Love ... " They all signed the card that I knew I'd have framed as soon as I got home. Aside from my cross, this was the best present I'd ever had. I looked up to see Kieran watching me. I knew he worried I wouldn't handle it without Em. Knowing him he probably even held back on the card deliberately, just for this moment. The longer we drove, the whiter the scenery became. Winter had arrived, and although a heavy frost was predicted overnight, snow fell thick and fast.

"I don't like the look of this," Liam said, looking up at the sky. He pulled into a space in the long-term parking lot and switched off the engine. When Liam had a bad feeling about something, he was usually right.

As soon as he said it, I felt it too. We waited for six hours in the airport for conditions to improve before finally finding out that our flight had been canceled. Weather permitting, the airline had rescheduled us on another flight tomorrow. Even with all that sorted, and the joy of knowing I'd have one more night with Em, something was still wrong. It was like the weather was a bad omen, and I could see by the look on everyone's faces that they felt it too.

We drove slowly down the motorway on the way back into the city. Cars backed up as the snow worsened, and the weight on my chest grew heavier and heavier. We were fifteen minutes from Nikki's flat when something just felt wrong.

"Kier, can you call Nikki? Make sure Em's okay?" I asked him.

"You don't want to wait and surprise her?" he asked me.

"No. I just want to know she's okay," I told him. Nodding, Kieran dialed the number, and it rang and rang.

"Don't worry. They'll be expecting us to be on a plane right now so they've probably gone for food or something," he reassured me. It didn't work. Despite what he said, I knew something was wrong. Liam drove faster as soon as the traffic started thinning out. We skidded to a stop outside Nikki's place, and I jumped out, slammed the door, and raced upstairs. I can't describe how I felt seeing the flat door slightly ajar. Fuck! I was a fucking idiot to think Em would be safe as long as she wasn't alone. Looking at Nikki's prostrate form lying on the carpet unconscious, I knew Frank had Em.

If he'd hurt her again after I had the opportunity to kill him and I let him go, I was gonna drive a motherfucking knife straight through his heart.

Tommy and Liam were hot on my heels. Kier checked on Nikki while Tom and I searched the flat unsuccessfully. Em wasn't there.

"I've called the police and an ambulance. I think she'll be fine but he must have given her a fair smack to the head," Kier said.

"Shit, Kier. I'm too late again," I said, pacing as I ran my hands through my hair.

"Hey, ain't that them down there?" Tommy said, looking out of the window into the flat's parking lot at the back of the building. Sure enough, Frank had an arm around Em's neck, a knife in his hand, and he was dragging her toward the cars. My girl wasn't going down without a fight though. She was biting, kicking, scratching, anything she could do to get away. If I wasn't careful, he'd knife her before I got there out of sheer desperation.

Kieran stayed with Nikki while Tommy and I raced down to the parking lot. By the time we burst through the door, the sound of sirens was wailing in the distance. As soon as Frank caught sight of us, the knife went up under Em's chin, and she froze. We all did.

"The police are nearly here, Frank. Run while you still have the chance," I said. I didn't give a shit about him. I just wanted my wife back alive. I've never been so scared in my whole life. She looked like an angel, with the snow settling on her beautiful blond hair, but one quick jerk of the knife and she'd be gone forever. If anything happened to her, he might as well stick a knife in my motherfucking black heart. I was done.

"Fuck you, O'Connell," Frank spat at me. "You're supposed to be on a plane right now. Everything is fucked! But I'm not going without Emily. I've had enough of waiting. This ends tonight."

This wasn't the calm, slick arsehole we'd seen in court. It was like he was losing his grip. Something had pushed him over edge, maybe even me.

"You can't take her," I told him calmly. "It's too late now, the police are nearly here. Let her go before it's too late."

"Why couldn't you just let her go? Why the fuck did you have to come back?" he screamed.

"Because she's mine. She's always been mine, and I will love her till the day I die. There is no one else for me, and there never will be." I wasn't telling that to Frank; I was telling it to Em. I was so proud of my girl. She was absolutely petrified, anyone could see that, but the fear was secondary to her hatred for the animal at her throat. I didn't want to anger Frank any more, but there was no way I was letting him leave with Em.

"She was never fucking yours!" he screamed. "We were meant to be together, and if it wasn't for the rest of you, she'd have been with me this whole time."

I heard a slight shuffling noise and the obvious click of a loaded gun. Looking around, I could see the police surround us, even looking down from the window I'd been standing in a few minutes ago.

"Armed police!" They called out. "Stay where you are and slowly raise your hands." This was not fucking good. Finally there were police witnesses to Frank's psycho behavior but, by the way his eyes panned across the parking lot, I could practically see his mind working. He wasn't getting away with it this time. When it was just me, I might have let him go to keep Em alive, but he knew the police wouldn't do that. They wouldn't shoot Frank unless he went through with it and killed Em. But there was no way they'd let him walk away either.

"If I'm going down, she's coming with me. None of you will ever know how much I love her. She doesn't even know because you all keep getting in the way. You won't let me show her—"

He never got to finish his sentence before he screamed out and his face contorted with pain. He let go of the knife, and Em dropped to her knees coughing. She scrambled through the shallow snow to get as far away from him as possible, and I raced toward her the minute she hit the ground. Lifting her up as soon as I reached her, I carried her to safety. There was a very thin red line around her neck where Frank had nicked her slightly, but other than that, she was safe in my arms.

"What the fuck did you do?" Frank screamed out. I turned to see him with his hands raised. Em's mum stood behind with a bloody knife in her hand.

"It was all lies, wasn't it? You told me you loved me. Time and time again you said it was all for me. For us," Margaret said, in a tone that was eerily calm.

"What are you talking about, you stupid delusional bitch?"
Frank said. He held his hands in the air, as Em's mum walked
around to stand in front of him.

"You swore to me the time you had sex with her was a
mistake. You said that she'd been flirting with you and you
gave in to temptation, and I believed you! I'm not stupid. I
could see how young and beautiful she was and how you
looked at her but that was just temptation. It was just sex.
It was me you were in love with. Me and you forever, that's
what you told me. Everything I ever did, I did for you."

"I do love you," he reassured her, like you would a child.
"I've always loved you."

"Shut up," she screamed, waving the knife wildly. The police hovered expectantly but seemed less inclined to engage
now that Em was safe. Her mum was unhinged, and they
were obviously nervous about intervening until she'd said
her piece.

"It's lies all of it. I heard you when O'Connell came over.
But I thought you wouldn't have stayed after Emily left if you
didn't love me. So I drove you here because you said we
were saying good-bye. Going somewhere to start a new life.
I've always done everything you've ever told me to. But you
brought her with you. It wasn't me you wanted to start a new
life with, it was her."

She was as fucked-up and obsessive about Frank as he was
about Em. The pair of them fucking deserved each other.

"Did you ever love me, Mum?" Emily asked. Her mum
turned with a jolt to face her, and it was almost like she'd
forgotten Em was there.

"Of course I loved you," she replied. "I struggled when you were born for a long time. They call it post-natal depression now, but your dad took care of you when I couldn't. By the time I started to feel better, you and he had a bond I couldn't share. Maybe I shouldn't have let Frank knock you around as much as I did, but you don't understand how much I needed him. I couldn't risk losing him, and when you found O'Connell, I saw a chance for me to have it all. I could be your mum again and still keep Frank. I know that you were upset when I lied in court but I knew you'd be okay. You had O'Connell to look after you."

"Oh Mum, why didn't you choose me? I needed you so badly when dad died. You let Frank beat and rape me and then let him get away with it. How could you?"

"You never needed me, Emily. And you never will now. I just want what you two have together. Is that too much to ask?" She looked at us both longingly but I felt nothing but revulsion.

"We do have that," Frank told her. "We can still have it."

"No, Frank. I can see what you really want now. It's too late for me, and I know Emily won't ever be able to forgive me, but at least I can do this one last thing for her."

"Don't do anything stupid. Now put the fucking knife down," Frank shouted angrily.

# CHAPTER 24

"Two twenty-three Brecan Road, Canning Town," her mum told Em.

"Margaret, no!" screamed Frank. I frowned, having no idea what she was talking about.

"It's the flat he took Em to. He wanted somewhere close to you, I guess. He rents it under my maiden name. He's been running a scam with some of his mates from the police there. They skim evidence from drug busts and seizures. Frank fences it through his probation clients."

"You stupid fucking bitch. After everything I've fucking done for you, you fucking betray me now?" he said, and she recoiled slightly.

"After everything you've done for me? You don't scare me, Frank. What have you done that was so great?" she asked.

"You think anyone else would have stuck with you as

many years as I have? You were always fucking jealous of Emily. You're right, it was always her."

With a wild animalist scream like nothing I've ever heard before, Margaret pulled her arms up over her head and plunged her knife into Frank's chest as a shot from one of the police officers cracked and echoed in the open space.

We all jumped as we watched Frank drop to the ground with Margaret on top of him, a crimson bloodstain spreading quickly across her shoulder. I turned Em away so that she didn't have to see any more and carried her up the stairs back to Nikki's flat.

\* \* \*

When we got there, Nikki sat on her bed rubbing her jaw as though she were still in pain, with Kieran beside her.

"It's done?" he asked, and I nodded.

"What happened?" Nikki asked.

"Frank used Em's mum to trick you into opening the door and he knocked you out," I told her.

"I remember that bit, thanks," Nikki replied sarcastically. "I meant, what happened after?"

"He took Em at knifepoint. Em's mum heard Frank talking about how he'd always wanted Em. Her mum lost it and knifed him in the chest."

"You're very verbose, you know that, Con? And you have a real gift for storytelling." I frowned at her fucking sarcasm. I told her what happened. What? Did she need me to describe it in Technicolor?

"I'm sorry, Con," she said at my frown. "I'm tired, my head hurts, and I'm feeling a bit testy." With everything Nikki had done, I had no reason to be pissed at a little sarcasm.

"It's okay," I told her. "I'm sorry for what Frank did to you. It wasn't fair of me to leave Em here and assume you'd be safe. That's on me," I told her. She shook her head no, but I knew it was the truth. "I need to get Em out of here," I told Kier.

"There's no way the police will let you go without taking your statements," Nikki warned me. I desperately wanted to get Em alone and help her process some of this shit. She hadn't spoken to me since it happened, and I had a horrible feeling she was going into shock.

"Take Lauren's bed," Nikki told me pointing to the bed opposite hers. "We'll explain to the police that you want a little time to make sure Em's okay. Maybe they'll let us give our statements first."

"Thanks, Nikki. I appreciate it," I told her as she stood up.

As I laid Em down, she started shaking. "It's okay, baby girl. It's all over now. You're safe, I promise. Everything's gonna be okay." I gathered her in close and grabbed a throw blanket from the bottom of the bed to keep her warm. Fuck knows if I was doing the right thing for shock but I had to do something. I rubbed her arms vigorously while holding her as close as I could without crushing her. I was really starting to get worried when she finally spoke to me.

"Is he dead?" she asked me.

"I think so, love. I can't imagine it's that easy to recover from a knife to the heart. Assuming he had one, that is," I said.

"Is it wrong that I hope he is dead?" she asked.

"No, baby. I'd think something was wrong if you didn't fucking want him dead," I reassured her.

"If he's dead, does that mean I should forgive her? She killed him for me. But I don't think I can forgive her." She sounded so utterly and hopelessly lost. Like she was alone in the wilderness without a compass. Well, I'd be her motherfucking north.

I held her chin gently in my hand and tilted her face up to look at me. "You listen to me, Sunshine. Your ma is one sick fuck. By the sound of it, she ain't been right in the head since long before your dad died. She killed Frank out of jealousy, not because she was protecting you. After what she did, there's no evening the score—not ever. So don't you feel like you need to forgive either of them for anything. I hope they both die and spend eternity burning in hell."

"When this is all over and your fight and my exams are done, I want to finish our home, close the door, and keep the world out for at least a week," she told me shakily.

"Sounds like a fucking good plan to me, love," I said with a chuckle. Em tucked herself in closer to my body. After a while, the shivering stopped, and her warm breath evened out as it blew gently across my neck. I knew that Em was finding all this difficult to process, but for me, it was like Christmas had come early. In all likelihood, Frank was dead, the evil poison in our life that was Margaret Thomas was looking at twenty years behind bars, that's if she made it at all, and my girl was lying safe in my arms.

\* \* \*

After making sure that Nikki was all right, we all piled into Liam's truck and headed home. Em didn't protest as I carried her up the stairs to our flat. After taking my keys out of the lock, I kicked the door shut and headed straight to the bathroom with her still in my arms.

"What are you doing?" she mumbled as I set her down on the toilet seat lid.

"Hot bath," I replied. "It will make you feel better." I knew she'd need to wash away the stink of Frank's touch, and I needed to be close to her, to feel like I was taking care of her. She liked baths hot enough that you could boil off a layer of skin if you jumped in too quick. Being only used to ice baths I was a complete fucking pansy arse about dipping my balls into the scalding water, but I did it for Em.

Pulling her to stand up, I carefully undressed her and folded her clothes neatly in a pile. She'd kill me tomorrow when she was feeling better if I chucked them all over the floor. When she was naked, I pulled my shirt over my head and made quick work of my boots, jeans, and underwear. She was so tiny that I lifted her effortlessly into the bath and then sat behind her, pulling her back against my chest. Pouring a ton of that smelly shit she liked onto a sponge, I washed her carefully as she laid against me with her eyes closed. When I got to her chest, I had to adjust my cock so it didn't impale her, but in all honesty, it had been at half-mast since I started undressing her.

"That thing's got a mind of its own," she giggled sleepily.

"It's not my fault. There's invisible string connecting my cock to your top. As soon as the top comes off, my cock salutes in approval." She giggled again, and it was such a fucking beautiful sound I wished I could bottle it and take it away with me across the world. I'd call it my jar of happiness, and it would let the sun shine into the dark.

There are days when men take their woman for granted. When you come through the door tired and hungry and don't see how tired she is or how the place is spotless and how, as you're hoovering your meal without really tasting it, she's spent ages in the kitchen making that just for you. There were probably days that I'd already done that to Em, and try as I might to make sure that didn't happen, it probably would, on occasion, happen again.

Today wasn't one of those days. My beautiful, gentle, loving wife was safe in my arms, and our bright and shining future was right in front of us. I sent a silent prayer upstairs for that. Fuck success and fuck the money 'cause everything I had right here and now was more than I ever deserved. More than I ever dared to dream. That didn't mean though that laying the world at her feet wasn't still on the agenda. Rico Temple's attitude pissed me off, and I had some shit kicking to do.

"I'm supposed to be back on a flight tomorrow night," I told her, "but I don't want to leave you."

"The university would probably let me bail on the exams if I asked them. They're only internal exams, sort of mocks for the finals. But I'm going to take them anyway," she told me.

"Why, if you can get away without doing them?" I asked as I rubbed the sponge gently up and down her arm.

"Because fuck Frank and his memory, that's why. Today he took the last piece of normality he's ever going to take again. The trial and worrying about Frank has messed around my final year so much, but I've worked hard for these exams and I'm going to sit them. And when I pass, I hope Frank gets my 'fuck you' message in hell."

"Baby?" I asked.

"Hmm…" she answered.

"Remind me never to piss you off, okay?" I loved that she giggled again. "I want you at the fight with me but I'm so fucking proud that you still want to see it through." I paused, feeling like I should cancel the fight to stay with her.

"Absolutely no way," she said without looking around to me once.

"What are you talking about?" I asked.

"I can practically hear your brain working, O'Connell. You are not canceling this fight. I'm going to stay with Nikki as planned. My last exam finishes on Friday, and there's a flight to the US early on Saturday morning. I probably won't make it for the fight but at least I'll be there to celebrate with you after."

"Please tell me there'll be sex. Lots and lots of sex?" I said.

"If you win, there will be," she teased. I tickled the sponge over her ribs making her laugh, then sucked gently on the side of her neck, making her moan.

"Not until after the fight," she protested without feeling.

"Spoilsport," I answered, but didn't push my luck. She

squirmed around a little to get comfortable, and the cheeks of her arse brushed against my already painfully hard cock, making me groan. I rested my forehead against her head and tried to remember that this was about taking care of Em, not twisting her around and bending her over the bath so I could take her wet, soapy curves from behind. *Shit! No!* She seemed a little less vulnerable now so sex was pretty much the only thing I could think about.

"Think about the national anthem," she said, tapping my leg.

"How come you're not as frustrated as I am?" I complained.

"Because I get to watch you all hot and sweaty in training then come home and touch myself," she admitted, and I swear to God I dropped the motherfucking sponge. The image of Em lying in our bed, maybe wearing my wraps and touching herself was burned on my retinas. After dropping that little bombshell, she started humming my go-to song for telling my cock to stand down.

"You know, one day I'm gonna fuck you to that song," I warned her.

"Promises, promises," she said and I smacked her arse as she climbed out of the bath. When she was safely covered from head to toe in my navy bathrobe and I had thrown a white towel around my hips, I pulled on her lapels to turn her around to face me.

"Seriously, Sunshine. I don't want you putting a brave face on this. What happened tonight was all kinds of fucked up and, I'll be honest, going to America and leaving you here feels wrong," I admitted to her.

"I won't tell you I'm fine," she told me. "It's probably going to take years of counseling before I can ever get to the stage where I'm not messed up about what happened. But I'll get there. Knowing that he's dead, though, feels like I've been let out of prison. I've wasted the last six months on Frank, but the next six belong to us." I smiled, because I knew that there was nothing about being a fighter that this strong woman couldn't teach me.

# CHAPTER 25

I was the last of our group to mount the stairs leading up to the plane. The sudden snow that covered half of London was slowly melting, and we were finally on our way to America, much to Earnshaw's relief. He'd worked hard to get me this fight, and I'm not sure that his stress levels could have taken it if I'd gone through with canceling it.

My hands were buried deep in my jacket pockets, and despite that fact that I had the fight of my life ahead of me, I still hated the idea of leaving Em behind. The night before a test, when she was going through her notes, I always made her tea and toast with chocolate spread. It was kind of becoming a tradition, but who would do that for her with me gone? I swear I worried about the stupidest shit whenever she was away from me. But that stupid shit was marriage. Always worrying about the other before yourself.

I nodded to the flight attendant as I ducked to walk in

through the door. We dominated the space as they directed us toward our seats, and all of us looked cocky and confident, as we tried to hide the fact that none of us had been on a long-haul flight before. Hell, most of us hadn't ever been on a plane before. Even Danny went back to Ireland by ferry. Earnshaw had that relaxed, bored look about him that said he'd flown a thousand times. Tommy managed to hit practically every passenger down the aisle with his duty-free bag, then argued with Liam when he went to put it in the overhead locker.

"What is all this shit anyway?" Liam asked, opening the bag.

"Stuff to do on the flight," he answered.

"Like what?" Liam replied. He opened the bag, and we all peered in. Inside was Tom's weight in chocolate bars and a hardback copy of *Gone Girl* by Gillian Flynn.

"What the fuck is this?" Liam asked, pulling out the book.

"Em read it and told me it was really good," Tommy explained. We all looked at each other wondering what it was about chick lit Tommy thought he'd enjoy.

"Jesus, Tom, I think you're actually becoming a bird by osmosis. You've shagged so many women that estrogen is actually being absorbed into your skin," Liam told him.

"At least it's got words instead of pictures. Be thankful it isn't a coloring book," Kieran added with a smirk as we settled into our seats.

"Oh, I have one of those," a pretty girl in the seat behind Tommy said, holding up an adult coloring book. Her friend leaned over the seat in front of her and pointed to the book Liam was holding.

"I love that book. Have you seen the film?" she purred

sexily at Liam as she spoke and leaned farther forward, giving him an eyeful of her rack. I chuckled as I sat back in my seat and closed my eyes. She was in for a long flight if she was hoping to seduce Liam. Tommy grinned and wiggled his eyebrows at us all. Apparently the female attention he was getting totally vindicated his choice of reading material. If he flashed about that chocolate later, he'd be attracting women like magnets.

As it happened, he was barely in his seat for most of the journey. Like some kid with ADHD, Tommy could never sit still for long. Kieran kept me company for a few hours, watching movies on the screen in front of us, until a kid started kicking the back of his seat. He gave me a look that said he was about to murder him before addressing the mother. "Excuse me," he said in his politest, most charming voice. "Your son is kicking the back of my seat, and it's getting really annoying. Do you mind stopping him?"

The bitch looked completely pissed off at been interrupted in the middle of whatever she was reading on her Kindle. "This is a family flight, and if you wanted more distance between the seating, you should have paid for a first-class seat." Even I turned around to look then.

"You're seriously going to let that little shit keep doing it?" Kier asked. She didn't get a chance to respond before he started talking directly to the kid. If this had been any of the gym kids, I knew what I'd do. Then again, I like to think they were too respectful for that. This little shit, who must have been about nine or ten, wore the smirk of a brat who always got what he wanted.

"Next time you kick my seat, kid, I'm gonna take my bottle of water and splash it all over your crotch. Then when you go to the bathroom to clean up, I'm gonna ask everyone to clear a path because my kid brother's had a little 'accident.' For the rest of the flight, you'll be the kid who pissed himself. You want that?"

"Really," said the mother, outraged.

"Yeah! Really," promised Kieran. The kid shook his head no and I closed my eyes again, smiling. Kieran really was something else.

A few hours later, the sun set and most of the passengers were quiet. The boys, having all gotten bored, had disappeared to the back of the plane. I sat listening to Kier's iPod as I ran through all Temple's previous fights in my mind, working out what my strategy was. It was the strong cloud of perfume filling my nose that made me open my eyes as a good-looking girl with long dark hair, perfectly manicured nails, and lots of makeup sat down next to me.

"Hi, I hope you don't think I'm being too forward. Your friends back there didn't think you'd want to join us but I didn't want you to feel left out."

I pulled off my headphones, not wanting to seem rude. "That's kind of you. But I've got a big week coming up, and I'm happy just sitting in my seat and relaxing until the plane lands," I told her politely.

"Maybe I could relax with you?" she suggested with a tilt of her head. She bit her shiny lip. Why girls did that I had no idea; it had zero effect on me. Actually that was a lie. Em always bit her lip—when she was working out math problems.

She had absolutely no idea she was doing it, and it was sexy as fuck.

"Look, I don't want to seem rude, and you're welcome to sit here if you're after a bit of peace and quiet, but I'm probably going to listen to music and try and get some sleep." I told her. Maybe I was being rude, not wanting to make idle chitchat with a stranger but being rude was pretty much what I was famous for. At least it used to be.

As soon as I went to put my headphones back on, she started talking again. "The guys told me all about your fight. They said that when you win you're going to be really famous. You must be totally pumped." Her perfect manicure was waving around excitedly as she talked about the fight.

"Yeah, I guess," I replied, trying to replace my headphones again.

"Listen, call it fate," she said, "but I'm in town for two weeks when your fight is on. Maybe we could hook up sometime?" She tucked her hair behind her ear and bit her lip again.

I looked at her and couldn't help but mentally compare her with Em. My girl hardly ever wore makeup, not because she didn't need it, which she didn't, but because I think it never occurred to her to wear any if she wasn't going out. She told me that waitressing made her nails all dirty so she kept them short and unpolished. Em was all natural, nothing false about her. There was no comparison. It wasn't this girl's fault. It was just that I gave my heart away the day I first clapped eyes on Sunshine, and I never wanted it back.

"Look, it's really nice of you to offer, but I'm married," I explained, holding up my ring finger. Leaning toward me, her weight on the armrest next to me, she looked down her shirt at her own cleavage, then raised her eyes to me to see if I'd caught the show and whispered, "I won't tell if you won't."

I leaned in next to her to give her my reply. "First time you come on to me, you're misinformed. Second time, you're disrespecting my wife. So how about you fuck off back to your seat before I decide to get offended?"

The look on her face told me this had never happened to her before. She flew out of the seat with a mumbled "arsehole," and I finally got back to my music. I let out a heavy sigh. No way was I traveling without Em again.

\* \* \*

The warm Las Vegas temperature was a welcome relief from the harsh weather we'd left behind in London. Of course, Danny sucked away all of my appreciation for the climate when he started pointing out that Temple had trained for months in this heat while I'd trained in the cold. Eyeing me up and down as we waited for our luggage like I was twenty stone and not two hundred twenty pounds, he grumbled about the amount of work we had to do. We queued for a taxi after getting through customs and when the driver asked what hotel we were staying at, Danny gave him the name of the gym, and the boys all grumbled.

"This ain't a feckin' free holiday!" Danny yelled at them. "You wanna go and lie on a nice beach? Fuck off to Spain. You wanna stay and see how winning is done, you pull your weight. Heath is gonna be busy with promotion, so Kieran, you're Con's sparring partner, and Liam and Tommy, you'll run circuits with him."

To be fair to Temple's camp, the gym they'd hooked us up with was small but decent. It wasn't in the best of neighborhoods, but as I shook hands with a few of the local fighters, I had to admit that Southside Gym had the same vibe to it as Driscoll's. As far as Danny was concerned, jet lag was just a myth, and, giving us ten minutes to change, we were up and working before we'd even learned everyone's names.

"Right boys. A lot of shit has gone down in the last week. Tough. This ain't the time for fucking distractions. For the next six days, you're all gonna eat, sleep, and dream boxing. When it's done—you get a day off."

That was it. The end of his groundbreaking motivational speech. Kier and I both grinned as we looked at each other. At least until Danny shouted, "That's it. What the feckin' hell you still standing around for. Get to work!"

I went with the same basic routine I followed at home. Only this time, some of the local fighters had in on the action. When I would run, Samuel, their head coach, made me run with a tennis ball. I'd squeeze it and then relax my hand, repeating the exercise for a mile and then swapping hands. I also didn't run alone anymore, mostly because it was easy to get lost and time was something I had precious little of left. I did ten miles in the morning but Danny replaced the afternoon run with sprints.

We shared the gym with Samuel's two bull mastiffs named Leonard and Dempsey. When the guys sprinted, they did too, adding a little extra competition. My days were filled with skipping, circuits, hitting tires with a sledgehammer, and punching sandbags. Unlike punching bags, the harder you hit sandbags the harder they flew back at you. Unless you wanted a smack in the head, you had to hit and learn to duck or dodge, fast. I wasn't used to training in the heat and my muscles knew it. By the end of every day, I was exhausted but felt like I could actually do this.

The friends we made at Southside should have been in Temple's corner. They were American, after all. But poverty and a certain respect for the sport and the old ways unified us, until they felt as much a part of our camp as the rest of the guys.

Samuel's wonderful wife, Odell, cooked for us all. She owned the diner across the road from the gym and was used to cooking for boxers. There was no give in the special diet I was on, not this close to a fight. She looked after us in a way a hotel never would. Pretty much the only time we even went back there was to sleep and grab fresh clothes.

Kieran continued to spar with me, but after a day, Samuel put me together with Leon. He was the nicest, gentlest guy I ever met, until you climbed into the ring with him. He was six feet eight inches and built like an absolute fucking tank. What he lacked in technique and footwork, he made up for in sheer blunt force trauma. Nine times out of ten, he couldn't get near me, and we could only spar for a few rounds before he'd worn himself out. But if he ever caught me, I felt his punch for hours. If ever there was a lesson in staying fast, it was Leon. Soft fucker was always the first one to stop and help me up when he knocked me down though. Made it kind of hard to hate the guy who hit you when he was so apologetic.

Tommy brought the famous soundtrack with him, and the Southside guys mocked us, but after a couple of days, even they were skipping to the rhythm of the same tunes that kept us pumped. Danny still made me do a criminal number of push-ups and hanging sit-ups. They weren't as much fun without Em to do the counting but she gave me something to think about as I worked through the pain.

Like most fighters, I led with my right hand. My right hook was famous, and Danny always let me lead with it. But he was learning as much as I was. Between him and Samuel, they decided to tie my right hand behind my back before putting me in the ring with Leon. Talk about a crash course in learning to lead with your left. I moved faster and harder between four ropes than I ever had before. Tying my hand was a risk. It fucked with my balance, and there was no need to read me. There was no question of which way I'd be punching, only where. In five hard fucking days, I learned to lead with both arms, and the first time I spared with Kier after that, I was all over him. He'd spent his whole life learning how to read me as a fighter. He knew my form, my technique. Shit, he knew how I'd fight depending on what mood I was in. Now he had no clue where I was coming from, and I knew then why they'd done it.

As I helped Kier up off his arse, we both smiled. Everyone did. There was electricity in the air, like something special was coming. Right now I was the underdog. The one statistically most likely to lose. But that also made me most likely to surprise people. I didn't need people to love me or believe me. I only needed it from those I loved. Because of Em and these guys, there was absolutely nothing that I couldn't do.

The only thing missing in all this was my wife. She would have loved meeting Samuel and Leon, and I could almost picture her perched by the ring cuddling and petting Leonard and Dempsey. No matter what I was doing, I called her every night before I went to bed. So far she said the exams were going well. I knew in Em's code it meant she was fucking acing 'em. She had a gift for math like I'd never seen before. It wasn't so much that she found it easy, it's that she could see a beauty in the numbers where other people couldn't. Maybe it's why she understood my sport so well. Those of us who loved boxing saw a beauty in the art of the sport, where others only saw violence.

Every day the hole in my heart from missing her grew bigger. By Friday, the tension between wanting more time to train and missing her badly became meaningless. The fight was tomorrow whether I was I ready for it or not.

# CHAPTER 26

Rest day was still spent at Southside. I'd have gone crazy just sitting in the hotel room, but the gym kept me centered and calm. Samuel taped fights almost religiously, and so we all spent most of the day holed up in a tiny little room at the back of the gym watching Temple fight. I only hoped he hadn't switched it up like I was going to.

"How are you feeling?" Em asked me that night. It was the last time I'd speak to her before the fight.

"Good," I told her honestly. "Confident. There's kind of a buzz like there is back home. You'd like it here."

"You probably won't want to work out after the fight but maybe I could come with you to see the place and meet a few of the guys?" she suggested.

Just the thought of having her there made me smile. "I'd like that," I said.

"How did today's exam go?" I asked, and I could see her

grin as she replied, "Good, I think. There were a couple of questions that I was nervous about but I worked through them when I got home, and I'm happier now with my answers."

"You all set for tomorrow?" I asked about her morning flight.

"Are you kidding? My bag's been packed for nearly a week. There's no way that I'm not going to be on that plane, I promise."

"Don't say that. Anything could happen to stop you getting here. Look at all the shit with the weather."

"Baby," she said, and I could hear the laughter in her voice, "how many times today have you checked that my flight is still listed?"

I didn't want to answer her because I knew she'd laugh. I mumbled into the phone.

"Cormac," she pressed. Which kind of shocked me because she never called me that.

"Fine. Fourteen!" I admitted. She did actually laugh at me. I needed to hear that sound in person.

"I will be on that flight, O'Connell, I promise. The snow is almost completely gone here."

"How are you getting to Heathrow?" I asked, worrying about her even now.

"Albie offered to drive me to the airport," she said.

"I made sure there's a car service at the airport to meet your flight. Earnshaw told me they'll hold up one of those signs with your name on it. Show them your ID when you get here and they'll bring you straight to the guys, okay?" Shit, I sounded so fucking nervous.

"O'Connell" she said to me.

"Yeah," I answered huskily.

"You've got this. When you get in that ring tomorrow, know that I'm on my way to you that very minute, and I want you to fight like I'm right in front of you. You've been training for this, so show me what my husband is made of."

Just like that, all the nerves and bullshit fell away, and I knew this fucking fight was mine. Now it was time to show the rest of the world that too.

\* \* \*

Fight day, like every morning here, was bright and clear, and I itched to go for a run. Kieran and the rest of the guys were in Odell's diner, stuffing down the American version of a full English fried breakfast. When I got back, I knew I was gonna sweet talk Kieran's ma into cooking me up a full Irish breakfast, soda bread and all.

Tommy questioned why I wasn't going along. They all knew I couldn't eat with them but guessed I'd want the company. Kieran knew better. He tossed me his headphones and iPod on the way out and left me watching Leon and his boys sparring. The music drowned out everything, and I let my head get where it needed to be. To a place it most definitely hadn't been during the exhibition match. Temple's cocky scowl was burned into my brain, and I knew, based on my last performance and the shit he'd been saying about me lately, he thought he had this in the bag.

As I looked around Southside, I realized just how different

Temple and I were. Sure, we were from opposite sides of the world, but both of us came from poor families and boxing had elevated us. What made us different was what we did when we got to the top. Temple surrounded himself with his "crew" as he liked to call them.

As far as I could tell, they were yes-men who changed from week to week. Sure he had a longtime trainer, like I had Danny, but the rest of them came and went. He was renowned in his downtime for attending clubs, celebrity parties, and high-profile events, his friendship with a few notorious rappers making him as infamous as the boxing did. There were always at least two models hanging off his arms. Shit, even at the weigh-in, he had half his entourage around him.

I listened to all of them, him included, talk shit about what I was bringing to the table. It was a time-honored boxing tradition to try and break each other mentally before a fight. My temper was usually on a hair trigger, but I'd perfected the art of looking bored shitless at weigh-ins, which usually succeeded in riling up my opponent. I think I might have even thrown a yawn in midway through Temple's rant.

I didn't want any of that shit. Sure, I wanted to be successful to give my girl a better life, so that I could take care of her. But I was the lucky son of a bitch who got to do that by doing what I loved. And I fucking loved the fight. Temple boxed with his head. He was what Danny called a "technical" fighter. His technique was flawless. Combine that with his size and fitness and the guy was a machine.

I ran my fingertips over the tattoo across my chest. "A

champion is someone who gets up when they can't.—Jack Dempsey." I wasn't a technical fighter. I was a wild card, always would be. When I got knocked down, when my ribs were bruised and every single part of my body felt fucking broken, I got back up. When the fight was over and all hope of victory was lost, I got back up. Heart is what got me a shot at the world heavyweight title, not fear or anger, but heart. In the end, it's why I would win. Because when his head told Temple it was all over, my heart would still be telling me to get back up. Losing was done when you listened to your head; winning was done when you listened to your heart.

The longer I watched Leon work his way through sparring partners, the more I imagined in my head how the fight was going to go down. I was fucking hungry for this. Temple had no idea what I was capable of, but he was about to find out. I was ready to hurt and keep hurting until Temple went down and stayed down. Whatever happened tonight, I was coming home with that title, not for Em, not for Danny or any of the boys, but for me.

* * *

"You ready, son?" Danny asked as he sat down on the bench next to me. He lit up a cigarette and inhaled deeply. Southside, like most gyms, was nonsmoking. Apparently that rule didn't apply to Danny on either side of the Atlantic.

"I'm ready, Danny. I can't explain why. A few weeks ago, Frank was all I could think about. Now it just feels like this is my time. Like everything that's happened has made me who I need to be to win this fight."

"That's good," he said. "Winning ain't about who deserves it, it's about who fights harder for it. So when you get in that ring tonight, you just remember that we're right behind you, and you keep fighting until it's done." I smiled at him, and he scowled back.

"This fight is mine, Danny. I'll make you proud of me. I promise."

"Kid," he said, standing up and taking another drag of his cigarette, "I've always been proud of you. Title or no title, that ain't gonna change." He patted me on the back and walked away.

There was a lump in my throat as I thought over what he'd said. When I was a kid and Danny had made us go to church, I couldn't help feeling resentful that God had given me a shitty mother. It never occurred to me until now that he'd actually blessed me with a pretty amazing father. One who never held me back or pushed me too hard, but one who also never lost faith in me and showed me the way. It was because of him I knew what kind of dad I wanted to be someday.

\* \* \*

There were so many people around that it was like being backstage at a concert. Everyone I passed seemed to want my autograph. When we finally made it to my dressing room, Kieran shut the door behind us, and no fucker was allowed in.

"Shit. This is a bit fancy, ain't it?" Tommy commented. Tom and Liam enjoyed the TV and leather sofa but the rest of us weren't interested. They turned the volume on the TV off as they settled in, and I appreciated it. Half the preparation in any fight was getting into the zone. I warmed up, stretched, and shadowboxed.

It was only once Danny started taping up my knuckles that he gave me the pep talk. "This ain't no exhibition anymore, son, and this guy ain't going down without a fight. Now you and me, we've come a long way this last year, but that don't change who we are or where we've come from. He's tough, but you're tougher. He's got the weight of the world on his shoulders and nowhere to go but down. Well, you're gonna help him get there real quick.

"This fight ain't gonna be pretty. But when you're done, you'll be the kid from the streets who came from nowhere to become the greatest heavyweight fighter in the world. So you ready to make history, Con?"

"Yes sir," I replied in all seriousness. I was done with watching Temple keep my title belt warm. This was my time and fuck Temple for not realizing that. When Danny was done with the tape, I stood up and shook out my legs as Kier got the pads ready for me to warm up. I was surprised when the television went off. Tommy and Liam looked restless and more nervous than I was.

"You okay?" I asked them.

"Shit, Con," Liam answered, rubbing the back of his neck nervously. "You're about to fight for the World Heavyweight title and you're asking me if I'm okay?"

"Yeah," I answered, making them chuckle.

"We're nervous. You tell me you ain't?" Tommy asked.

I thought about it for a second as I cricked my neck from side to side. "No. I'm not nervous. I don't think about the title or who's watching. Once the bell goes, there's just him and me anyway."

Tommy rolled his eyes and went back to pacing. A sharp knock sounded at the door, pissing Kieran off. "What do you want?" he said, yanking it open.

"Well, is that any way to talk to a man of God?" an Irish voice replied.

"What are you doing here?" Kieran asked, as he let Father Pat in the door.

"Didn't seem right letting you fight without following tradition," he told us as he gave me a quick hug.

"You flew halfway around the world for confession? What's the real reason?" I asked with a smile.

"The congregation and I bet five hundred pounds on you, so I'm here protecting our investment," he answered.

"Very Christian," Danny chuckled.

Another knock sounded at the door, and one of the managers put his head around it. "Ten minutes, Mr. O'Connell," he said.

"Well then. We don't have time for a full confession, but how about a quick prayer?" Father Pat asked, and Danny nodded his permission. We gathered around in a circle, even Danny, and bent our heads.

"Dear Lord, we ask you not for victory, for somehow that seems wrong. But only for Con's protection and the courage for him to be strong. Strength not to conquer, but just that he fights well. And proves himself a sportsman at the ring of the final bell."

"Amen," we all said together, and a contemplative silence fell about the room. There was no whooping and hollering and no talking smack about Temple. The time for talking was done. Now there was only doing what needed to be done.

Kieran held up my green silk robe and helped me slip it on. Shit was a lot fancier when you fought at this level. I'd keep it for Em if I won. She'd get a kick out of that. Her flight would be landing any minute now, but I knew by the time she got her bags and made it here, the fight would be done and dusted.

I bounced from foot to foot to keep limber and because I was so wired that I could barely keep still. Stopping for a moment, I spoke quietly to Danny, out of earshot of the others. "I wish Sunshine could have been with me for this," I admitted.

"She is here, son. She always will be," he replied, and I nodded, knowing that he was right.

"In case I forget to say it later, thanks for everything, Danny. I wouldn't be here now if it wasn't for you."

"You're welcome, son," he replied, squeezing me on the shoulder. "Now, tear this arrogant little fecker apart so we can go home," he said, making me grin. The venue didn't allow smoking and had alarms practically every two feet. Not being able to have a cigarette for hours on end was making him twitchy.

I closed my eyes briefly and thought about Em. Right then

I knew she'd be looking at her watch and thinking of me too. This was the moment I was going to prove to her and every other fucker in the world that her faith in me wasn't unfounded.

\* \* \*

The music playing in the stadium stopped. After a brief pause, the opening bars to my introduction music boomed through the speakers, making the floor shake. The door opened for the last time.

The crowd roared as the spotlight caught and followed me to the ring. My heart was racing so fast, it felt like it was going to explode in my chest. But with every beat, I became more and more pumped. With every step, I breathed deeply, sharpening my will to end this, to end Rico Temple.

"Hurricane, we love you!" I heard a woman's voice scream from the crowd. They didn't love me. They didn't fucking know me. There's only one woman who knew me, who'd love me with or without these gloves, one woman who owned me. The crowd was fickle. They loved a winner, and tonight that meant they would love me.

The rest of the screams were white noise, and the sea of faces was lost behind the flash of bulbs. I reached the ring and walked up the steps, climbing between the ropes with the boys behind me.

Kieran took off my robe as my music ended. After a brief pause, Rico Temple's stupid-arse song rang in my ears. "I see his shit taste in music hasn't improved," shouted Kieran, making me smirk. I did a lap of the ring, ignoring the smoke machines and other stupid shit his entourage had going on. I wasn't intimidated by his crap, the size of this place, or anything else. Like my girl had once said to me, the only thing I had to fear is fear itself.

Liam and Tommy sat in the front row, an empty seat between them. It didn't matter that Em couldn't make it on time. There would always be a seat for her wherever I was fighting. Whatever happened, however the next twelve rounds played out, this fight was for her. I would give the very best of myself, knowing that she'd taught me how. This was my tribute to the woman who'd changed my life. To the woman who'd changed me.

# CHAPTER 27

I rotated my shoulders and shook out my arms as I waited for the bell. The emcee climbed into the ring and circled around as he waited for the crowd to settle. I'd met him a couple of times before, and he seemed like a really nice guy. He even came to wish me luck earlier on. Maybe I wasn't the only one who thought that Rico Temple was an arsehole.

When the crowd finally calmed down enough for him to speak, he raised his microphone, and his booming voice echoed across the arena. "Ladies and gentlemen. I'd like to welcome you to the MGM Grand Garden Arena, in Las Vegas, Nevada, USA. AL Promotions presents the main event of the evening. Twelve rounds of boxing for the WBO Heavyweight Championship of the World. And now the officials are ready. The fighters are ready. Are you ready?" he called out, getting the crowd all riled up again.

"Boxing fans, ARE YOU READY?" he called out, and the

crowd screamed back at him. "For the sixteen thousand eight hundred fans here in attendance at the MGM Grand Garden Arena and the millions watching around the world, courtesy of HBO, ladies and gentlemen, let's get ready to ruuummmbbble!" The whole arena was electrified, his words switching them on and bringing them to life.

"Introducing first, fighting out of the red corner, standing with his head coach Danny Driscoll, wearing green-and-white shorts and officially weighing in at two hundred twenty pounds. Tonight with honor, he challenges for the World Heavyweight title. The fighting pride of Ireland, Cormac 'The Hurricane' O'Connell." The crowd erupted, and I raised my hand in the air in silent thanks.

"And his opponent across the ring. Fighting out of the blue corner, with his head coach Aaron Beaumont, wearing red-white-and-blue shorts. His official weight being two hundred twenty-three pounds, ladies and gentlemen, introducing from Detroit, right here in the USA, the current WBO Champion of the World, Rico 'Double Tap' Temple." His fans screamed and hollered as people cleared out of the ring. Kieran removed my robe, and Danny put the gum shield into my mouth.

"I hope you took a picture, 'cause that face ain't gonna be so pretty when you come out," Danny joked.

"Well he's fucked then, 'cause if he fights Temple like he did last time, his looks'll be the only thing he's got going for him," Kieran replied with a chuckle.

"Your confidence in me is fucking overwhelming," I mumbled at them through my gum shield.

"Ah, put your big girl pants on," Danny barked at me. "Last time you fought this fucker, I told you to make him work for it. Now I'm telling you the same thing. I want five or six rounds nice and easy. Make him think you're nervous. Make him throw and miss his punches. When he starts getting tired, but figures he's got you on points, I want you to let him have it. I want you shocking the hell out of this crowd and lead southpaw."

I nodded my head to let him know I understood. I knew the game plan, and I was following it this time. I would be disciplined and precise, but fucking brutal. Rico Temple wouldn't know what hit him.

When we came to the center of the ring, the referee called for a clean fight. Temple smirked at me, and I regretted that I couldn't give him the finger. I held out my gloves like last time, knowing he'd ignore them. Fuck him if he wanted to be a bad sportsman.

He knocked my hands away then laughed when the crowd jeered at him. I flexed my shoulders and shook out my arms as I waited for the glorious sound of the bell to ring. When it did, I came out ready to dance. Temple didn't expect it. He knew I was hungry for this, and my bet was that he thought I'd follow the same play as last time. The cocky, inexperienced kid who thought he had a shot at the title at twenty-four. This time I did *exactly* as I was fucking told. I wouldn't be letting Danny down twice. I'd given Temple a shit performance last time, so I could forgive him for not knowing what a fucking amazing boxer I could be.

The first minute or two, he watched me bob and weave

my way around the canvas, almost taunting him to take a shot. I wasn't being edged into a corner or against the ropes. If this fucker wanted me, he could come and get me. He threw out a couple of wild jabs to goad me into attacking, but after a couple of minutes, he knew the fight wasn't going to go down like he expected. That might have been the point that I winked at him. Of course Temple didn't appreciate my newfound take on anger management. In fact, I'm pretty sure from the way he grunted and charged at me, that the wink pissed him off. He threw combination after combination at me, but I kept my guard up. I imagine it would have made a great news story to say that he knocked me out in the first round, but today wasn't Temple's day. It was mine. I let him wear himself out until the bell rang, then winked at him again. Fuck him.

"Well, I like your style, Con, but I don't think Temple's a big fan of your work," Kieran told me as I sat down on the corner stool.

"Shame, that. I think we could 'ave been mates," I gasped, before Kier filled my mouth with water.

"You're doing good, Con. You're doing real good. Just keep out of the way of that monster right hand of his. Don't get sloppy and leave yourself open, or this thing's gonna be over before it even starts." I nodded, taking Danny's advice before I was standing and the bell rang out again.

For the next four rounds, my feet barely touched the canvas. I was fast but not invisible. Even with my guard up high, this fucker hit like a wrecking ball. The whole fight was playing out almost like a complete reversal of the exhibition bout. The calmer I was, the angrier he became. I dropped my guard a few times, and he caught me with a couple of jabs, one of which cut the corner of my left eye.

When the bell rang, signaling the end of round five, I was about done with this passive bullshit. "Dan, he ain't tiring out as quickly as we thought. If I don't get him on a knockout, I might end up losing this thing on points," I panted, as Danny treated my bloodied eye.

"He's getting frustrated, but ain't letting go of this title easy. You've done enough to wear him down, now you start showing me some magic. But no going southpaw yet. You hold that back until you need it at the end," Danny advised me.

When he'd finished with my eye, I swilled around some water then spat it back out. The minute the bell rang, I was off that stool and looking for an opening. Temple threw a couple of jabs, expecting what I'd been showing him for the last five rounds. This time I didn't let a single jab connect.

As I ducked and sidestepped a second time, he dropped his guard, and that was it. Like the whole thing was happening in slow motion, I saw my window of opportunity and took it. Years of push-ups, pull-ups, and bench presses and a lifetime of pain and discipline went into that punch. My right jab caught his attention but I followed it up with a left hook that connected with his torso. I know he felt that down to his foundation. A perfectly executed body shot is a thing of beauty. The head shots look bad, but I just caught this fucker in the liver. From the look on his face, the pain was crippling.

The crowd went crazy. If I'd hit any other fighter like that, he'd be on his knees or flat out on the canvas by now. As cocky as he was, I had to give him credit. He was hard as fucking nails for taking that shot and still standing. For the thirty seconds left in the round, I tried to capitalize on the hit, but he was too good. He stayed out of my way and protected himself. I gave him a pummeling but there was no second opening. As the round ended, he slumped into his corner. He might recover enough to catch his breath in the next few minutes, but as he stared across the canvas at me, all cockiness gone, I knew he understood just how dangerous I was.

The next three rounds were the most difficult I'd ever fought in my career, each one more brutal than the next. The cut to my eye was getting bigger with every punch.

"What do I do about my eye?" I asked Danny during a break.

"Don't get hit again," he replied with a chuckle. "Protect the eye and look for an opening. Keep your guard up and don't fight defensively. He didn't go down with the liver shot, and that punch was feckin' perfect. We need the points now so start getting 'em on the scorecard."

He finished just as the bell rang. Temple immediately went for my face, forcing me to keep my guard up. After a while, he worried more about my face than his own body and I got him again in the torso with a hook. It wasn't a direct hit. It wasn't even a good punch but his liver had taken such a blow the first time that even the judges had to see him flinch in pain.

Round ten was an all-out street brawl. This was my wall, the point where I was fatigued and my body wasn't doing what my brain was telling it to. We were both flagging. The body shots had cost him heavily on points but I was still making up for the early rounds. At this point, nobody could call it, so we both just kept hitting.

My right jab caught him square on the jaw, but I dropped my arm doing it, and he caught me solidly with a right hook. *Fuck!* My face was probably a fucking mess by now, and my eye felt like it was about to explode. We staggered and were unsteady on our feet, but the ringing of the bell saved us both. I sank onto my corner stool and closed my eyes as Danny cleaned me up and Kier hydrated me. The sound of the crowd was ringing in my ears when I heard her voice. I must have been hit in the head harder than I realized.

"I'm here, I'm here! O'Connell, I made it." The voice was getting louder. I whipped my head around to see a red-faced Em being ushered up the steps by Kieran.

"Quick, he's got seconds," Kieran warned.

"I made it. Baby, I'm here," she said, laying her palm against my cheek through the ropes.

"You okay, Sunshine?" I asked her through the gum shield, the coppery taste of blood still filling my mouth despite the water.

"I'm fine," she answered with a laugh, though there were tears in her eyes. "How we doing?" she asked me, looking toward Temple.

"Killing it," I said, making her smile. Danny climbed out of the ring as she removed her hand.

"I love you," she told me. Just like when I was doing hanging sit-ups, she was like a shot of adrenaline to my system. My girl was here. She's made it, and there was no way I was losing now. If I had to bring everything in me to the table, so be it. I wanted to be the only man she saw in this ring, the only one she saw, period.

The bell rang, and I stood in time to see Rico Temple make his fatal mistake. He looked over at my wife, then turned to me and licked his lips. From that moment on, it was all over. Stupid fucker just didn't know it. I had wanted to win this for Em. Now I wanted to end him for me.

He was expecting me to come at him with all guns blazing, but I didn't. I shook out my shoulders, bounced around the canvas, and looked like I didn't have a care in the world. Temple came at me after a few seconds of dancing and threw a jab, followed by a fairly decent hook, or it would have been if it had connected. I was gone before the punch landed.

Switching to fighting left handed, like the boys from Southside had taught me, I completely disorientated him. My combinations before now had probably been as predictable as his. Now I had him against the ropes, and there would be no rope-a-dope this time. His core was taking an absolute pounding. After disrespecting my wife, hell, after even looking at her, I was gonna make him piss blood for a week. There was no break and no letup. I hammered him with every single fucking thing I had.

Sweat and blood dripped down from my eye, but I didn't pause. This guy was an absolute fucking machine, but so was I. It was a tossup between whether the referee would pull us apart or the bell would ring, when I saw it. That magical opportunity that Danny was always talking about. There were few things in this world that I was good at. Loving my wife was one and boxing was the other. The control I had over my temper was shit, but between those four posts, it was like I could slow everything down and see those gaps in a defense that anyone else would miss.

That was how I knew that my left hook to his body would make him drop his guard to protect his liver. As soon as he did that, I brought my fist up in an uppercut to the face that lifted him off the floor. I stood back, knowing what I'd done.

Temple bounced off the ropes and staggered across the ring before landing on the canvas. From the outside, he looked in much better shape than me, my face bearing most of the cosmetic damage. But where I carried my pain on the exterior, he carried his inside. That last uppercut was enough persuasion for his body to surrender.

As I watched the referee count, I thought of Danny telling me that it didn't matter if I went down, only if I stayed there. I'd been to that point where you feel like you can't get any lower. What defines the person you'll become is whether you get back up when everyone thinks the fight is over. It didn't matter how many times I went down. I would *always* get back up because I was a fighter, like Em.

I used to think that being a boxer and a fighter were the same thing. Now I know different. Being a boxer is what I did. Being a fighter is who I was.

When the referee reached seven, Danny stood on the

ropes, with Kieran pressed up behind him. By eight, I knew that Temple was done. When the referee reached nine, the whole arena held its breath, and at ten, it erupted. It was over, and the only thing I could think about was having my wife in my arms again.

It amazed me how quickly the ring filled up as soon as the fight was over. People seemed to pour through the ropes like ants, and it pissed me off. Television cameras and microphones were thrust in my face, and despite how I felt about winning, I was going to knock a second person the fuck out if I didn't get to my wife and the guys soon.

Kieran got to me first, and we threw our arms around each other. "You did it! You fuckin' crazy Irish bastard!" he screamed.

"We did it," I told him, and he hugged me again.

From over his shoulder, I could see a shock of blond hair from behind some guy that made me smile. When Em got to me, she held my face in her hands and, with tears streaming down her face, kissed me fiercely. "I'm so proud of you, O'Connell. I knew you could do it!" she said. Throwing my sweaty arms around her waist, I lifted her high so she had to lean down to kiss me again. Then Liam, Tommy, and Earnshaw tackled me so hard that I nearly took Temple's spot on the canvas. "Where's Danny?" I asked, but they didn't know. Kieran removed my gloves, and all six of us held on tight as we made our way to the center of the ring. Rico Temple was on his feet now, looking dazed and more than a little pissed off. I'm betting he'd never lick his lips at another guy again. I didn't bother trying to keep the enormous grin from my face as the emcee's booming voice echoed through the microphone.

"Ladies and gentlemen. After eleven rounds of boxing here at the MGM Grand Garden Arena in Las Vegas, Nevada, I give you the winner by knockout and new WBO World Heavyweight Champion, Cormac 'the Hurricane' O'Connell." I looked at Em and the guys as my hand was held high, and I couldn't believe we'd all made it. The kids who everyone had written off, who wouldn't amount to anything even if they survived, were standing here with me. They got me here, and I couldn't have done this without any of them. No matter what happened, I would no longer be remembered for my fucked-up past, but as the kid who went from nothing to becoming the Heavyweight Champion of the World.

I handed Em my title belt, which seemed way too big for her little arms, and kissed her deeply, making the guys catcall at us. She, Kieran, and all the boys stayed by my side as I answered question after question in front of the cameras. Out of the corner of my eye, I could see Rico Temple doing the same thing. He was the toughest guy I'd ever fought, and that deserved some respect. Leaving Em with my guys, I made my way to his corner. His trainer held out his hand to me, and I shook it firmly.

"Well done, son. You earned that," he said, tipping his head toward the belt in my corner.

Temple turned around to face me and looked like he wanted to keep the fight going. Then, with a wry smile, he shook my hand and gave me a bro hug. "It was a good fight, O'Connell, but just so you know, I'm getting my belt back."

I grinned back at him and knew then that there'd be a rematch in my future. "Bring it on," I told him.

He laughed and turned back toward his trainer as I looked for Danny. Through the crowd, I could see that the front row was empty, save for one man who looked around the arena like he had no idea how he had ended up there.

# CHAPTER 28

"I can help you get that weathered old arse up into that ring if you like," I said to Danny as I sat down in the empty seat next to him. The cameras were following my every move but Kieran and Liam were keeping them out of my face while Tommy gave them my life story.

"Feck off, ya' cocky little shite," he replied, making me chuckle. "Your face looks like crap. Thought I told you not to get hit again."

"Yeah, but since when did I ever listen to you?" I answered. We both paused as we stared, disbelievingly, at the ring in front of us.

"You did it, kid," he said to me, his eyes a little stunned and watery.

"You gave this to me, Danny. You put me on this path, and without you, I wouldn't be here. Shit, without you, I'd probably have gone down the same path as me ma," I told him.

"Don't sell yourself short. Boxing is in your blood. You've got some kind of magic in that ring that I ain't never seen before. And you weren't never going the same way as that gin-soaked, sour-faced, bitter old bitch. You just needed a kick up the arse that's all. Maybe we both did. If anyone's responsible for all this, it's that girl of yours."

We both looked up to see Em answering questions from some reporter. I could tell how nervous she was by the way she kept tucking her hair behind her ear.

"She ain't never getting rid of me," I told Danny, like it was a vow. Em was mine for life. That would never change.

"Poor girl," he said with a chuckle that turned into a laugh. Honest to God, in all the years I've known Danny, I'd never seen him laugh. Even Kier and Liam turned around to watch. It was pretty infectious, and we were all grinning and laughing along with him as the gravity of what we'd done began to sink in. Pretty soon tears of laughter were running down his cheeks, and Danny wiped them away with the back of his hand. He patted my knee in amusement, then stood up.

"Where are you going?" I asked him.

"I'm gonna find a good Irish bar and see if I can help Father Pat put a dent in the church central heating fund."

More camera crews were getting pretty persistent, and eventually I caved in and gave them the interviews they were looking for. When it was done, I saw Em, still standing in the ring and chatting with some of Temple's entourage. Knowing her, she was probably trying to console them over their camp's loss.

"Sorry, boys, I'm taking back my wife," I interrupted, and without waiting to hear what they had to say about it, picked her up bridal-style and carried her to the ropes. I dropped her over the side, and she screeched as Kier caught her.

"Fuck, why are you hitting me? He's the one who dropped you," Kieran complained as she smacked him on the arm.

"Because he's been hit enough for one day," Em told him. They both wore stupid-arse grins that I expected we'd all be wearing for the next month, or at least until I had to start training again. Jumping down myself, I jogged over to take Sunshine from him. Call me possessive as fuck, but I didn't want her in anyone's arms but mine.

When we got back to the locker room, the hallway was filled with people all wanting a piece of me. Earnshaw was in his fucking element, so we left him out there to deal with them and shut the door behind him. He was PR's golden boy now. The kid in his twenties who'd left a big firm to sign with an unknown, who'd come from nowhere to win a World Heavyweight title. There were probably as many people out there who were trying to poach him as those who wanted a piece of me. I liked the guy but it would be a good test of his loyalty to see whether he stuck with us or jumped ship.

I crossed the length of the room in seconds and as I got to the door of the bathroom, I called back to Kier who was turning on the television as the boys handed out beers. "Tell the doc to give me five minutes," I told him.

"You sure you won't need longer?" he asked, smirking at Em and making her blush.

"I need a fucking week, but after two months of no married time, I'm pretty sure two minutes would do it."

"O'Connell!" Em exclaimed, outraged as she covered her face in embarrassment. The boys laughed and upped the volume on the TV. Closing the door behind me, I turned on the shower and stripped off my boots and shorts as the water heated.

"Baby, your face. Shouldn't we wait until you've seen the doctor before we fool around?" she told me.

"I'm not planning on fooling around. I'm pretty serious about what I want to do. Honestly, I'm fine." I closed my eyes as she delicately stroked my injuries and opened them again to see the worried look in her eyes.

"Mrs. O'Connell, do you know how fucking happy I am that you got to see me fight?" I asked.

"Not as happy as I was to make it in time. Remind me to call and thank the car service before we go. They took my bag and delivered it to the hotel so I could get to you quicker."

The fucking tape on my hands was taking ages to get off. As soon as I saw Em slide down her skirt, I knew the tape could wait until later. Grabbing her roughly like some kind of caveman, I lifted her effortlessly to wrap her legs around my waist while plundering her mouth. Fuck, she tasted like heaven. Her tongue tangled against mine as she pressed herself as close to me as possible. Slipping one hand down her panties, I squeezed the smooth globe of her arse cheek. She sat perched on my cock that was hard as a diamond, but I couldn't bear to let her go long enough to strip her.

"Let me down, O'Connell," she said huskily. It killed me to do it but I reluctantly did as she asked, groaning because she brushed past my dick on the way down.

"Start singing the national anthem," she ordered.

"I don't think that's going to work this time," I replied, looking at her breasts as her hands moved up to her bra. One strap slid down her arm and then the other. When she reached around to unclasp it, my mouth went dry.

"You promised me once that you were going to fuck me to it," she said with a glint of mischief in her eyes. I started singing, but a few bars in, when she slid down her panties, I was done. Dropping to my knees, I palmed one of her tits. When I slid the nipple into my mouth and swirled my tongue around it, she moaned and slipped a hand into my hair to steady herself. I wanted to make this last so fucking badly, but we had forever to take our time. This was going to be hard and fast.

Sliding my hand up her silky soft leg, I reached between us to part her folds. I didn't exactly have a plan, but spotting the bench and towels behind us, I found a way to make her at least a little comfortable for what was coming next.

Standing abruptly, I kissed her hard, then reached over to spread the towels out over the bench, lifted her up, and laid her down across them. Before she could protest, my head was between her legs, and I was feasting like a man possessed. She was already so fucking close. Her little gasps and moans were making me even harder, and I knew the only place I wanted to celebrate my victory was in bed with my wife. I felt like I'd finally proved my worth to her in the ring, and now I was reminding her why I was the only man she'd ever need to satisfy her outside of it.

She writhed and wriggled beneath me, trying to make it over the edge. Sliding two fingers inside her as my tongue worked its magic, I gave her the blissful oblivion she was looking for. With her hand gripping my hair and riding my fingers hard, she cried out loudly as she came. Half the guys in my dressing room probably heard it, but I didn't care. While she was still quivering and contracting, I sat down on the bench and lifted her to straddle me. She was soft and relaxed, like a woman completely sated. She was so wet that she slid down slowly but easily onto my waiting cock. I buried my head in the crook of her shoulder and stayed completely still, scared that even the slightest movement would trigger my release. I was still struggling with my control when she grabbed the hook on the wall above me and used it as leverage to rock her hips up and down. Her tight little hole milked me with the aftermath of the orgasm I'd just given her.

"Fuck, Sunshine, I'm not gonna last long," I told her.

"Me either, baby," she moaned. I reached between us to stroke my thumb lightly over her clit and angled my pelvis higher to hit the right spot. Still trembling from the last orgasm, she came again loudly on my dick. What little control I had completely snapped. Grabbing her hips, I lifted her up and down hard and fast. Tomorrow I probably wouldn't be able to move but tonight I was pumped full of adrenaline, and every muscle in my body was primed and ready to make this woman mine. I wanted to brand myself so deeply into her soul that my name would be the first and last on her lips, forever.

"O'Connell," she moaned in pleasurable agony and the sound of my name vibrating through her lips was enough to set me off. The violence of my orgasm rocked us both, and I held her close to me, her forehead resting gently against mine. My heart was beating so loudly that I was sure she could hear it.

"I fucking love you, Mrs. O'Connell," I said. There isn't a single day that went by that I didn't thank God that she chose me. I didn't need her to fix me and all the fucked-up shit that followed me. I just needed her to love me and have faith in me while I fixed myself. She was so far out of my fucking league that having her love me back seemed like an impossible hope once. But striving to be worthy of that love had changed me. It made me a better man. Now I knew the man I was capable of being and the man I was.

"I love you too, Mr. O'Connell. So much," she whispered back, and closing her eyes, she gently kissed her way down my injured face. We showered each other, tenderly, and then threw on some sweats. I imagined the boys had organized a victory party at the hotel so we could change there. I loved that she reached for my black hoodie to keep her warm. The minute I saw her in it, I was hard again. At this rate, neither of us would be able to walk tomorrow. Five minutes I'd told Kieran, but it was forty-five before we came out of the bathroom giggling and holding hands. Everybody stared pointedly at the television and avoided looking at us, though Tommy was humming the Irish national anthem.

"Don't worry, the doctor waited," Kieran told us without turning away from the screen. Sure enough, the middle-aged doctor sat on the sofa between Liam and Tommy, clutching his medical bag on his lap and looking absolutely terrified.

"He wants to know if you're okay, Sunshine," Tommy asked. "You sounded like you were in pain." Unable to hold a straight face any longer, they all burst out laughing and started whooping and hollering. When Tommy started making arse-spanking gestures, the doc looked like he was gonna piss himself. Em pulled the neck of her hoodie to cover her face and buried her head into my side.

"Laugh it up, arseholes," I told them, rubbing her back reassuringly and not giving a single fuck who heard us.

"Sorry to keep you waiting, doc," I told the doctor and led him to the back of the room so he could do his stuff. Em sat down in the seat he'd vacated, and I smiled as they carried on ribbing her. A couple of small stitches and some ice packs for the swelling, and I was given the all clear. Despite the soft tissue damage, which would heal, my vision was fine. I'd have a hell of a black eye tomorrow though.

Em and I held hands on the car journey back, me playing with her fingers and teasing them gently through my own. Every touch was foreplay. The bathroom had taken the edge off but we still had months to make up for. Right now we were slow dancing, building the anticipation for what was going to be the end of a fucking epic night. When we got back to the hotel, I decided to skip my ice bath, even knowing I'd be in agony in the morning. I shaved and changed into jeans and a black shirt, then sat flicking through the television channels while I waited for Em. When she came out of the bathroom, I dropped the remote control.

"Fuck me," I whispered, making her smile.

"Are you sure it looks okay?" she asked nervously. She stood in the doorway wearing a short, body hugging black dress and black stiletto heels. She looked like every wet dream I'd ever had. When she turned around to show me that the dress was backless, my jaw hit the floor.

"O'Connell, say something!" she complained, rubbing her hands anxiously down her dress. I was speechless, willing my brain to put together words to form a sentence.

"You look amazing." It was the fucking lamest thing I could ever had said, and it didn't do any justice to the breathtaking, heart-stopping way she affected me, but it was enough to make her smile.

"I know it's not really me, but this is Las Vegas, and Nikki and Katrina have been nagging at me to try clothes that are less conservative," she told me by way of explanation. Trying to use my words only ever made me seem like a fucking moron so I crossed the room, grabbed the nape of her neck and, with one kiss, showed her exactly how I felt.

For one rare and magical evening, we both got to act our age. The hotel party was epic, and I don't know how the guys organized it, but everyone we knew, including the Southside guys, were there, together with a load of people that we didn't know. We danced and drank for most of the night, and then I got to fall into bed and get hot and naked with my wife.

When Em woke me up at noon the next day, I felt like

I'd only been asleep for five minutes. My head was pounding, and I was pretty sure that I was paralyzed from the neck down. I tried moving my arm and cried out like a little fucking girl when the seized-up muscle started to spasm. Not only did I have the hangover from hell, I'd missed my ice bath and was paying for it dearly.

"Come on," Em told me as she helped me up, "I've run you a warm bath." It did help but I still felt like shit when we reached the lobby. The guys were already waiting, and with most of us decked out in mirrored aviators to protect our fragile eyes from the sun, it looked like a casting call for *Top Gun*. Not a word was said as we took a taxi to Odell's diner. When we arrived, we all shuffled into a booth and waited in hungover silence for a waitress.

"Have you ever seen a more sorry lot in all your life, Danny?" Father Pat asked as he grinned at us all.

"They're feeling a bit delicate today," Em told him. I didn't need to ask why Em wasn't suffering. She'd only had a few drinks last night, still feeling uncomfortable about losing control in public, even with Frank dead. Old habits die hard, I guessed. Although we didn't say a lot, the food really helped, and we demolished our meals in no time, feeling a bit more human after.

"Can you pass the sugar, please?" Earnshaw asked Tommy, who pushed the bowl toward him. I watched, mesmerized, as he loaded up his coffee with sugar after sugar. When he'd finally made it to the party, he had a grin from ear to ear. Despite the late start, I still think he partied harder than all of us. We'd talk properly when we were back home but he'd told me last night that there was some pretty exciting stuff on the horizon.

"Are you going back to the hotel after this?" Danny asked us.

"No. We've got something to do first. We'll meet you in the hotel lobby at seven o'clock," Kier told him. Danny didn't ask what we had planned. It might have been because he knew better, but more than likely he just didn't give a shit.

"What do you have planned?" Em asked me.

"Leon and the Southside guys are taking us all out for dinner tonight and showing us some of Vegas. This afternoon we've got something to do though." She found out what two hours later when I ushered her into the door of the tattoo shop Leon had recommended. We'd all agreed, Earnshaw included, that if we won the fight we were getting tattooed. Everyone got to pick what they wanted but I wouldn't let Em see mine until it was done. She ran her fingers reverently over the raised script across my ribs.

> *The only thing we have to fear is fear itself.*
>                                              —FDR

She bit her lip, trying to hold back the tears, as she read it. I pulled her in for a quick kiss, knowing exactly what she was thinking. We had two more blissful days of doing tourist shit in Vegas before we had to fly home, and I was relieved that we managed to get Em a seat on the same flight. It was like a mini-honeymoon, only I'd been beaten up and we had five chaperones. None of that mattered though. Having her there with me, when she should have been half a world away, was a gift.

We wore our stupid grins for the whole flight. Everything still hurt, and I'd heard the weather back home was shite, so the only thing I planned on doing was getting back to the flat and falling into bed with my girl, at least until Christmas.

We had no idea how many paparazzi would be waiting for us at the airport. Apparently my ugly mug made for a good story. I barged through them without so much as a smile, making Earnshaw roll his eyes. Fuck it. I was on the grid now. Ireland's bad boy of boxing.

The papers would no doubt dredge up details of my tragic upbringing and Em's horrific past, but as long as Em was good, I didn't give a shite. If everything we'd endured up to this point was necessary to bring us to where we were now, to the man I was today, then I'd still do it all over again.

Life isn't about settling for what you have and making the best of it. It's about getting back up when everyone else around you is counting you out, and fighting for what you want. As I walked out into the cold winter's night, surrounded by my family and with my wife's hand in my own, I knew exactly what was worth the fight.

# EPILOGUE

## EMILY O'CONNELL

My graduation ceremony was much more boring than I thought it would be. It was blind luck that the seat allocated to me was one of only a few seats with a view of O'Connell and the boys. I thought O'Connell looked good in pretty much everything, but seeing him in a tailored steel-gray suit had me weak at the knees. As if he was wasn't eye candy enough, Danny, Liam, Kieran, and Tommy were all decked out in their best as well. Seeing so many hot guys sitting together had definitely set tongues wagging. I didn't mind that. I was definitely used to women staring at O'Connell. I was married to him, and even I wanted to stare today.

The last seven months had gone by so quickly. Despite O'Connell's concerns, Earnshaw hadn't jumped ship after his win and was as much a part of Driscoll's as ever. In fact, the endorsement deals he'd set up after O'Connell's win meant that, if we were very careful, O'Connell wouldn't have to work again if he ever got injured. He had his whole career ahead of him and would probably end up striking it rich, but I'd rather live cautiously comfortable than extravagant and reckless. As much as he loved boxing, I wanted to make sure he could give it up at any time. His health would always be more important to me than the money.

I bounced my knee up and down impatiently while I waited for my name to be called. Like most of the families here, we were all heading out for dinner after this. I let the boys decide where we were going so chances are it would be a steakhouse.

It was my surprise after that I was most looking forward to. Our house was finally finished. O'Connell promised to let me drag him around for the summer so that we could pick all the decorations and furnishings together. He made out like it was a chore until I found a stash of interior design magazines under the bed. No one was more excited to move into our own home than he was.

Over the last few months, O'Connell had split his time between training and working on the house, with a lot of help from the boys. We were all going back there after dinner so they could show me what they'd done. I don't think there is anything I could ever do that would repay the debt I owed to them. This big, loud, brash group of burly, tattooed fighters were my family. Before them, I didn't even know what that meant. Now I couldn't live without them.

I wish I could tell you that happy ever afters wash away the sins of the past, but they don't. I still couldn't sleep without making sure the door was locked, I wouldn't drink if we went out and O'Connell was drinking, and, from time to time, I still had nightmares about Frank. I kept up with my counseling sessions. O'Connell would always take me if he was home and often came in with me. And there were still demons to battle.

O'Connell hadn't seen his mother since before I was kidnapped, and now that he knew Frank had paid her to get me away from Kieran, I figured there would be a reckoning there if they ever saw each other again. My feelings toward my own mum were complicated. Shortly after we got back from Vegas, the policeman friend of Danny's paid us a visit to return my wedding and engagement rings to me. They'd raided Frank's flat in Canning Town and had seized evidence as they put a case together against the people he'd had been working with. They would have kept it as evidence, but Frank was dead now so they had no need of it.

O'Connell had them cleaned and polished by a jeweler and blessed by Father Patrick before he put them on my finger again. He was romantic that way. As I stared down at them now, glistening in the sunlight, they didn't remind me of what I'd been through, but of how far I'd come and how well I was loved. As for my mother she was still alive though I didn't know where. I figured the police would have told me if she had died. At this point I didn't really care. I had all the family I'd ever need. One day, God willing, we'd add to it with a baby of our own, but even if that was never in the cards for me I had a life I never dreamed I'd have, and I thanked God every day for it.

"Emily O'Connell." The dean called out my name at last,

and I walked to the front of the auditorium and climbed the stairs to get my first-class degree in mathematics. After this, I was taking the summer off with O'Connell, who'd just weeks ago won his first title defense.

I was going to become a teacher. That disappointed a lot of professors who encouraged me to take a master's degree. I knew they thought I was throwing away so many opportunities. But the truth was, I didn't want a think-tank job or one in the city earning six figures. Money wasn't important to either of us. When I talked things over with O'Connell, after meeting with my tutor and worrying that I'd made the wrong decision, my husband told me to pick the option that I thought would make me happy. It was as simple and as uncomplicated as that.

"Congratulations, Mrs. O'Connell," the dean said to me as I shook his hand. I took my degree and turned to the audience, as we all did so families could take our picture. Kieran, Liam, Tommy, and O'Connell all whooped and hollered as they clapped, with Danny noisily swearing at them to pipe down because they were embarrassing him.

I grinned from ear to ear, having never felt so proud. My life wasn't a fairy story, but the people I loved taught me that I chose how it ended. And if there was one thing I was sure of, it's that it would be a hell of an ending.

# A NOTE FROM THE AUTHOR

Dear Readers,

Now that we've heard from both Em and O'Connell in their own voices, I wondered who else readers would want to learn more about. And I suspected that it would be a sexy boxer, of course!

Many of you have asked for Kieran's story—thank you— but I would like to do him justice in a full-length novel, and I wanted to use this opportunity to provide some insight into someone new and interesting, but a character that we may not get to hear as much about.

So, especially for my American readers and any reader who can appreciate a hunky Yank, here's an inside look at Heath Earnshaw. He's a recent addition to Danny's gym, but I'd like to think that he spiced up my second novel. And you are about to see him in action in a way you never imagined . . .

R.J. Prescott

# HEATH

I paused at the heavy metal door, briefly contemplating what I was about to do, before raising my fist and knocking twice. It was so cold that I could see my breath in front of my face, but I didn't feel it. I was too jacked-up on adrenaline. Alive, for the first time in months. A panel slid back sharply, and a pissed-off face looked back at me.

"What do you want?" he said.

"Peter Hall invited me. He told me he'd add me to the list for tonight," I replied. The guy looked down, and I figured he was checking the list for my name. When the panel shut sharply in my face, I cursed Pete, guessing that this had been a monumental waste of fucking time. Before I had a chance to turn around, bolts slid back from behind the door, and it opened.

"You coming in or not?" the guy asked. He was shorter than I thought, maybe five feet ten inches at the most, and his face looked like it had been used as a punching bag on a regular basis. Bad boxers don't age well. I hitched my training bag higher on my shoulder and walked through the door, letting him slam it behind me.

"Follow me," he said, leading the way through the corridor and down several winding metal staircases. From the outside, this place looked like a warehouse, all locked up for the night. It wasn't surprising that it remained hidden since everything happened so deep underground.

Eventually we got to another heavy metal door, and as he opened it I was hit by a wave of noise and heat. In the middle of the concrete floor was a battered, old boxing ring, the canvas spotted with stains of rusty orange. The place was completely packed, and the stench was as bad as the heat. Men, like the mystery guy who'd let me in, lined the metal walkways, looking down on the proceedings like prison guards. Most were built like linebackers and all of them were armed. Not for the first time, I questioned the stupidity of what I was doing.

I had gone for inconspicuous in dark jeans and a T-shirt with a high-neck leather jacket, but most of the guys on the floor were still wearing suits. The guys running the show looked down on them with disdain, and why not? They probably did, for real, what these bored corporate suits only played at. Brad Pitt and Edward Norton had a lot to answer for.

A small storage room served as an office, and my guide nodded his head toward the man behind the desk before leaving me to it.

"How did you hear about this place?" he asked me.

"Like I told the guy at the door, Peter Hall invited me," I replied.

"And how do you know Mr. Hall?" he said.

"We train at the same gym," I answered. He nodded like this was what he wanted to hear.

"You have the entry fee?" he asked. Reaching into the inside pocket of my jacket, I pulled out a stack of notes and placed two hundred and fifty dollars in front of him. He picked it up and counted it before passing the stack to the man behind him.

"I take it that Mr. Hall has explained how things work here."

"You put me in the ring with a guy, and if I don't want to fight or if I lose, then I forfeit my entry fee. If I win, then I stay on to the next round. Last man standing gets two thousand dollars," I said.

"Each fight will be three two-minute rounds. And there are rules," he said.

"Rule number one, no one talks about fight club?" I answered, like a smart-ass. His face was stoic, and I guessed that every man who'd sat at this table probably used the same line.

"No weapons, no eye-gouging, and no biting. Any man who tries to interfere with a fight is out the door. Your opponent goes limp, calls out for you to stop, or he passes out, then the fight is over. I have the right to stop the fight at any time, if I think either of you is seriously hurt or too fucking pussy to carry-on. You clear?" he said.

"Yes," I said, and nodded in agreement. Now that I had

committed, I was itching to get on with it, restless in a way that I couldn't begin to describe. I had everything I'd ever worked for. A great degree from an ivy-league school, a high-flying job with one of the premier sports agencies in the country, nice suits, and money in the bank. I had everything. And it wasn't enough.

He noticed my restlessness and eyed me up and down. I assumed he was assessing my chances in the ring. At six feet five inches, I was a big guy, but I was gym-hardened, not battle-tested. Aside from the shiny, new punching bag in my corporate gym, I hadn't boxed since I was a kid. There was a very good chance that I'd end up in the hospital by the end of the night, but it would be worth it.

"Marco here will take you to the changing rooms. If you have shorts and a T-shirt, I'd wear that. You fight barefoot, and no Vaseline or oil allowed. You're up in ten minutes," he told me.

"Who am I fighting?" I asked.

"Does it matter?" he replied. I guessed not.

I followed Marco down to the changing rooms, which was basically a shitty communal room lined with chairs. There was a small bathroom off to the side that smelled as if something had died in there.

"I'll be back for you in ten minutes," Marco said and left.

I changed quickly into loose training shorts but left my chest bare. A top would only inhibit my movement. Folding my clothes neatly into a pile, I placed them on the chair beside me, thankful that I'd left my wallet at home. At least I wouldn't have to worry about it getting stolen while I was in the ring. At a loss for what to do while I waited for Marco, I did a few push-ups and shadowboxed for a bit to warm up my muscles. When he finally appeared at the door and said, "You're up," I was anything but relaxed.

The sea of suits parted as I strode toward the ring. I wondered if I knew anyone here or if anyone would recognize me. Nothing about this setup was legal or sanctioned, and the prospect of getting fired if my firm found out was a very real possibility. I just didn't have it in me to give a shit though.

The only time I'd ever felt any semblance of purpose and control was between those four ropes. I lacked the natural talent to go professional, so I figured that becoming an agent would give me a good career and keep me close to the sport I loved. I couldn't have been more wrong. When I wasn't flying from state to state, living out of hotel rooms, and driving rental cars, I was putting in a minimum of twelve hours a day, six days a week at the office. Half my clients were assholes who wanted premium endorsements before the ink was even dry on their contract, and the other half I had far too little time for.

The soul-eating monster that was my career had devoured my social life. Every minute of every day was accounted for, and before I knew it I'd drifted apart from most of my friends from college. I'd wandered so far off the path I'd envisaged for myself that I had no idea how to find my way back. Maybe this wasn't the answer, but for now it was enough to feel something again. To remember what I wanted in the first place and why.

I climbed between the ropes, and jumped up and down a bit to try to loosen up. All around men were swapping money and eying me like hungry hyenas. I wondered if any of them had the balls to get up here, or whether they just loved the violence and the thrill of being on the wrong side of the law for a night.

Across the ring my shirtless opponent climbed in wearing sweatpants. I had a couple of inches on him and his gut hung over those pants a little, but I could see from the self-satisfied smirk on his face that this wasn't his first time. Like a shark, he could smell fresh blood in the water, and I was the chump.

Marco rang a crappy little bell in the corner, and the guy charged at me. Determined not to get caught on the ropes, I met him in the middle. He swung at me a few times, and I could tell he had some power. If even a couple of his jabs caught me, I'd be in trouble. But he lacked any sort of technique. You only had to watch his shoulders to see where his next hit was coming from.

My ducking and weaving was stilted, and it was patently obvious that, as far as boxing was concerned, I was out of shape. But reading this guy was as easy as reading the newspaper. He was predictable and impatient, and a minute into round two I had him. After blocking a few of his favorite jabs, he dropped his guard and I landed a powerful left hook to his face. His nose splattered on impact, and, after staggering a little, he fell to the floor on his knees and covered it to stop the bleeding.

Just like that it was over. Marco, who'd been acting as

referee, ignored my opponent. With little ceremony and a bored look on his face, he raised my arm to declare me the winner. A chorus of boos and cheers erupted from the crowd, and more money changed hands frantically. It was right then—my chest heaving from exertion and my head giddy with the thrill of victory—that I had an epiphany. I was never going to be a fighter, but I also couldn't carry on this mundane trudge through the monotony of my life. I needed something more, something bigger. Hell, maybe even something smaller. Now I just needed to work out what.

* * *

On a red-eye flight to Chicago three weeks later, I found what I'd been looking for. A tiny ad in the back of a boxing magazine read SMALL LONDON GYM SEEKS SPORTS AGENT/MANAGER FOR RANGE OF FIGHTERS FROM AMATEUR YOUTH TO IRISH PROFESSIONAL HEAVYWEIGHT. SALARY NEGOTIABLE DEPENDING UPON EXPERIENCE. There was no address or e-mail, just a number for applicants.

I put down the magazine and closed my grainy, sleep-deprived eyes. God, I was tired. I had less than twelve hours in Chicago before I had to turn around and come straight back home again for another meeting. There was little chance of sleep though. Something about the ad called to me. My sister was starting an internship in London in a few months, and the big brother in me liked the idea that she wouldn't be there alone.

There was only one professional Irish boxer that I knew

of who was training out of London. Cormac "The Hurricane" O'Connell was an up-and-comer with a serious amount of promise. This could be the opportunity of a lifetime or career suicide, but for the first time in a very long time, I was excited. The idea of staying in one place and putting down roots, of working with one professional at the start of what could be an amazing career and with kids who still loved the sport for its purity, untainted by the bullshit that came with success, was heady. I didn't know anything about the Danny Driscoll who was the contact in the ad, but pulling my iPad from its sleeve, I spent the next two hours digging up every bit of information I could. An hour after I walked off the plane, I made the call.

* * *

I tugged nervously on the sleeve of my thousand-dollar suit, waiting for Danny to make his way around the desk before sitting myself. I might as well have turned up in jeans for the look of contempt he gave me. I was massively overqualified for this job and we both knew it, but the guy had insisted on meeting me in person. Leaving me no other choice, I had cashed in a couple of rarely used vacation days and caught a flight to London. I was there for one night only and back on a return flight the next day. I must have been crazy to agree to it, but Danny was a hard-ass of the highest order.

"You nervous?" he asked me, as he lit up a cigarette.

"Yes," I replied, with an uncomfortable cough.

"Why?" he asked.

"It's a job interview," I said. In truth, I had no idea why I was so nervous. This place was a world away from the gleaming offices of my firm, a beacon to potential clients of the gaudy glamour and wealth that could all be theirs if they only signed with us.

"I've read through the CV you sent me," he said, glancing over my résumé with the same look of disdain he'd given my suit.

"So who are you running from or what drugs are you taking?" he said.

"Excuse me?" I replied.

"Look, kid. When I placed the ad, I expected a guy at the end of his career looking to wind things down. You're applying for a job halfway around the world for a fraction of your current pay. If you're not on drugs or running from something, then I want to know why." He sat back and waited for an explanation.

I had a gift for walking into a room and owning it. In less than fifteen minutes, I could convince bright, young athletes at the top of their game that the world was their oyster the minute they signed on the dotted line. I could do all that, yet here I sat like a nervous school-kid, cracking my knuckles as I searched for an answer.

Finally I lifted my head and looked him square in the eye. "I want to be inspired. I don't want to be a suit or a number, just another guy in a long line getting his slice of the pie. I want to be a part of something bigger. More than anything, I want to feel pride in my work again." I answered honestly and from the heart, and still the hard-ass looked completely unaffected. If anything, he scowled a little harder.

"You any good?" he asked. I listed off some of my biggest clients and the endorsements I'd secured for them. Sports careers were short lived, but with the contracts I'd arranged, most of my top names would be set for life. Of course, it was pretty soul destroying to see a few of them doing their best to blow the lot as quickly as they could. I set up the deals, and what they did with the money was up to them. I didn't have time to play agent, counselor, and life planner. I hoped that would change.

"What about setting up the fights? Negotiating the purse? You got any experience in that?" he asked.

"I cover a range of sports, and I have a lot of contract negotiations behind me. It's my contacts here and in the US that will be of most value to the job."

He stared at me, clearly unfazed by my evasive answer. Promotors generally set up fights; I just made sure the money was right. The longer he said nothing, the more I squirmed. Jesus, it was like sitting in front of the principal at school.

"This place is my home," he said finally, as he sat back in his chair and made himself comfortable. "These boys ain't just fighters, they're family. From the youngest of the kids to the eldest. Everyone pulls their weight. Everyone takes care of the family. I give you this job, then I'm trusting you with that responsibility. O'Connell's got a kind of magic I ain't ever seen before. He'll give this everything he has and still he'll keep on giving. I don't have the contacts or the savvy to get him the fights he needs. But that kid could be world champion one day. He's that feckin' good.

"You deliver what you say you can, and I think you'll find what it is you're looking for. Don't be expecting the lads to give you an easy time of it though. You're a college boy and a Yank, neither of which will go down well. They'll expect you to look down on them, and they'll be a pain in the arse to work with. Earn their respect and they'll give it to you," he said.

I nodded, acknowledging the wisdom he was imparting. My parents would have me committed for even thinking about this. Who gives up a high-flying career and moves to another country to work with people who don't really want them there? My fear must have been written across my face.

"Look, kid," Danny said as he stubbed out his cigarette into an overflowing ashtray, "the job's yours if you want it. I'm offering the salary I gave you on the phone, plus you get five percent of any endorsements you set up for the guys. Go back to America. Take some time and talk with your family. Really think about this. If you decide you still want it, let me know, and we'll set this up."

Standing up, he leaned forward on the desk menacingly. "First and last warning, mind. You fuck over any of my kids in any way, try taking money off the back end, then there ain't no place you can go that I won't find you."

I swallowed audibly. I wasn't really scared of Danny—well, maybe just a little—but this wasn't like any job interview I'd ever had. I felt completely raw, like he could see right through to the heart of me.

"Danny," I mumbled, as I walked toward the door he held open for me, "thanks for giving me a chance."

"Kid," he said, slapping me on the back, "you were the only one who applied."

\* \* \*

The gym was completely quiet as I walked through, taking in my prospective new place of employment. The early morning sun shone through the small windows to light up the ring in an almost reverent way. Danny talked about his boys with such loyalty that I felt slightly shamed at the thought of going back to my life, where my loyalty was bought and sold like a commodity.

The seed of want that was sewn so many weeks ago had grown into full-blown hunger. I could be a part of this, and what's more I could be fucking great at it. My head told me it was complete madness, but it was my heart that told me to give it a try. Maybe it would be a big mistake, but I'd rather regret the chance I took than the one I didn't. With that happy thought, I picked up my bag and walked away, feeling lighter than I had in years.

They are polar opposites who were never meant to find each other. But some things are worth the fight.

Please see the next page for an excerpt from

# *THE HURRICANE.*

# CHAPTER ONE

*Oh, my God, I am so late!* I ran down the street, my heart pounding. The early morning commuters trying to make it into the office were oblivious to my plight as I dodged in and out of people. My thin summer shoes offered nearly no protection against the bitter bite of the frosty morning. By the time I opened the back door to Daisy's Café, my teeth were chattering and my fingers were stiff with what I was sure was the onset of frostbite. I had no idea what I was going to do when winter really set in. I was barely scraping together enough money for rent and food, let alone having to worry about gloves and a winter coat.

"Mornin', Em." Mike, the owner, smiled as he turned the bacon over in the pan. For the last few weeks, I'd been pulling extra shifts at the café and then studying when I got home. I thought I could handle it, but after waking up at my desk half an hour ago, I knew I was wrong.

I wasn't surprised that Mike didn't seem mad. I'd never been late for a shift before, and more often than not, I was the last to leave. Daisy's had heating, after all. Heating and company. Two of the things I was in need of most at the moment.

"Sorry I'm late," I mumbled to Mike. I avoided making eye contact and raced to hang up my coat and tie my apron. Tapping down the pocket, I made sure I had my pad and pencil and quickly scraped my hair back with one of the elastics kept permanently around my wrist. Wrestling it into a messy bun, I weaved through the kitchen and grabbed a pot of coffee.

I passed Rhona who'd been at Daisy's since the doors first opened.

"Slow down, love," she said with a warm smile. "You just need to do the refills and take the order for table two." She breezed into the kitchen without waiting for a reply.

Daisy's was one of the only cafés around that offered unlimited tea and coffee refills with a meal, which meant the place was usually packed for breakfast. After running around topping up coffees, I said hello to Danny as he sat down at his usual table. We chatted for a bit and, promising him a fresh pot, I headed to the kitchen to pass Mike the order for table two.

As I walked back out, I froze. Sitting next to Danny, and glancing at me over the menu, was hands-down the hottest guy I had ever seen. His nose had a slight crook in it, which made me think it was once broken, but that was the only flaw in his otherwise perfect face. Razor-sharp cheekbones, tanned skin, and dark hair added to the beauty that seemed completely at odds with his stature. If it weren't for the broken nose, he could be a model, but I knew that whatever this man did was dangerous, because everything about him exuded violence. I had no idea who he was, and the fact that he was sitting with Danny should have eased me, but it didn't. My internal alarm was going off big time. From the set of his shoulders, to the sheer size of him, he looked like nothing but trouble. Whoever he was, it looked like Danny was raking him over the coals about something.

Danny was a small, wiry man, who couldn't have been much younger than seventy-five. The deep grooves in his face and leathery skin spoke of hard living, but he was no frail pensioner. Mike was twice the size of Danny, but even he was a little bit scared of him. From my very first shift at Daisy's, he'd strolled through the door a few minutes past opening, plonked himself in an empty booth in my section, and beckoned me over—which soon became our morning ritual.

But that first day was different; I'd been absolutely petrified of everything and everyone. Most regulars had gravitated toward the other girls' sections, wary of the new girl messing up their order. Danny had no such compunctions, though. He'd sat straight down and called out, "Hey, Sunshine, come and get me a cuppa coffee. I don't bite."

Shaking like a leaf, I filled his cup and, by sheer force of will, avoided spilling the scalding liquid all over his lap. If he noticed my nerves, he'd never said anything. He rattled off his order then unfolded a crisp, clean newspaper and read silently until I brought out his breakfast. When he was finished, I removed his plate and refilled his coffee.

"Thank you, Sunshine," he said, without smiling and without looking up from his paper.

Things went on that way for a few weeks, and when I finally stopped shaking, he spoke to me. It was never anything too personal, just remarks about the weather, questions about school, and what I thought of my professors. In the beginning, I did my best to find one-word answers, but just over a year later, Danny was the closest thing I had to a friend.

I wanted to run and hide in the kitchen. But hiding wouldn't do me any good, it never did. Ten horrific years of my stepfather, Frank, knocking me around had taught me not to speak unless spoken to and not to make eye contact. Whenever I felt threatened, those were the rules I fell back on.

Moving quickly through the tables, I wiped down a couple, gathered up a few dirty dishes, and after dropping them off at the kitchen, I could procrastinate no further and headed to Danny's table.

"Two full fried breakfasts please, Sunshine," Danny croaked, with his usual scowl. If he ever did smile at me, I was a little worried that his weather-beaten face might crack.

Lowering my eyes, I gave him a small nod but didn't reply. It was our usual routine, and he was familiar with it. Without asking him, I filled up his coffee cup, and my hands trembled. It had been months since that happened, and I knew if I had to ask Danny's companion if he'd like coffee, my voice would crack. I turned toward him with the coffeepot in my hand, and my eye caught on the sleeve of his white T-shirt. The biggest biceps that I'd ever seen strained the seams, and beneath, the edge of a tattoo was visible. It looked like a series of intricately woven Celtic designs. From what I could see, the artwork was beautiful.

"O'Connell, do you want coffee or not?" Danny snapped at him. I flinched at the sharpness of his tone, but he did, at least, save me from speaking.

"Yeah, sure," the guy replied lazily, almost bored. I shook badly again, and I was sure that I'd spill it, but I didn't. Gathering up their menus, I all but whispered, "I'll be back with your order soon," and fled to the kitchen to hide. The guy's eyes were boring a hole in my back as I walked away.

Ten minutes later, their order was done. Taking their warm plates through to the café, I placed the identical breakfasts down in front of them and escaped.

"You keep your eyes off that, boyo. That one's not for you," I heard Danny warn quietly.

Danny was born and raised in Killarney, Ireland, and I very much doubted that the forty years he'd spent here in London had softened his accent much.

"Why was she shaking so badly?" the man Danny had called O'Connell asked in a deep, husky voice with a slight Irish lilt that was just about the sexiest thing that I had ever heard.

Danny sighed deeply before answering. "You probably scare the shite out of her. That one's special, but she ain't for you, so you'd best mind yourself and leave her to her business. Now, stop looking after something you can't have and think about what I said, 'cause if we have one more conversation about you drinkin' and fightin', you eejit, then you and me are gonna have words!"

The rest of the conversation was lost on me. The idea of Danny threatening this mountain of a man with anything would be enough to make me smile, if he hadn't mentioned the fighting. Truth be told, you only had to look at O'Connell to know that he was dangerous. It was hard to tell how tall he was, but by the way he was crammed into that booth, I'd guess he was big. Broad shouldered and ripped, he looked every inch a fighter, but it was that relaxed, almost bored, indifference about him that sold the package. He could take care of himself, and he knew it.

A few more of my regulars made their way over to my section, and after doing my rounds with the coffee and rushing back and forth with orders, I realized that the seat across from Danny was empty. I let out a deep breath and began clearing the table.

"Give my compliments to Mike," Danny told me, as I stacked up the plates.

"Sure, Danny," I replied. "Can I get you another coffee?"

"No, thank you, Sunshine. My bladder control is not what it used to be, and I'm gonna find it hard enough to get back to work as it is."

This was more information than I needed to know. I was

sure that he threw it out there just to get a rise out of me, and I humored him by rolling my eyes.

"Make sure you wrap up warm, then." I gestured toward his coat and scarf on the bench. "It's bitter out."

I dealt with ringing up his check, and before he'd even closed the door behind him, Katrina Bray was up in my face. With her shirt pulled tight against her impressive cleavage and a skirt rolled higher than her apron, she stomped her way toward me.

"What the hell was Cormac O'Connell doing in your section?"

I gave her the one-shouldered shrug. "I have no friggin' clue, and you're welcome to serve him next time," would be my response of choice, but I kept my mouth shut. Katrina was the last person that I needed to start an argument with.

"You have absolutely no idea who he is, do you?"

She obviously deduced this for herself, given the vacant look on my face. Without waiting for an answer, she flounced off in a cloud of cheap perfume. Rhona, having heard the whole exchange, shoulder bumped me on her way back to the kitchen.

"Go on, girl. 'Bout time that madam had a bit of competition, and once upon a time, I wouldn't have minded a piece of that boy, myself. I wouldn't be turning a blind eye if I was twenty years younger."

"Need some help?" I motioned to the dishes in her hand, trying to change the subject. It had completely escaped her notice that I was neither flirting, nor being flirted with. I was no expert, but I was sure that you actually needed to talk to someone to start a relationship.

"No thanks, love, I've got it. Your section is getting pretty full."

She nodded back toward the café. Seeing she was right, I hurried back to take orders. People were pretty slow about coming into my section to begin with, but once they saw me waiting on Danny every day, they slowly started drifting over. The breakfast and lunch shifts flew by, punctuated by evil looks from Katrina. I guessed from her attitude that O'Connell was on her hit list and she hadn't scored with him yet. Which would put him in the minority, from what I heard.

When Katrina wanted a guy, he usually didn't offer much resistance. She had nothing to worry about from me, though. If O'Connell came in here again, she was welcome to him. However good-looking the package, I didn't need that kind of trouble in my life. It wasn't as if he'd ever give me a second look anyway.

By the time my shift ended, I was glad to be heading to class. Waitressing was okay, and it was nice to have some company, but school was where I really lost myself. Getting a place at UCL had been the scariest and most exhilarating thing that had ever happened to me. None of it would have been possible without my former teacher Mrs. Wallis. I had been wriggling around in my seat, trying not to let the chair touch any of the fresh bruises hidden under my sweater when she had approached me. With tears in her eyes, she had told me she knew I had a difficult home life, and as I was nearly eighteen, there was a way of escaping. If I wanted her help, I would have it.

That was the nearest that I ever came to breaking down. Part of me wanted to scream at her that, if she knew, then why didn't she tell social services so they could get me? I think we both knew that would only have made things worse though.

I didn't scream at her or cry, but actually setting out the bare bones of a plan was terrifying. The fear of being caught, and of my stepfather, Frank, discovering what I was doing, had me feeling sick every minute of every day. Using Mrs. Wallis's address, I had applied for university places and identification. When I turned eighteen, I changed my surname legally. I accepted a place studying applied mathematics at University College London, and now, eighteen months later, the only person who could ever connect Emily Thomas from Cardiff, South Wales, with me was Mrs. Wallis, an elderly home economics teacher who was the only person I'd ever trusted.

I'd breezed an access course in accounting over the summer, but my heart was in math. It was clean and pure, and in my world of gray, it was black and white. If I had any chance at building a future, then I needed qualifications.

The dread of being caught was always ever present though. I guessed that Frank was looking for me but getting my degree was worth the risk. If I committed to staying in one place long enough to finish university, I had to keep a low profile. It was my best chance of evading him. So I did what I'd always done. I made no eye contact and never initiated conversation.

It had worked in high school, but university was a completely different kettle of fish. The guys here were relentless. Politely turning down unwanted advances, without causing offense, had become an art form that I'd perfected. It was the safest way to live, but I was lonely. There were days that I desperately wanted someone, anyone, to call a friend. In lecture room three, on that frosty Tuesday afternoon, I got just that.

"This seat taken?"

I looked down at cherry red leather boots with a killer heel and looked up to see that the voice belonging to them liked to coordinate her cherry red hair with her outfit. Clearly I was more than backward when it came to accessorizing. My hair didn't go with anything.

"Um..." I looked around, desperate to say yes, hoping to remain as anonymous as possible. The lecture theater was only a third full, at best, and there was no reason why this girl would want to sit next to me. She wore a denim miniskirt, a fitted black top, and a leather jacket that I would have given my left arm for. With the killer boots and her glossy hair layered artfully around her face, she looked edgy and hot. No wonder half the man-geeks were drooling. My first thought was that she was in the wrong place.

"No," I replied. Could I have been more socially inept? If she was in the right place, it looked like she'd be beating off the guys with a stick, so what better place to take cover than beside the only other girl in the room.

"Nikki Martin," she said, sliding into the adjoining seat.

"Sorry?" I mumbled.

"I'm Nikki Martin," she stated, expectantly awaiting a response.

"Oh, hi," I replied, as I went back to copying down the equation from the projector.

"Oh, my God, you really are one of them," she laughed, teasingly.

"One of them?" I answered, glancing up in confusion.

"The freaks who only speak in numbers and have no social skills whatsoever."

"Wow, rude much?" Oh, my God! I've never been confrontational, *ever*, but with this girl, it just slipped out.

She laughed again, probably at the look of sheer horror on my face. "So the kitten has claws. You know, you and me are going to get on just fine."

I had no idea what to say to that. This girl was like a beautiful steamroller.

"Okay, a name would be good about now, unless you want me to call you Mathlexy all term."

"Mathlexy?" Yep, I was getting good at repeating everything she said back to her as a question.

"I can tell you're a math fiend by the stack of handwritten notes you've got there, and you're the sexiest thing this lot has probably ever seen."

She gestured around the lecture hall, and I wasn't convinced that the guys would actually wait until the end of class to pounce on her. The wide-eyed looks of disbelief, appreciation, and finally hunger reminded me of starving hyenas, eyeing up their appetizer. I giggled at the image and snorted through my nose at the absurdity of the name. Snorting was neither sexy nor attractive.

"Emily McCarthy," I offered up in return, hopeful of rejecting that ridiculous nickname before anyone heard it. The last name was new. I'd only had it for a year, and I was still getting used to it. But I figured that keeping my first name wouldn't hurt. Emily was a pretty common name, and people got suspicious if you didn't answer to your name when called because you didn't know it.

"Well, it's nice to meet you, Emily McCarthy," she answered.

By the end of the lecture, I had three sides of crisp clean notes, and Nikki had half a page and some lovely heart and floral murals.

"What's your next class?" she asked, as we were stuffing things into our bags.

"I don't have another one for a couple of hours," I replied. "I was just going to the library to study."

"Perfect, I have a couple of hours free. Let's go and grab a coffee. My treat."

She looped her arm through mine and all but dragged me out, clearly not caring about my plans.

*Latte, espresso, tall, fat, mocha, grande.* The board in front of me laid out the endless possible taste sensations, and I agonized over my decision. I loved coffee, but on my budget, regular coffee at Daisy's was about as good as it got. So if this was my treat for the month, then I was going to make the most of it.

"Come on, Em," Nikki moaned, "I'm growing old here!"

"A cappuccino, please," I ordered quickly. The barista handed me my drink, and I pulled out the chair next to Nikki.

She took a long sip of her coffee, sighed deeply, and turned to me. "So...the whole social hermit thing. Is it just for a term or are you committed for life?"

# ACKNOWLEDGMENTS

Writing a book is like walking through the wardrobe into Narnia. For the writer, it feels like while you delve into this fantasy world, no time at all has passed. Then, when you finally leave, you realize that, for your loved ones, months have passed in which they haven't seen you. To my husband and best friend, Lee, you will never know how much I love you, not only for waiting outside that wardrobe door for me to return, but for encouraging me to walk through it in the first place. To my sons, Jack and Gabriel, I love you both so much, and I couldn't be prouder of you. It amazes me how pleased you are when I release a book, and I live in perpetual fear that I will teach you swear words as you read over my shoulder.

There aren't words to describe just how amazing and wonderful my family really is. Mum and Dad, you take it for granted that I can do absolutely anything in the world if I put my mind to it. If I told you I was going to the moon, it wouldn't surprise you. To grow up knowing that you are loved enough that you can follow your dreams wherever they take you is a precious thing. Gerry, Faye, Laura, Sarah, Boo, Gareth, Daniel, Ben, and Dave, I love you all so much. You support me, encourage me, and believe in me always, and that makes me believe in myself.

I owe a massive debt of thanks to my baby brother, David, who buys paperbacks of my books that he won't read because he can't face sex scenes written by his sister, and who turns up unannounced on his weekends off just to type copy or entertain the boys when Lee is working so I can write. Thank you just doesn't seem enough.

Marie, what can I say? I needed you so very much with this book, and you were always there for me. I wouldn't be living this dream without you, and I wouldn't want to. Your friendship means more to me than you will ever know.

To my other best friend, Ria, you are patient, kind, and generous, and I am forever grateful for our friendship. Thank you so much for all your help, and thanks to your awesome husband, Vin, for all his expert technical advice and for letting me pick his brain.

Thank you so much to author Rachel de Lune for everything. Your constant support and steady supply of pictorial man candy saw me through to the end. For your next book, I promise to return the favor.

Louisa Maggio, you are a rock star of cover design. You create covers that bring my stories to life, and I love that I get to call you my friend. You are quite simply one of the most talented people I've ever met.

To my agent Marisa, from the very first time we spoke, I

was moved by your passion for what you do. Your steadfast belief in me and your encouragement and support inspires me. Thank you so much for everything.

To Alex, you are a phenomenal editor. You challenge me as a writer and always encourage me to do the very best that I can. I am grateful for your humor and for your limitless patience with my appalling grammar. I have no doubt that the story of how I called my own hero an arsehole will haunt me forever. Thank you for seeing something in Cormac O'Connell—and in me—worth taking a chance on.

To my beta reader for life Rachel V and authors L. A. Casey and James Oliver French, who are never too busy to offer support when I really need it.

Thank you to all my friends in Cardiff and Bristol for your support and your friendship. You have all helped and encouraged me in ways that I'll never forget. Thank you also to Ashleigh and Andrew for your never-ending patience with me and anything book related.

Publishing *The Hurricane* changed my life in so many ways. It gave me confidence in myself and in my writing, but more important, it has led me to meet so many great friends all over the world. Thank you so much to every book blogger, author, and reader whom I have met along this crazy journey. You have somehow made O'Connell real, and I love you for it. Just know that every kind review, comment, or post makes my day.

My last and biggest thanks will, always and forever, belong to you, the reader. Just by reading this book you continue to make my dreams come true!

# ABOUT THE AUTHOR

R. J. Prescott was born in Cardiff, South Wales, and studied law at the University of Bristol, England. Four weeks before graduation, she fell in love, and stayed. Ten years later, she convinced her crazy, wonderful firefighter husband to move back to Cardiff where they now live with their two equally crazy sons. Juggling work, writing, and family doesn't leave a lot of time, but curling up on the sofa with a cup of tea and a bar of chocolate for family movie night is definitely the best part of R. J. Prescott's week. She loves to hear from readers so contact her at:

Facebook: www.facebook.com/rjprescottauthor

Twitter: @rjprescottauth

Website: http://rjprescott.com

E-mail: r.j.prescott@hotmail.com